To The BREAKING POINTE

by

CINDY MCDONALD

To The Breaking Pointe

For information call: 304-995-1295
or Email: cindys.mcdonald@gmail.com

This book is a work of fiction. Names, characters, places, and incidents are products of the author's imagination or are used fictitiously. Any resemblance to actual events or locales or persons, living or dead, is entirely coincidental.

Designed by Acorn Book Services

Publication Managed by Acorn Book Services
www.acornbookservices.com
acornbookservices@gmail.com
304-995-1295

On the cover: Stuart Tomlinson
Photographer: Gilles Crofta
Cover designed by Todd Aune
Spokane, Washington
www.projetoonline.com

IISBN-10: 0991368029
ISBN-13: 978-0-9913680-2-0

Printed in the United States of America

INTO THE CROSSFIRE

BOOK #1 OF THE FIRST FORCE SERIES

A notorious killer leaves Jack Haliday's world in shambles.

It has been four years since ex Navy SEAL, Jack Haliday, had an explosive run-in with a biker gang wounding their leader, Gunner. During those years Jack had acquired everything he ever wanted: a beautiful wife, an adorable daughter, and a lovely home in the suburbs—everything was just about as perfect as it could get, until Gunner returned to twist Jack's world inside-out with a vengeance that he could never have prepared for.

Now Jack has a score to settle and he's got some friends to help him do it!

Into the Crossfire is the first book of Cindy McDonald's suspense series, First Force, available in print or ebook at amazon.com, BAM, barnesandnoble.com and where all fine books are sold. For more information on *Into the Crossfire* and all of Cindy's books, please visit her website: www.cindymcwriter.com

The reviewers love INTO THE CROSSFIRE!

"*Into the Crossfire* is a powerful story that will leave you breathless."~**Jersey Girl Reviews**

"If you're looking for a quick read that will get your adrenaline pumping, pick up *Into the Crossfire.*"~**Moonlight Reader Reviews**

"An ending so powerful, electric and dramatic only author Cindy McDonald can deliver it."~**Fran Lewis**

*I would like to dedicate **To the Breaking Pointe** to the cast of my 2005 production of **Coppelia**. The memories of my dance school burn warmly in my heart—it was a precious time of my life for which I will always be thankful for.*

ACKNOWLEDGMENTS

There are many people I wish to thank who had a hand in the publishing and pre-publishing process of *To the Breaking Pointe*. My dear friend and confidant, Linda Taylor, who always reads my manuscripts before they go to my editor—thank you for all of those wonderful "suggestions" of yours—I don't know what I'd do without them!

I wish to thank my wonderful publishing manager, good friend, and fellow author, Lauren Carr, for her constant support and insightful editing; and the creative genius behind this fabulous cover, Todd Aune.

Thank you to those at Acorn Book Services that worked behind the scenes on my behalf. Last but certainly never least, I want to thank my husband, Saint Bill, your love and support always takes my breath away—you are my everything.

On the cover: Stuart Tomlinson, Professional wrestler with the WWE & UFC. Former footballer for championship teams: Burton Albion & Port Vale, UK

Photographer: Gilles Crofta, Loughborough, England

Cover design: Todd Aune/Projeto Communications

TABLE OF CONTENTS

To The BREAKING POINTE

BOOK TWO

Happiness is having a dream you cannot let go of and a partner who would never ask you to.

Robert Brault

If you lead with your heart, you will go to the most amazing places.

Cindy McDonald

CHAPTER ONE

Yekaterinburg, Russia

E asing her sore, aching, and abraded feet into a tub of hot water, Silja (Sil-ya) Ramsay let out a gratifying groan. She laid her head against the sofa, allowing the Epsom salts to soothe the pain from the bloody welts on her toes. The toenail on her left big toe was discolored and cracked. *Yuck.*

For the past five weeks, she'd danced the principle role of Swan Hilda in the ballet *Coppelia.*

The ballet tells the enchanting story of an old inventor named Dr. Coppelius who has created a lovely, life-size doll named Coppelia. He displays his exquisite invention on the balcony of his shop, intriguing all the townspeople. They try and try to get Coppelia's attention to no avail. The doll simply sits on the balcony, supposedly reading her book, ignoring everyone. Franz, Swan Hilda's fiancé, falls completely in love with the beautiful maiden and brushes Swan Hilda aside, believing the doll to be a real girl. Swan Hilda becomes enraged and sets out to prove that Coppelia is nothing more than a fake.

Coppelia is a fun ballet adored by all. Yet, the role of Swan Hilda had always proven to be truly demanding. Silja was rarely off stage during the course of the performance, and she seldom stood by while the other dancers danced. She was engaged in nearly every movement of the ballet. Although the muscles in her body begged for mercy and her feet felt as though they would fall off, she wasn't complaining. She was living her dream of being the principal ballerina for a small yet prominent ballet company. She'd left everything behind, even the man she loved, to follow her dream. Oftentimes she had regrets, but not this night. Oh no, her performance had been flawless, bringing the audience to their feet for three curtain calls!

Silja closed her eyes and her lips curled up in bitter-sweet contemplation. She missed her home in the United States, and she missed Grant. It was so long ago, why did he even seep into her mind anymore? It had been five years since she had seen him and only a few emails were exchanged each year. He had his life, and she had hers, period. End of story. Leave it be. *Gawd, Silja, he's probably with someone else.*

Silja had come to Russia five years previously to dance with the Novikov Ballet Company. Even though she was born in Russia, she'd been raised in the United States after being adopted by an American couple, the Ramsays, twenty-five years ago. Her adoptive parents were wonderful. She was provided with a loving home. When Silja fell in love with ballet, her adoptive mother saw to it that she had the very best instruction.

Her eyes welled with tears. She so wished that her parents could have seen that night's performance. Then again, she had longed for that on so many nights. She missed them desperately. A car accident had claimed them several years earlier.

When the opportunity presented itself to audition for the Novikov Ballet Company, Silja knew that it was what her mother would have wanted.

Grant encouraged her to follow her dreams. He was a gentleman. He loved her, but, mostly, Grant Ketchum was a selfless man.

She could still remember his words to her when he left her at the airport. He had brushed a stray hair from her cheek, kissed her lips, and whispered, *"I'm so proud of you, Sil. I know you'll be great."* His eyes were shadowed with sadness, but his words were genuine. He turned and hurried away.

Silja's lips curled at the memory of his pet name for her: Sil.

Now she was the principle dancer for the company, and her feet were reminding her of that fact with burn and ache.

"Are you all right, Silja?" Natalia Novikov's heavy Russian accent pulled her from her thoughts.

Silja opened her eyes to find the owner and director of the Novikov Ballet Company standing over her. She was a tall wisp of a middle-aged woman with dark, wavy hair that was swept up in a loose French twist. Her inky eyes were outlined with heavy black liner. She wore a black pantsuit that accentuated her lean figure, topped off with dangly rhinestone earrings that almost touched her shoulders. The former ballerina was an attractive woman dipped in a domineering flavor.

Natalia cradled a bouquet of two dozen red roses in her arms. She smiled. "Ballard Crafton sent these for you. He said to tell you that your performance this evening was the most impressive that he has ever seen. He is fond of you, Silja." She held out the bouquet for Silja to take, but instead Silja gestured for her to lay them on the sofa next to her.

Wrinkling her lips, Natalia set them down.

Closing her eyes, Silja folded her hands over her flat tummy.

Natalia pointed out, "There are worse things in this life than to have a wealthy man yearn for your affections, Silja. Ballard Crafton could provide you with anything that you desire in this world."

Silja swished her feet in the warmth of the water. Peeking out from under her half-closed lids, she said, "He's also old enough to be my father, Natalia. What is he? About fifty? Maybe fifty-five?"

"So you would be young widow. You are so beautiful. I'm sure you would still have your looks, and you would be wealthy, too."

"I'm not attracted to him at all, Natalia. I wouldn't marry a man for his money. I want to marry for love, thank you. By the way, I don't accept his gifts because I don't want to send him the wrong message."

Natalia went to the dressing room door. "You should put the roses in water before they wilt—like memories of someone that you left behind."

Silja's eyes jerked open. Her jaw dropped a bit as she sucked in a breath.

Natalia chuckled. "You are very transparent, Silja—like most American women."

"I'm as Russian as you, Natalia."

"I think not. Soak your feet. You have another performance tomorrow afternoon. I have things to tend to. Good night, Silja." Natalia eased out of the room and closed the door behind her.

Silja glanced at the crimson roses lying on the seat next to her. Ballard was always sending her flowers, cards, and sometimes jewelry. He was a powerful man who was used to getting whatever or whomever he wanted. He attended almost every performance—sitting in the very front row, dead center. Occasionally he would show up at the studio to watch her rehearse.

Stalker.

With a sweep of her hand she knocked the roses to the floor.

"Another bouquet from your rich admirer?" Eleni Babinski asked as she picked up the discarded flowers from the carpet. Holding them to her face, she breathed in their glorious scent. The bouquet practically covered Eleni's upper body.

The dancer was a tiny girl with barely any breasts to speak of and narrow hips that eased into long, athletic legs. Her dark hair was still pulled back in the severe bun that she'd worn during the performance, and the glitter eye shadow still twinkled on her lids and brows. She was wearing a tightly fitted red sequin cocktail dress, red stilettos, and red lipstick. Eleni shifted from one foot to the other.

Surely her feet must be sore, too, especially in those torturous heels. Wincing at the thought, Silja asked, "Where are you going?"

Eleni took the flowers to the decorative table across the room. Gently, she laid them down next to the vases filled with the flowers that Ballard had sent after each performance of *Coppelia*—ten thus far. Against Silja's wishes, Natalia had put the flowers in the vases rather than return them as she had requested.

The diamond stud earrings in Eleni's delicate lobes glinted when she turned to catch Silja's attention. The prima ballerina's eyes narrowed.

"I have things to tend to," Eleni said. "I will see you before the matinee tomorrow."

"Everyone seems to have something to tend to tonight. All the girls were dressed up, like you. Am I missing something?"

"It is Saturday night. I suppose we have places to be. I'm sure you could, too, if you would just give Ballard Crafton a chance. He is American, like you, yes?"

Silja rolled her eyes. "Let's review: I was *raised* in America, and yes, I am an American citizen, but I was *born* in Russia, which makes me *Russian*."

Lifting a shoulder, Eleni glanced at her watch. "I will be late. I must go." With that, she rushed out the door.

Silja was left alone in the dressing room suite. The room was filled with the succulent smell of roses. The vases on the tables were filled with an array of colors representing their not-so-subtle connotation:

Red for love—check.

White for purity—she wasn't sure where he was getting that information. Regardless—check.

Pink for grace—check.

Yellow for friendship—check.

Purple for majesty—check.

And orange for desire—wouldn't want to leave that one out. Check.

Silja supposed that Ballard didn't want to leave out any emotion or subliminal message, so he simply covered all the bases by sending different colors or a combination of the colors every night. She noted that there were far more red and pink and orange roses than any of the other colors.

Whatever.

She could hear the janitorial staff vacuuming the hallways and the auditorium. The audience was gone, the orchestra was gone, and Eleni was the last of the dancers to leave.

She pulled her feet from the tub to dab them gingerly with a towel.

Yep, it was Saturday night and all Silja wanted to do was catch the bus to her apartment, take a hot shower, sip some hot tea, curl up with her cat, and get some much-needed sleep.

* * * * *

In the basement of the Mockba Theatre, a crowd had gathered in the reception room. While not particularly spacious, it was quite elegant with red velvet swags hung in the archways, gilded crown moldings, and crystal chandeliers hanging from the ceiling. A bar was set up in one corner. A violinist provided soft background music in another.

"It is ridiculous! An outrage! Dominik Potrovic should be included in the auction!" Ivan Belsky bit out in Russian. "A choice, that's what the contributors' should have! We spend a lot of money at these parties!"

Natalia waved at the bartender for a glass of wine while digging two pain relievers from her pocket. "I have already explained this to you, Ivan. Dominik is in a relationship with our choreographer, Edvar. He is not available for the auctions."

"Several of the dancers are married! Yet here they are—to be auctioned as the rest. I understand why Silja Ramsay is not present—she is an American. But there is no excuse for Dominik!"

"I do not understand. You always choose from the box filled with the ballerina's shoes, not the male dancers' shoes. So why do you fuss?"

"I enjoy the girls very much. But Dominik—"

"If you are not happy with our selection of dancers, pull your bid and be on your way."

Red-faced with frustration, Belsky let out a loud harrumph, and then stalked into the party just as Ballard Crafton rounded the corner.

"Where is Silja?" he asked Natalia while he searched through the party guests.

The room was filled with men, a few older women, and most of the dancers from the Novikov Ballet Company. Only one dancer in particular was missing ... Silja Ramsay.

Natalia picked up her glass of wine from the bar. "Silja is not ready to attend our little soiree yet. She hasn't been informed of my ... financial situation."

Ballard pulled a bracelet from his suit jacket. "Silja doesn't like diamonds?"

Natalia huffed at the sight of the bracelet that she thought she had convinced Silja to keep.

"She had this returned to me by messenger this afternoon," he said. "Doesn't she ... don't you understand just how wealthy I am?"

Natalia tossed two ibuprofens into her mouth, washing them down with the cabernet. "She still believes in love, Ballard—"

"I *am* in love with her!" he bellowed.

Taken aback by the outburst, the crowd hushed and turned in their direction.

Forcing a laugh, Natalia waved her hands carelessly at the crowd. She spoke to them in Russian, "Mingle, mingle, get to know our beautiful dancers."

With hesitant glances at Ballard, the crowd returned to their conversations. The women in attendance ran their hands up and down the male dancers' muscled arms while the men flirted mercilessly with the ballerinas.

"You told me that she would be here tonight, Natalia," Ballard said in a more hushed tone.

"As always, there are plenty of lovely ballerinas here to choose from this evening, Ballard. Forget Silja for now. I will keep working to make her come around. She still ... how do you say ... *pines* for another."

"Who?"

"I do not know this. Be patient. Pick another for this evening. Here ..." Natalia gestured to the bartender. He retrieved a box from behind the bar. Natalia took the box and offered it to Ballard. Lifting a brow, she said, "You may have first pick tonight, yes?"

"No, I am tired of spending time with ballerinas that I don't want. I only fantasize that she is Silja. I want *Silja!*"

Natalia set the box on the bar. Slowly, she dragged her gaze to meet his. He was like a spoiled child who had not received the gift that he desired on Christmas morning. No, he was worse—much worse. Finally, she decided to put Ballard Crafton in his place. "I am quite aware of what it is that you want, Ballard. But I must wonder ... will Silja meet the same fate as your other lovers?"

His eyes widened in raw indignation, except Natalia did not allow his glare to dissuade her. "The opera singer from New York who no longer sings—instead she sits in a home with head injuries so severe that she can barely speak, or the concert pianist whose fingers are now crippled from the hammer that was used on them? What could these women have done to make you so angry, Ballard? What kind of monster lies within? I am desperate to save the Novikov Ballet Company, this is true. But I won't let you destroy a beautiful dancer in her prime. How do you Americans say ... we understand each other, yes?"

Ballard's hands curled into fists of righteous agitation. The red flush started above the Armani tie that he wore around his neck and crept to his cheeks. He spun on his heels and marched out of the gathering.

Letting out a relieved breath, Natalia peered into the box which was filled with pointe shoes. Each shoe had the signature of the dancer from the Novikov Company to whom it belonged. Her nerves tightened the knot in her stomach and shame swelled in her chest. She took another long drink of the wine, and then she managed a faux smile for the crowd, who anxiously anticipated the beginning of the evening's event.

Natalia called out in Russian, "Who will be first to choose a pair of shoes tonight?" She held the box up high, shaking it. "Edvar! Where is Edvar?"

From the far corner of the room the ballet company's dance instructor and choreographer, Edvar Kozlovski, brushed his fingers through ballet dancer Dominik Potrovic's hair. After a whispered promise of return, he raised his hand calling back in their native Russian, "Here I am! Are you ready, Natalia?"

The crowd buzzed with excitement. The dancers exchanged nervous glances. All eyes were on Natalia.

"Yes!" she sang out. "Who is our highest bidder this evening? Who will get first pick of the shoes?"

Edvar fished a paper from the pocket of his jacket, and then he announced, "Ballard Crafton!"

Searching the room, everyone waited for Ballard to come forward to choose a shoe for his evening of sultry delight with the dancer whose name was on the shoe.

Natalia shook her head. "He had to leave. Who is the second?"

Edvar squinted in a big show of reading the next name on the list. He proclaimed, "Belsky!"

From the back of the crowd, the tubby man merrily trotted forward to where Natalia stood. The ballerinas were exchanging curled lips of derision—hoping that he would not pull their shoe from the box.

He wiggled his fingers in a show of anticipation of what lovely, well-toned ballerina would be his for the night. With a smirk on her lips, Natalia offered him the box filled with the male dancer's slippers. Glowering at her, he pitched the box aside. Natalia snorted when she offered him the box of pointe shoes. He reached into the box and snatched a pair of worn European pink pointe shoes. The crowd tensed while waiting for a name to be called when he handed the shoe to Natalia.

"Anna Antkowiak!" Natalia called out.

The young girl from Poland's shoulders drooped. Her face dropped. She was the newest member of the company. She hadn't signed on for this. She had heard whispers among the dancers that Natalia's ballet company was almost broke and about the after-performance requirements: prostituting the dancers for contributions to keep the ballet company above water. The only dancer exempt from the proceedings was the company's principal dancer, American Silja Ramsay.

This evening was her first time to be summoned by Natalia to the contributors' party. The call also came with a warning: not a word to Silja about the parties or you will be dismissed without a recommendation from the ballet company.

Anna could barely breathe when she saw Belsky's eyes scanning the crowd for her.

Locking eyes with the innocent girl, Natalia crooked her index finger at the ballerina to come forward to claim her date.

Trepidation filled Anna's face. Her stomach twisted into a tangle of knots when she saw the other dancers silently urge her to do as Natalia requested. Noticing the bulge in Belsky's trousers, she kept her head bowed while she crept through the crowd.

Belsky grabbed her by the hand to hurry her out the door.

Natalia clapped her hands. "Another happy contributor to the Novikov Ballet Company! I'm sure

Anna will make his night!" She shook the box again. "Who will be next to choose, Edvar?"

* * * * *

Silja stepped off the bus into the hoary night. She tightened her knit cap over her ears for the two-block trek to her apartment. With each step, her feet were screaming to be released from the boots that squeezed and tortured the blisters on her toes. They would begin to heal overnight, only to be pressed into her pointe shoes and ripped open once more during the matinee performance of *Coppelia* the next day. It was a definite possibility that she would loose a toenail. She was convinced that she would have the most disgusting-looking feet when she grew to be an old woman.

The snowflakes caught on her lashes while she made her way along the sidewalk toward her apartment building.

It seemed that it was always snowing in Russia. Even the summer months were chilly.

She loved Russia, but the truth was that if it weren't for her position in the ballet company she would be back at home in West Virginia sitting in front of a crackling fire with Grant. Well, not exactly—Grant now lived somewhere in Pennsylvania.

She stopped.

Wow. There he was again—Grant Ketchum— heavy on her mind. She hoped that it wasn't bad karma—that he was okay. The ex-Marine worked for some kind of covert security firm, and his job took him on some pretty precarious missions.

Trying to cast the thoughts out of her mind, she hunkered down into the collar of her wool coat while digging through her purse for the swipe card to get into the apartment building.

She pushed through the doors and made her way up two flights of stairs to her tiny residence. When she opened the door she was greeted by a soft meow. Purring, a calico cat welcomed her home from her curled-up position among the cushions on the sofa.

The cat jumped down from her cozy nest to rub her body along Silja's legs while she unwound her scarf and unbuttoned her coat. After stuffing her scarf, cap, and gloves into a sleeve and tossing the coat on a chair, Silja gathered the cat into her arms to tickle her tummy. The kitty had been a going-away present from Grant when she left for Russia five years ago.

"Well hello, Greta. Are you hungry?" Greta purred while leaning into the gentle caresses over her ears. "I'll bet you are. I'm starving. Let's see what we can do about that."

Greta climbed onto her mistress's shoulder. Silja opened a cabinet to fetch a can of cat food. The cat jumped to the floor while she opened the can and emptied the contents into a bowl. Greta set straight to eating her dinner.

Letting out a weary sigh, Silja looked around the small kitchen. Opening the fridge, nothing among the shelves looked very appetizing. She settled for one of the apples in the bowl on the counter.

Munching on the apple, she pulled the pins that held her bun in place to let her golden brunette hair spill down over her shoulders. She raked her fingers through the long tresses to loosen them from her scalp. Taking another bite from the apple, her eyes fell upon her laptop resting on the small desk near the window. *Grant.*

She hadn't communicated with Grant in over six months. She was too busy. She was always at rehearsal—or was it that communication was too much of a commitment, too awkward, or honestly, too painful? Without realizing it, she was making her way with measured steps toward the desk, the laptop, and the email function. Suddenly, there she was—standing right in front of the desk.

He had been in her thoughts all day.

She pulled the chair out.

He would love to hear that she was dancing the principal role in *Coppelia*.

She sat down.

A quick, short email couldn't hurt.

Biting her lip, her fingers hovered over the keys.

Three curtain calls—Grant would be thrilled to know that she'd had three curtain calls.

Oh, what the hell...

31

She typed:

> *Hi Grant,*
> *I hope this note finds you well and in good spirits...*

The cursor came to a stop. It blinked and blinked and blinked urging her to continue typing. Her fingers froze in place above the keys. Now what was she supposed to say? *I miss you? I'd love to see you? Are you dating anyone?*

She pressed *cancel.* Most likely he was on a mission somewhere dangerous or tropical wooing a beautiful spy for some pertinent information to save the good ol' USA or some other country from sure disaster. Her lips curled at the thought.

That's my hero.

Greta jumped onto the desk. She padded across the keys of the laptop. Taking the cat into her arms, Silja sat back against the chair.

Natalia's words from earlier that evening played over in her head. *"There are worse things in this life than to have a wealthy man yearn for your affections, Silja. Ballard Crafton could provide you with anything you desire in this world."*

Maybe Natalia was right. When she left home she foolishly thought that dance would be enough for her.

Since arriving in Russia she had taken only one lover, Dominik Potrovic. He was so handsome, and his body was so beautiful, much different than Grant's body. Grant was six foot three and one hundred ninety-eight pounds of solid, meaty muscle, with chiseled abs and arms. Dominik was slightly shorter and thinner. His muscles were tight and lean—he had the physique of a dancer, graceful, limber. Grant had the body of a warrior, hard, solid. Both were incredibly sexy in their own right.

She had spent three years with Grant. Within six months of the relationship with Dominik she'd discovered that he was only using her to make Edvar jealous. When the company's choreographer finally noticed Dominik, their relationship was over.

Poof!

She was so stupid, she'd felt humiliated, and she never took up with another dancer. Dancers were the only people who she really had any contact with.

She was so lonely. Except Ballard Crafton was not the man she wanted—she didn't know how to get the man she wanted.

Not anymore.

CHAPTER TWO

Malibu, California

In the darkness of the night, First Force operative Dan Garrison hunkered down in the brush on a hill high above a compound that belonged to porn film director Richard Roman. Dan listened intently for any radio communication from Grant Ketchum or Jack Haliday, who at that point had to be inside the compound. With night vision binoculars pressed to his face, he watched the estate for any and all movement from the small security staff on the premises. He was most impressed with their complacency. The two guards wore forty-fives strapped to their hips. He smiled. From the looks of them, they probably barely knew how to use them.

Dan, Grant, and Jack had been observing the compound from the hill for two days. The rent-a-cops stopped vehicles—mostly limos—at the gate, and then casually waved them through after they found their name on a clipboard. From the team's perch, they also watched their mark sunbathe on a balcony. Oh yeah, this was a tough mission.

The daughter of a high-ranking diplomat from Colombia was a dark-haired, well-endowed, caramel-skinned beauty. Anita Salazar would wander onto the balcony every afternoon, peel off her satin robe, grease up her incredible naked body with tanning lotion, and then ease onto a lounge to provide the operatives with a thrill for several hours. Hooyah!

Much to her daddy's disgust, Ms. Salazar had taken up with the middle-aged porn filmmaker and was starring in his dirty flicks, which were filmed inside the compound. The first objective of First Force's mission was to destroy the editing room where the movies were created before any of the diplomat's errant daughter's films were made public.

The second objective was to grab Ms. Salazar and take her to First Force headquarters in Harverton, Pennsylvania, where her father's security team was waiting to return her to Colombia.

The young woman was about twenty-three. She was old enough to make her own decisions; however, being the daughter of a diplomat didn't leave much room for such iniquitous indiscretions.

Dan checked his watch. Communication had been silent for over an hour while Grant and Jack made their way through the canyon pass, crept along the walls, and then rappelled into the back section of the estate. The security guards were a joke. They were only a formality, really. They were a presence in case amateurs attempted to break-in. Dan, Grant, and Jack were not amateurs—they were professional operatives who worked missions with focus, stealth, and agility. Especially this mission: it was an easy extraction, in and out, like a cakewalk at a kid's party.

"Explosives are set in the edit room. I'm in the east corridor. No security anywhere. Explain to me again why the CIA or Secret Service couldn't handle this job?" Grant whispered into his radio.

"Can you say, *'international incident?'*" Dan asked.

"So we're the scapegoats?"

"Very well-paid scapegoats. So don't screw this up."

"Cakewalk, Garrison. Easiest op in months."

"Famous last words," Jack warned through his radio. "There are two very large bodyguards watching TV in the living room. I haven't seen Richard Roman anywhere. He might be in the bedroom with the sex kitten. I'm at the end of the hall.

I've got your six. Go get the girl, Ketchum, and let's get the hell outta here."

"I'm not looking for her to go very willingly, so keep as quiet as possible," Dan added.

"No worries. We have a great diversion in the explosives downstairs, which are set to go off in ... four minutes and thirty-two seconds," Grant whispered. He crouched down beside a long decorative table outside the master suite.

"Not enough to bring the house down or kill anyone, right, Ketchum?" Dan inquired.

"I wouldn't want to be in the editing room when they go off. Otherwise, we're good. I'm goin' to visit Miss Salazar now." With that, Grant dashed to the door, quietly twisted the knob, and opened it just a bit for a peek into the suite.

Through the slight gap, he could see an elegant sitting room. He listened. Hearing no voices or movement, he slipped through the door, gingerly closing it behind him. Staying close to the wall, he crept toward another door that was partially open. He could hear movement inside the room.

"Heads up, Ketchum. Boyfriend coming toward the bedroom," Jack's voice filtered through his earpiece.

Shit. Grant ducked into a closet filled with negligees, feather boas, and sex toys—whips, crops, handcuffs, and things that he neither recognized nor wanted to know about. A feather from one of the boas floated from a hanger to tickle his nose. He stifled a sneeze.

"Anita ... what are you doing, baby?" he heard Richard say while stepping through the bedroom door. Grant peered through the tiny gap that he'd left open.

The beautiful Colombian woman stepped into the sitting room—wearing a red satin teddy, thigh-high stockings held up by rhinestone clips and black stilettos. Whoa. Her full, plump breasts bulged from the top of the teddy. Her smooth, curvy hips were completely bare.

"Oh baby," Richard moaned, "Didn't you get enough during filming this afternoon?"

Anita's Colombian accent was sensually husky. "Did you like my performance for the cameras this afternoon? Do you like how I look for you now? I want to reenact the scenes with you, baby."

He took her into his arms and kissed her. She raked her fingers roughly through his hair while his hands wandered lower over her firm, bare buttocks. Grant leaned back—fearing that he'd be in the closet longer than the three minutes till things started going boom!

Richard moaned, and then said, "We will do every scene, baby. But I want to take a shower first. Wait for me in the bedroom, and don't take any-thing off—I want you to strip nice and slow when I come out."

Grant let out the breath he'd been holding when he heard the spray of the shower crashing against the walls. Hmmm, Roman got in the shower rather quickly. Grant couldn't blame him. Easing the closet door open, Grant slipped into the sitting room, and then, with measured steps, he made his way to the bedroom.

Anita was dousing her breasts with body spray when he crept up behind her. She gasped and her eyes widened when she saw the reflection of a man wearing camo pants and a Kevlar vest in the vanity mirror.

Grant put his finger to his lips. "Don't be frightened, Miss Salazar. I'm here to take you home to your father," he explained.

Anger instantly filled her eyes. She let out one loud shriek and then another. Whipping her hand up, she sprayed him in the eyes with the perfume.

Immediately, his eyes burned and watered. He staggered back.

Screaming, she stepped past him to run toward the bedroom door.

"That's just perfect." he heard Jack wryly say in his earpiece. "Here come the bodyguards."

Two minutes until the explosives go off!

Grant dove on top of Anita—driving her to the floor.

The water in the shower came to a halt. He could hear Richard Roman calling from the bathroom, "Anita! Anita! Is everything okay?"

No, everything was not okay. The cakewalk had gone totally FUBAR! He could hear Richard shuffling in the bathroom like he was getting out of the shower and fumbling for his clothing. Grant struggled with the half-naked woman while she kicked and screamed and scratched. Finally he managed to hoist Anita over his shoulder while Dan yelled in his ear, "What the hell is going on in there? The guards are running toward the house!"

A spurt of gunfire exploded in the hallway. "Come on, Ketchum!" he heard Jack yell. "I'm holding them back! Let's go!"

With Anita kicking him madly in the gut with the pointy tip of her shoes, Grant dashed down the hallway toward Jack's voice. The young woman yelled and cursed at them in Spanish while dangling over Grant's shoulder with her bare derriere in the air. She beat him in the back with her fists.

Ducking behind a wall, Jack held the bodyguards at bay with a spray of gunfire.

Pulling his Glock from his shoulder holster, Grant rounded the corner. "This way!" he called to Jack, "Thirty seconds until she blows!"

Jack turned to follow. "Where's her freakin' clothes?" he shouted when he found himself staring at the beauty's exposed backside.

"What? You think I had time to go through her wardrobe?" Grant yelled over his shoulder while they raced down a wide corridor with Anita still screaming in Spanish and kicking and clawing at Grant's Kevlar vest.

As they approached the back entrance of the mansion where they had entered, two security guards stepped through the door. Trepidation filled their faces. Not knowing exactly what to do about the two men dressed in camo with blackened faces and their boss's half-naked girlfriend slung over one of the men's shoulder, they froze.

Grant let off a shot from his Glock above their heads. Terrified, both men dove for the floor.

Grant and Jack kept right on running for the door.

Kaboom!

The floor beneath them rocked.

The bodyguards, who had just arrived at the top of the corridor, sprawled to the floor. They covered their heads with their arms as if the entire house was crashing down around them.

Grant and Jack were now out of the house in the open yard. They sprinted across the lawn, past a fountain, and down a small embankment to where the service entrance for the compound was located.

A black SUV burst through the wrought iron fencing with Dan at the wheel.

Alarms sounded into the night at the breach in security.

"That's gonna wake the neighbors," Dan said when Jack yanked the back door open. Grant shoved Anita into the seat and hopped in next to her. Jack jumped into the front passenger's seat. Anita proceeded to punch Grant.

When he grabbed her hand, she bit him. "Dang!" he yelped.

Dan spun the vehicle around and speeded out the gate and onto the road.

Spitting out a long sentence in Spanish, the beautiful young woman pushed her long, dark hair away from her face to reveal the venom in her eyes.

"I have no idea what you're saying, sweetheart," Grant informed her.

Dan translated. "She said that she will make sure that her father boils our balls in hot oil for what we have done to her. I'm pretty sure she meant while they're still attached."

"Well that's gonna hurt like hell. Did you tell her that it was her father who sent us?" Jack asked over his shoulder.

"I did," Grant said, tersely.

"You will have to kill me, because I will not let you rape me!" Anita screeched in English.

"Oh, good God," Jack said, rubbing his eyes. "Would ya' cover her up, please?"

Grant reached behind the seat and grabbed a blanket. He tossed it in her face when she attempted to slap him. "Calm down, darlin', no one wants to rape you. We just want to get you back to Daddy so you can explain why you were making dirty movies. That should be loads of fun."

Anita covered herself with the blanket—pulling it all the way to her ears. "Richard was going to make me a star. All the stars start out this way," she bit out.

"Really? Who says?" Jack asked.

"Richard. He is a great American director."

"I'll bet," Jack muttered.

Dan's eyes flicked to the rearview mirror. "Hey, what happened to her head?"

A nanosecond later, Anita's fingers were dabbing her forehead above her right eye and getting covered with beads of fresh blood. Her eyes filling with rage, she punched Grant in the shoulder. "You! You did this to me! Now I am injured! My father will punish you first!"

Grant put his hands up in surrender. "Easy, let me see." She allowed him to examine the wound. "It's only a little cut. You probably hit your head on the wall when I tackled you. I think it'll be fine. We'll have Dr. Lee look at it when we get to headquarters."

Again, Anita spewed malevolent words in Spanish. Eventually, she fell silent—until she noticed Jack take a Hershey Bar from his camo pants. Her eyes brightened. "Chocolate?"

"Ahhh, the universal female language ... chocolate-ese," Chuckling, Jack broke off a section and handed it back to her.

As if Jack had just soothed a wailing baby, Grant let out a relieved breath, wiped a bead of sweat from his brow, and settled into a comfortable position.

Dan picked up his cell phone, thumbed a number, and then put it to his ear. "Little ... we'll be at the helipad in fifteen."

* * * * *

It had been a long flight from the helipad in Malibu, California, to Harverton, Pennsylvania, where the First Force headquarters were located. The helipad was privately owned by an old friend of Walt Wabash, First Force's leader. The helicopter had to stop several times along the way to refuel.

The team's four men—Dan, Grant, Jack, and the pilot, Stewart Little—were thankful for the noise from the rotors because they couldn't hear Anita's constant threats and cursing in Spanish. She was relentless. Watching her endless venting was tiring.

They took to nodding and smiling politely at the fuming woman, who was still clad in the satin teddy. The thigh high stockings hadn't fared well during the getaway.

Stewart Little did not smile or nod at the beauty. He scowled and growled under his breath while keeping his eyes firmly focused on the sky and the dials of the helicopter's dash. It was his best attempt at patience.

After a few refueling stops where Ms. Salazar was not permitted to exit the copter, Dan grew weary of the tantrums. He lay his head back and fell asleep. Jack and Grant were left to watch over the spoiled ex-porn star.

Hours later, they landed on the helipad at First Force headquarters. It was eight o'clock in the morning.

Anita had fallen asleep only an hour prior. Unwilling to deal with the woman for one more moment, Stewart jumped from the copter to file his flight report.

Only three men remained to wake the sleeping time bomb.

"I—I'm a dad and ... and Rayne's not going to like it," Jack said.

"What's your girlfriend got to do with anything?" Grant demanded.

"I don't know ... I just thought I'd put it out there. I mean look at her ... she's dressed in a freakin' ... whatever that is. What's Rayne gonna think if I walk in with ... *her?*"

"Wait a minute, dude. You watched her on the balcony with your tongue hanging out, just like Garrison and me."

"Yeah, but she was so far away, and she seemed so harmless."

"Gimme a break, Haliday." Grant turned to Dan Garrison. "C'mon dude, she's punched me, kicked me, and bitten me. You wake her up."

"I have anger issues with women."

"You do not!"

"I do now."

"Who put me in charge of the crazy porn queen?" Grant demanded to know.

"You're the one who carried her out of the house," Dan pointed out.

"It was the mission!"

"That's right," Dan said, "Now it's your mission to wake her up and get her into the house so we can hand her over to those poor schmucks who have to take her to her father."

"Shit, Dan, it might take all three of us to get her into the house." Grant gauged the distance between the helipad and the back door of the Georgian-style mansion that housed First Force. It was approximately three hundred feet.

Dan's spine stiffened. He exchanged glances with Jack. "He's right. Okay, Grant, you wake her up, and Jack and I will help get her into the house. Fair enough?"

Grant let out a disgruntled breath. With a shake of his head and indecipherable grumbling under his breath, he climbed into the copter and shook the sleeping beauty by the shoulder. "Miss Salazar...

Miss Salazar, we're at headquarters. Can you come with us, please?"

Anita slowly opened her eyes. Dragging her fingers through her hair, she sat up. Her Spanish accent was raspy from sleep when she asked, "Is my father here?"

"No, Ma'am," Grant said, "His security team is here to take you to him."

"Eh! It is story of my life. He is never there. He sends someone in his place to care for or fetch me," she explained. "Do you have parents? Mister ... What did you say your name was?"

"Yes, Ma'am, I have parents. They live far away. I don't see them much."

She blew out a breath. "My mother is a governess, and my father a diplomat. I was raised by nannies and security officers. I finally find a man who cares for me, a man who only wants the very best for me, and they ruin it. They send American soldiers to bring me back. They care nothing for me."

"Please come with me, Miss Salazar. Dr. Lee will want to do a routine exam to make sure you're all right, and of course we will provide breakfast." Grant offered his hand to her.

She grabbed the blanket to wrap around herself, and then she hesitated. With a curl to her lips, she tossed the blanket to the floor, took Grant's hand, and let him lead her from the copter.

When she stepped out, Jack's eyes widened. "Where's the blanket?" He almost panicked.

"It's a lovely morning. I don't need it," Anita said.

Jack looked at Grant, who shrugged. "You sure as hell do," Jack insisted. He went into the copter to retrieve the blanket. He wrapped it around her shoulders. Tossing him a dirty look, she held it in place and walked toward the house with the three men surrounding her.

With a duffel bag slung over his shoulder, Stewart Little caught up with them to bring up the rear.

Dr. Rayne Lee greeted them at the door with Jack's four-year-old daughter, Lil. They were flanked by two men who made up the Salazar security team.

While Grant ushered Anita through the door, she let the blanket fall to the floor. Rayne's eyes widened at the sight of the woman dressed in nothing but an extremely revealing teddy. She had lost the rhinestone clip that held the left thigh-high stocking in place. It was pooled at her ankle. The right stocking was still secured by its clip, but it was in shreds, with runners and snags. The cut above her eye was crusty with blood and her dark hair was askew. Nonetheless, Anita Salazar was stunning.

Brushing the blonde curls that had fallen into her eyes while cocking her head to one side, Lil asked, "Why is that lady wearing a bathing suit, Dr. Rayne?"

Taking in Rayne's censure, Jack quickly stepped past Anita and swept Lil up into his arms. He sang out of his shoulder at her, "Honey, I'm home."

As if he were a teenager who'd just arrived home with his parents' wrecked car and a drunken hooker in the back seat, Jack removed himself and his daughter from the room. Grant and Dan smothered a chuckle. Little saw nothing funny about it. He tossed his duffel bag aside and headed straight for the kitchen, where he could smell bacon cooking.

Nostrils flaring, Rayne pitched Jack a dirty look. Then, pulling her composure together, she managed a svelte smile and an almost hospitable tone. "Welcome to the First Force Headquarters, Miss Salazar. I'm Dr. Rayne Lee. I'd like to perform a routine exam, and then we can get you some ... um, clean clothes, and a good breakfast."

"That man is your husband?"

"No, he is not."

"He is very handsome."

"With a twisted sense of humor, I'm afraid."

"He cares for you, Doctor. I can see it in his eyes," Anita said.

Rayne's brows arched. She stared at Anita for a moment. Clearing her throat, she responded, "Please come with me, Miss Salazar." With the subject dropped like a hot rock, Rayne led the scantily clad woman down the stairs to the medical unit.

Wearing impassive expressions, as if Anita was dressed in a turtle neck sweater and jeans, the Salazar security team fell in line behind the two women.

Making their way into the kitchen, Dan slapped Grant on the back. "Well that went a helluva lot easier than we thought it would. It was a freakin' cakewalk."

Grant blew out a breath. "Yeah, she's their problem now."

The kitchen was thrumming with hungry men. After filling their plates with sausage, eggs, and pancakes, Jack handed them down the line while the other members of the team poured coffee into mugs. Grant and Dan took their seats at the table when Lil came bounding into the room sporting a black leotard, pink slippers, and a bright neon green tutu.

High up on her tippy toes with her arms over her head, she bourreed across the kitchen to where her father had taken his seat. "Look, Daddy! Look at my ballerina outfit! I'm gonna start ballerina lessons this week!" the child joyfully announced.

"Whoa, that was a quick change," Jack pointed out with a chuckle.

The room was filled with ooohs and aahs. The curls on her head whipped about as she twirled while watching the sequins on the tutu catch the light. Her innocent joy was simply infectious.

Wearing an ear-to-ear grin across his bristly face, Jack clapped his hands. "That's fantastic, baby! You look beautiful!"

Whirling around, Lil bumped into Grant's chair. He grabbed her arm before she tumbled to the floor. The little girl gazed up at him with wide eyes. She asked, "I'll have to practice more before I can be a real ballerina, isn't that right, Mr. Grant?"

He smiled and swallowed hard. "I think you'll make one of the prettiest ballerinas I've ever seen."

She beamed up at him.

"He's right," Jack agreed. He patted the chair next to his. "C'mon, sit next to me and have some breakfast."

Lil climbed into the chair between her father and Stewart Little. While Jack forked a pancake onto her plate, she said to Little, "You'll come to my recital, won't you Little Big Man?" Stewart let out a grunt. Dipping her finger into the pool of syrup on her plate, she said, "Good."

The corners of Grant's lips curled while he watched the exchange between the tiny girl and the big man over the rim of his coffee mug. Lil had dubbed Stewart "Little Big Man." She said it was because he was so big, yet his name was Little—she found that most interesting. Stewart found it most annoying—or so he pretended.

Grant couldn't help but think how all little girls dream of becoming a ballerina. At one time he was so very much in love with one such girl who made that very dream into a reality.

Silja Ramsay—Sil.

CHAPTER THREE

Grant was happy that the escapade with the crazy porn queen was over. Dressed in a pair of Rayne's scrubs, Anita Salazar and her security team drove to the airport where a private jet waited to take them to Colombia.

He felt a tinge of pity for her. She actually thought Richard Roman had her best interests at heart. She believed he loved her. How could she reason that a man who would film her having sex with different men loved her? Whoa. That was just crazy. It was sad. As beautiful as Anita Salazar was, she must have been so very lonely to be that desperate for a man's love.

Grant wondered what her father was going to say to her when she arrived home. Would he be angry? Or would he dismiss the entire incident and carry on business as usual? It was messed up.

Too tired to drive back to his apartment, Grant decided to stay at the mansion that served as head-quarters for some rest. He tossed his go-bag onto the bed in one of the guest rooms. The mattress dipped when he sank onto the edge of the bed. Dragging his fingers through his hair, he could feel the burn of fatigue in his eyes. He lay back across the bed, laced his fingers behind his head, and stared up at the ceiling.

Yeah, he could identify with Anita. The loneliness that his job incurred could be suffocating. He didn't have time to find or develop a relationship. His job wasn't relationship-friendly.

None of the guys on First Force were married or in a serious relationship, except maybe Jack.

That was different.

Jack and Rayne had been brought together under extenuating circumstances. Rayne was the head medic for First Force. She had lived at the mansion for several years before Jack came along after his wife was murdered. Walt hired him, and he and his daughter, Lil, lived at the compound with Rayne when he wasn't on an op.

There was no definite relationship between the two. Oh, there was a lot of flirting—especially on Jack's part. One could see the spark in Rayne's eyes when he was in the room, but she was hesitant to show any real affection toward the ex-Navy SEAL.

The team had a running bet—it was only a matter of time. Lucky bastard. Sooner or later Jack would have a good woman who loved and cared for him.

Grant couldn't picture that happening for him any time soon—perhaps never. Could've. Would've. *Should've.*

Oh, it wasn't that Grant didn't participate in a casual hook-up every now and then. Hey, he had a needs like any other man—the need to hear a woman's silky sigh and feel her warm body moving in rhythm beneath his.

Nonetheless, no matter how attractive the woman was, she never compared to Sil. Yeah, it was pretty unfair to the women—measuring them to Sil that way, but it was just the way he felt.

His left hand searched for the bag lying near his hip. Pulling it to his chest, he opened it to get out his iPad. Turning it on, he scrolled through the pictures of the one woman he could've had it all with, Silja Ramsay. The right side of his mouth hitched up when he admired the photos that she'd emailed him over the past five years slowly scroll by.

The first photo she'd sent shortly after moving to Russia. She was dressed in a beautiful purple sequined tutu. She had danced the part of the Sugar Plum Fairy in the Novikov Ballet Company's production of *The Nutcracker.* She looked incredible.

The second was a photo she'd sent of her ballet company with their arms wrapped around each other in the studio. And his favorite photo: A self-taken shot with her cell phone. She was in her apartment snuggling with Greta—the cat he'd given her as a going-away present.

He wondered if she still had Greta. He wondered if the ballerina ever thought of him. Probably not. He hadn't heard from Silja in over six months—or had it been a year? She was so beautiful. He had no doubt that she was probably involved with someone. He couldn't blame her. He certainly had nothing to offer her.

What could it hurt to send her a quick message? Just a short hello, how are you?

Rolling over on his stomach, Grant typed on the iPad:

> *Hey, haven't heard from you in a long time.*
> *How are you? What ballet are you dancing in?*
> *I—*

The curser bobbed and blinked urging him to continue, except he didn't know what else to say. I miss you? I made a terrible mistake by letting you go? Please come home? Not a chance. He hit *cancel*, turned the device off, and tossed it aside.

Most likely Silja was dancing the lead role in a ballet, receiving flowers from admirers, and bowing for curtain call after curtain call.

That's my girl.

Surrendering to those visions, Grant pushed up from the bed, pulled off his T-shirt and kicked off his boots, pants, boxers, and finally his socks.

He went into the bathroom to get a hot shower—maybe a cold shower.

He needed to wash it all away: The memory of Anita Salazar, the woman who was blessed with unbelievable beauty, yet cursed with a loveless existence. The memories of the ballerina he loved, and yet who he had let dance out of his life five years ago.

Stepping into the shower, he let the water wash over him. The steam engulfed him while the spray flattened his hair to his scalp. The water ran across his broad shoulders, his sculpted chest, down his lean hips, and over his tight buttocks.

He dipped his face into the spray, hoping it would clear his overactive thoughts. Silja danced through his mind's eye. He ached for her. Oh how he wished that she were in the shower with him right now. Leaning further under the spray, he imagined her long legs wrapped around his waist and her naked breasts pressing against his chest. She would press her lips to his as he eased inside her, and together under the heat of the water, they would climb to that place where nothing mattered except the feel, the touch, the ecstasy—oh yeah; he doubted that the rest he so desperately needed would come any time soon.

Grabbing the temperature knob, he turned it to cold.

* * * * *

Mockba Theatre, Yekaterinburg, Russia

The cast of *Coppelia* was busy prepping their muscles for the performance, set to start in ninety minutes.

The booms holding the backdrops had been raised. The scenery and props had all been pushed to the backstage area to create an open space for the dancers to warm up before the matinee performance of *Coppelia*. Ballet barres had been set up along the entire length of stage left. Dancers were stretching their legs on the barre while others lowered into deep grande plies. Center stage was left open for floor stretching and pirouettes.

Her legs stretched out in a wide straddle, Silja sat on the ballet mats—flexing and pointing her aching feet. She had decided to forego the lamb's wool today and try gel pads inside her pointe shoes. Slowly, she lowered her chest to the mat while stretching her arms over her head. Her upper body lay flat on the mat with her legs extended out to the side. It felt good.

While stretching her spine and her legs, she heard Natalia call out, "Eleni ..." and then she spoke a long sentence in Russian that Silja did not understand, although she heard Anna Antkowiak's name mentioned among the foreign words.

Eleni replied, "No."

Letting out a huff, Natalia asked, "Silja, have you seen Anna?"

She looked up to see Natalia cup her chin in her hand while scanning the stage area with a worried look in her dark eyes. "Not since last night's performance, no," she told her.

"Where could she be? I will have to replace her if she isn't here within the next thirty minutes." Natalia nodded toward the edge of the orchestra pit where Ballard Crafton was watching. "You have a visitor, Silja."

Silja's eyes followed the hitch in Natalia's chin. She let out a sigh.

Natalia urged, "Go to him. What will it hurt to talk to him or spend a short time with him? But make it quick, you have makeup to apply."

Behind her, Dominik landed a triple pirouette. Then, he strutted over to Silja to offer his hand to her as she pushed up from the mat. "Yes, go, Silja. He is of your type."

Once on her feet, Silja pulled her hand from Dominik's with a puzzled look on her face. "What's it to you, Dominik, what kind of man I need?"

"Pfft ..." was his only remark before he strutted away with a shrug.

Begrudgingly, she made her way to the edge of the stage.

Ballard was a handsome man, very distinguished, with salt-and-pepper hair. He was tall and thin and wore a suit very well. He smiled wide when Silja approached.

Handing her a single red rose, Ballard said, "I'm looking forward to the matinee. I've enjoyed all the performances immensely. You are a wonderfully talented dancer, Silja."

She took the rose from his hand, and then, dragging her gaze to meet his, she said, "Thank you, Mr. Crafton."

"Please, Silja, call me Ballard. I was hoping that you would do me the honor of having dinner with me after the matinee?"

What part of "no" did Ballard Crafton not understand? Then again, perhaps Natalia was right—what would it hurt to spend a short bit of time with him? What harm could come from having dinner? He would probably take her to a lovely restaurant, and she'd have a decent meal instead of the soup and peanut butter sandwich that was waiting for her at home.

She favored him with a svelte smile. "All right, Ballard, you can pick me up at my apartment around six. I live at—"

"I know where you live, Silja. I will be there at six sharp. Now I have so much more to look forward to than just the ballet. I will have the pleasure of a lovely companion at my dinner table." With that, he turned and left.

Wait a minute. He knows where I live? That gave her the total creeps. Maybe having dinner with Ballard Crafton wasn't such a good idea. She might get more than a decent meal. She might get more than she bargained for. It was too late for second thoughts. She had already agreed to the date, and Ballard was already making his way up the theatre aisle with a nip in his step.

When Silja turned to head for the dressing suites, the stage crew was clearing the barres away and the booms that held the backdrops were slowly lowering into place. Only a few dancers remained milling about the stage.

She flinched when someone nudge her. Turning, she found Eleni smiling at her while adjusting the clip on her left diamond stud earring.

"You have decided to give Ballard a chance, yes?" Eleni inquired.

"It's only a dinner date. I haven't agreed to bear his children or anything like that, Eleni."

Wrapping her arm around Silja while leading her toward the backstage area, Eleni tossed her head back with a laugh. "You never know, Silja. You never know."

* * * * *

A young dancer from Moscow who had only been with the company for four months won the opportunity to replace Anna as one of the Chinese dolls in the matinee. The young girl was thrilled, but the rest of the dancers seemed edgy during the performance. After the show had ended, the dressing room suite was unusually quiet.

Wiping the glitter eye shadow from her lids and brows, Silja measured the jittery women in the reflection of the mirror at her lighted vanity. Some of the girls whispered among themselves as they stripped from their costumes and hung them on the racks. Silja couldn't understand what they were saying.

Finally, Eleni sat down at the vanity next to hers and pulled the pins from her hair.

Silja asked, "What's wrong? Why is everyone so on edge?"

Eleni didn't look at her when she plucked the fake eyelashes from her lids. "You did not notice that Anna never showed up this afternoon? They are worried that something has happened to her."

"Like what?"

Still Eleni did not look at Silja. Her eyes remained focused on the mirror. "I do not know. Perhaps something happened to her last night after the show. No one has seen or heard from her. She does not answer her cell phone."

"That's terrible."

Eleni finally turned to her with eyes as cold as winter, and a tone that was just as frigid. "Yes, Silja, it is."

CHAPTER FOUR

Knowing that Ballard would take her to an elegant restaurant, Silja dressed in a cocktail dress that was dazzling yet conservative. She made sure that she had spared the cleavage—the neck line ran along the bottom of her throat, dipping low in the back, drawn up with long sleeves. Made of pink satin, the dress had an overlay of black lace. It showed off her slender physique and clung to her curves. Her long legs were bare.

She managed to hide her bloody toes by wearing a pair of closed black stilettos. Needless to say, her feet burned and ached and screamed for mercy all evening.

Silja was thankful that the theatre was closed on Monday. Ahhh, a day off. She planned on soaking her feet, curling up on the couch with Greta, and watching the American television shows that she'd recorded all week long on her DVR.

Only five more performances of Coppelia remained. Afterward the company would enjoy a two week hiatus before returning to prepare for the next production. She was seriously considering a trip to the United States. Maybe look up some old friends. Hmmm, maybe she'd drop in on Grant Ketchum ... maybe.

"Silja ..."

Ballard's voice brought her back to the present. By the look on his face, he must've been trying to get her attention for a few moments. She blinked back. "I'm sorry ... you were saying ..." She suddenly realized that the chef was standing next to her chair.

Ballard said, "I come to this restaurant quite often, so the chef indulges me with some of my favorite New York foods, like cheesecake. He wants to know what kind of sauce you'd like over yours: raspberry, chocolate, perhaps cherry?"

"They all sound wonderful, you choose."

Smiling, Ballard fell back against the seat with his hands over his heart. "Ahhh, a girl after my own heart. She's actually going to have dessert. Most women bypass it because they are so afraid to gain an ounce."

"Are you kidding? I'm thrilled to death to have cheesecake. No way am I going to pass it up."

He turned to the chef. "We'll both have cherry topping, thank you, Nikolai." After the chef hurried away, Ballard turned to Silja. "What are you thinking? You're miles away."

"I'm sorry. I'm rather tired, and to be honest my feet are killing me."

"Do you have blisters?"

"Dozens."

Ballard pushed his chair out to kneel next to her. "Let me see."

Thrown off and embarrassed, Silja's eyes flicked around the restaurant to find people staring at them as if Ballard were about to propose. She didn't know what he had planned, but she was very uncomfortable with whatever it was. "Oh, no, that's really not necessary ..."

Ignoring her request, he gently took her by the knees and swiveled her legs out from under the table.

Silja swallowed hard. It was silly, but she felt panicked. She insisted, "Really, they're fine, Ballard."

But he wasn't listening. With a velvet touch he removed her left shoe. Holding her foot in his hand as if it were as fragile as fine china, he examined the broken and swollen skin. His lips fell into a thin line. Silja didn't know what to do. The women at the surrounding tables were watching with expressions of pure adoration, like it was a fairytale moment unfolding before their eyes.

Then, Ballard did something that she was completely unprepared for—he lifted her foot and kissed each swollen toe and each brilliant red blister. Frowning, he ran the pad of his finger over the toenail that was cracked and discolored.

The women at nearby tables drew their hands to their chests in awe. Silky sighs and hushed comments could be heard throughout the room. Even the wait staff stopped mid-chore to take in the sight.

Silja cupped her hand over her mouth in complete shock. She was not only taken aback by his actions, but also by the reaction that her body was having to it—everything female was clenching with a tinge of arousal. *What?*

Tenderly, Ballard set her foot to the carpet and repeated the sensual healing ritual with the other foot.

He dragged his heated gaze to meet her wide-eyed stare. In a husky whisper, he said, "I worship you, Silja. I would kiss your feet every day if you were mine."

She let out a quiet gasp before she could call it back. She was surrounded by the gentle moans of envy from the women in the room.

Measuring her with his intense gaze, Ballard's mouth lifted into a salacious curl. Silja could feel her lips returning the favor without her permission—she had no control, they simply responded.

Picking up her shoes, he returned to his seat. He placed the shoes on the empty chair next to him, just then the chef arrived with their dessert.

Silja was utterly speechless. Her mouth was suddenly dry. She couldn't deny how incredibly sexy the entire moment had been. Was Ballard Crafton beginning to rock her world? She swallowed hard again. Unable to think of anything to say, she picked up her fork and dug right into the cheesecake. It was the best she'd ever had.

* * * * *

At the restaurant, they talked for hours.

Silja told Ballard how she had been born in Russia and spent her first two years in an orphanage. She was then adopted by the Ramsays and was raised in West Virginia. She also talked about how her wonderful parents had been killed in a car accident. Silja couldn't deny how she missed the States, but Russia was her home—for the present.

Ballard told her he'd only been living in Russia for a little more than a year and longed for all things American.

"What brought you to Russia?" she asked.

"I moved Crafton Technologies to Russia because I found brilliant engineers and scientists that I wanted to employ, but they refused to leave Russia, or perhaps they were not permitted to leave," he explained. "In any case, I moved in order to get the best experimental results for our serums."

"Oh, what kind of serums does your company produce? Nutritional? Body building?"

The left side of Ballard's mouth lifted. "You're very close. We are involved in cutting-edge scientific technology funded by the Russian gov—" Biting his lower lip, he hesitated, and then he half-smiled. "If I continued it would truly bore you and, if nothing else, I don't want to be a boring older man."

Silja looked up to realize that the restaurant was empty—except for them. Her cheeks flushed. She whispered, "Ballard...everyone is gone. We should leave so they can close the restaurant and go home."

Taking note of the empty tables that had been re-set for the next day, Ballard couldn't help but chuckle. "I was so immersed in our conversation that I didn't even notice everyone had left. Come ... I'll take you home. I know that you are tired from your wonderful performance this afternoon." He got up to pull out her chair.

Silja pointed out, "I need my shoes."

"No, you don't. My car will be parked right out front."

"But ..."

"No worries, Silja. I always have everything under control—always."

After slipping her coat over her shoulders, he palmed her elbow to lead her out of the restaurant. When they reached the lobby Ballard's body-guard was waiting inside the door. With a nod from Ballard, the large Russian man opened the door. Ballard swept her up into his arms to carry her through the snowy night to his waiting limo. The chauffeur smiled and tipped his hat as Ballard carefully set her into the vehicle and then slipped in beside her. Again, Silja was taken aback—literally swept off her feet by this handsome older man.

Twenty minutes later, the limo pulled up in front of her apartment building. The chauffeur opened the back door. She could see the same security guard slide from the black SUV behind them and hurry up the steps to stand next to the door. Ballard took her swipe key, and, without asking, he carried her up the stairs, opened the door, and then gently set her down inside.

He turned to the very large, very no-sense-of-humor-looking guard who had escorted them. "Wait here," Ballard instructed.

Carrying her shoes, he walked her up the two flights of stairs to her apartment door.

"I had a wonderful evening, Ballard. Thank you so much," Silja said.

"No ... thank you for blessing me with your companionship. Every man in the restaurant hated me this evening."

Silja felt her cheeks flush. Nonetheless, she asked the question that had been on her mind all the way back to her apartment. "Do you always have a bodyguard with you?"

The right side of his mouth lifted. "I'm a very wealthy man in a foreign land, Silja. One can never be too careful." He added, "I hope you will have dinner with me again very soon." He lowered his lips to gently caress hers. The kiss was brief, as if he were being very careful of unspoken boundaries that she might have. With a svelte smile, he handed her the shoes, and then he left her standing at her door.

She listened until she heard the front door of the building close before letting herself into her apartment. Greta jumped down from the sofa to greet her. Tossing her coat to a chair, Silja gathered the cat into her arms and stroked her head.

"I think I may have misjudged Mr. Crafton, Greta. Maybe I should accept his gifts, and maybe I should leave my past where it belongs ... behind me." She nuzzled the cat.

She carried Greta into the bedroom and set her on the bed. After stripping from the dress, she left it lying on the floor. She looked down at her mutilated feet. A smile slithered across her lips at the memory of the handsome, sophisticated older man kissing each foot so tenderly, so ... lovingly. How could he want to touch such ugly feet with his mouth? *Ick.* A sultry shiver found its way down her spine. Whoa.

It was late, 1:30 a.m., and even though she didn't have a performance or a rehearsal tomorrow, she needed to get to bed, although she was quite certain that rest wouldn't come any time soon.

* * * * *

Monday was going just as Silja had planned—quiet, peaceful, restful.

She couldn't help but think about Ballard Crafton. While soaking her feet in the Epsom salts, the memory of how he'd caressed her feet with his lips wandered into her mind. Pinching back the lace curtains, she sipped hot tea and watched the snowflakes cascade past her window. She thought of the delicious coffee that had been served with the cheesecake, and how Ballard had carried her through the snowy night to his limo. The evening couldn't have been more perfect if she had scripted it herself. Only she would've never planned an evening with Ballard—she would've chosen Grant.

What a delightfully unexpected turn of events.

Later in the afternoon, she decided to watch the television programs that she'd recorded when another thought crept into her mind: *I wonder if anyone has heard from Anna?* She hoped that nothing had happened to the young dancer who hadn't shown up for the matinee the day before.

Anna couldn't have been older than nineteen or twenty. She was a lovely girl who was quiet and rather shy. Anna danced the part of one of the Chinese dolls in the ballet—she made an adorable doll, and she danced the part so very well.

Perhaps she'd overslept. The rehearsal and the performance schedule for *Coppelia* had been so grueling that Silja could understand if she had slept through an alarm. She didn't know how Natalia or Edvar would react to that. Anna may not get her part back. She may very well be demoted to one of the groups of town folk who danced in many of the scenes. That would be a shame.

Silja's thoughts were interrupted by a knock at her door.

Pausing the DVR and setting Greta aside, she hurried to the door. A young Russian man stood in the hallway holding a gift bag.

Through his broken English he managed, "Silja R-R-Rumsie? I deliver for you."

Silja took the bag from his hand and then went to her purse on the counter. She gave him a tip, and then after closing the door, she took the bag to the sofa while pulling out the colorful tissue until she came to something that was wrapped in yet more tissue. Greta climbed up onto her shoulder to bat at the delicate paper as she tore it from a furry white teddy bear. Sporting a bright purple bow, the fluffy creature held a box of Band-Aids.

Silja smiled. She didn't have to guess, she knew who had sent the darling little bear—Ballard. Peering into the bag, she found a tiny card that read:

I hope this bear will warm your heart, and the Band-Aids will protect your pretty little toes.

All my love,
Ballard

Her heart swelled. It had been so long since she'd been courted in this manner. So long since a man had cared for her the way Grant had.

Hokay, Ballard Crafton was older than her—yet not as old as she had first thought. Ballard was quick to disclose that he was only forty-eight during dinner. Older, but not horribly so to her twenty-seven years—while Grant and Dominik were both twenty-nine. Ballard obviously had strong feelings for her, and she could feel something inside growing toward him, too.

It was wonderful to feel that warmth inside again after so much time, after so much heartache, and after so much loneliness.

Snow fell steadily from the gray sky as the day gave way to early evening. The scene below her window was like a postcard. People huddled in heavy coats and scarves scurried through a city park to get to the warmth of home.

Silja turned the TV off to read when another knock at the door brought her to her feet. Through the peephole she could see Ballard standing in the hallway.

She turned away from the door—panicked.

Her hand immediately went to her hair, which was drawn up in a cheap plastic clip, and she was wearing the most god-awful pair of sweats. She looked a complete wreck.

From the hallway, Ballard's voice called, "I know you're fussing about how you look, Miss Ramsay. But here's the big news: you would look gorgeous in a gunnysack. Besides, I come bearing gifts of pizza and cheesecake. Won't you please let me in? It's cold in the hallway."

Okay, how could she turn down that offer?

Her lips curled as she opened the door to find the handsome older man looking surprisingly stunning in a pair of jeans and a leather coat. His cheeks and nose were red from the nip outside. Indeed he held a box of pizza in one hand, a box with a cheesecake in the other, and a spicy smile on his lips.

"Pizza and cheesecake, evidently you've wooed women before, Mr. Crafton," she teased.

He liked it. "Every evening, Miss Ramsay, but only after six. I have my business to tend to."

"Come in." She stepped aside. "I got the adorable little bear, thank you."

"No returns?"

Silja felt ashamed for the way she'd treated him. She replied, "No returns."

Scanning her tiny apartment, he set the boxes on the counter. His eyes fell upon the cat cuddled in an afghan on the couch. "Who do we have here?" he asked while Silja took the leather jacket from his shoulders, and carefully laid it on a chair.

"Oh, that's Greta."

Upon hearing her name, Greta promptly jumped down from her cozy bed and made her way over to check out the stranger in their kitchen. Ballard scooped her up into his arms to stroke her head and ears. Purring, Greta tilted her head into the caress.

Feeling rather excited that he'd dropped in unexpectedly and watching him askance, Silja took plates and glasses from the cupboard. Mid-chore, she remembered that she had a bottle of wine in the pantry. Quickly, she retrieved a corkscrew from the drawer and the bottle of rosé that she found tucked toward the back of the pantry. She uncorked the wine to let it breathe. *Hmmm, are you supposed to let a rosé breathe? Should it be chilled?* Heck, she wasn't even sure if it was the proper wine to serve with pizza—or cheesecake—but she was certain of one thing: Ballard Crafton would be too much a gentleman to mention a mistake. That in mind, she figured that she was good to go.

With the rosé breathing on the counter and Ballard still making a fuss over Greta, she set the table with the plates, paper napkins, and the two wine glasses that she owned. Brushing a few loose tendrils from her eyes, she leaned a hip against the counter, unable to suppress the arch that flirted with the edges of her lips.

Greta was really eating up the attention that Ballard was dishing out. "You like cats, I see," she said with a smile in her voice.

"I like all animals. Greta is very sweet and loving. Like her mistress, no doubt," he said, tossing her a wink.

Sexy.

"Everything is ready—I hope you like rosé. It's the only wine I had on hand. I'm not sure it's the proper wine to go with pizza."

Gently, he placed the cat on the chair with his jacket and went to the tiny table set for two. "Any wine goes with pizza, as long as you are enjoying the company that you are drinking it with." He poured a generous portion of wine into the glasses.

As they ate the pizza and the cheesecake, Silja was mesmerized by how striking Ballard looked in a casual setting. He didn't look around at her simple dwelling with his nose out of joint, as if it weren't good enough for him. Instead, he sipped the wine, chatted freely, and flirted even more freely. His sense of humor was delightful. Yep, it was alluring. After all, she was accustomed to seeing Ballard in fine suits and silk ties, imposing, stunning. Yet this evening, here he sat in her kitchen in faded Wranglers and a soft green cotton shirt that he had left untucked. The Rolex on his left wrist was the most extravagant piece of his wardrobe and yet it, too, had a relaxed, laissez-faire persona of its own. This man had a style and a scent—and a sensual demeanor that was stimulating her libido moment by moment.

In a desperate need to escape her thoughts and craving, Silja pushed away from the table. "Oh, I'm stuffed. Thanks so much for the pizza and cheesecake. Would you like to sit in the living room? It's a bit more comfortable."

Ballard stood and poured two more glasses of wine before he followed her the very short distance into the living room. Setting the glasses on the coffee table, he noticed a framed photo of Silja with a young man in a military uniform sitting on a porch swing. He picked the picture up to examine it for a moment.

"Who is this handsome young man?" he inquired, trying to sift out the bother in his voice.

Smiling, Silja replied, "A very old friend. At the time of the picture he was in the Marines."

"He looks like more than a friend in the photo."

"At the time he was."

Natalia's words from Saturday evening came rushing back to him, *She still ... how do you say ... pines for another."* His upper lip wrinkled in agitation at the reminder while he set the frame on the end table—face down. "And yet there he is," he muttered under his breath. He was unwilling to accept any form of competition.

He pulled the clip from her hair to let it spill about her shoulders.

Silja was taken aback, except she wasn't frightened or threatened. With all her doubts and reservations, she felt that she'd misjudged this older, handsome, and oh-so-charming man. She wasn't sure where the evening was heading, but she was most certain that she would follow right along. It had been so long since she'd been with a man—a man who was truly passionate about her—and she was having no problem finding that passion in Ballard's deep brown eyes.

Yet, something else flashed in those eyes once again—a dangerous heat that she hadn't noticed the night before. For a second, she found it unsettling.

Disrupting her thought, Ballard crooned. "I never get to see your hair down, Silja. It is so beautiful. Everything about you is beautiful, right down to your very sore toes," he whispered as he brushed a wisp of hair from her cheek with the pad of his thumb. He leaned in to press his lips to hers. When he discovered that she was willing, he deepened the kiss—pushing his tongue into her mouth. She tasted of the wine. He welcomed her as she pressed her body closer to his and wrapped her arms around his neck.

He could feel the ache of his erection when she slowly retreated from the kiss. Her eyes dragged open, and the corners of her full and swollen lips arched. Her hair fell around her face in loose tendrils. The pupils of her almond-shaped eyes were dilated, filled with a longing he had hoped to find. A fresh spade of hunger dug into him. He ran his fingers through her long tresses to swallow her into his arms once more.

"I want to make love to you, Silja. I want to take you to bed and make you cry out my name, and then I want to hold you through the night," he whispered into her hair. His hands found their way under her sweatshirt. Ever so lightly, his fingers caressed her spine, hesitating at the clasp of her bra. He pressed his mouth to hers. He wanted her and he felt that she would give herself to him.

Yet, it was too soon.

He didn't want to risk scaring her away. His hands fell to her hips. He withdrew from the kiss.

Expelling a deep sigh, he said, "But not tonight. Not now. I want to wait until we know each other a little more. I want you to know that you are not a passing fancy or a one-night stand."

He could feel her droop in his arms as if he'd just kicked her cat.

It was a good sign. He would bed her the next time they were together. With a quick snort, he cupped her chin in his hand and looked into her sultry gaze. "One more glass of wine, and I'll be on my way before I change my mind." With that he picked up the glasses and placed one in her hand.

She said nothing, although within the graceful frame of her slender body, he could see that she was almost pouting.

"Are you sure you want to go?" Silja asked.

Quickly, she cupped her hand over her mouth. Had she said what she thought she said? Embarrassed and stunned by her own brash, shameless question, she took a swig of the wine. Maybe it was the wine talking. It had to be the wine.

She was not in the habit of asking a man for sex. Not Grant. Not Dominik—certainly not Ballard. Except, yes, indeed, that's exactly what she had just done.

Mortified, she slid her gaze to meet his through her lashes. He was smiling at her—or was it a smirk? It didn't matter. She deserved whatever expression Ballard Crafton tossed at her.

There it was again—that flash of heated intensity—danger.

Silja wasn't accustomed to drinking more that one glass of wine in a sitting, and justly, the wine was educing heady sensations. She licked her lips— wanting to taste his mouth again, wanting more than the evening had offered.

What was wrong with her? When was the last time she'd felt this way? Obviously, it had been too long. On some level, the whole thing didn't feel right. Was the age thing still niggling at her? Was there something in his eyes that was sending a warning?

Perhaps.

Somehow, she didn't care. She wanted him to touch her, to strip her naked, and to make love to her, heated skin sliding over heated skin. She wanted to let him do whatever he had in mind that would make her call out his name while her back arched away from the sheets as the orgasm exploded through her body.

His Adam's apple bobbed while the wine made its way down his throat until finally the glass was empty. She found that simple, involuntary movement tempting.

Measuring the self-reprimand that was taking place behind the ballerina's eyes, Ballard placed the empty wine glass on the coffee table. He said in a husky voice, "No, I'm not sure that I want to go, but I promise you this: when I make love to you, Silja, you will not want another man." He pulled her to him again and kissed her hard, primal, possessive. When he pulled away, he murmured, "Good night, Silja."

She was dazed—unable to move from her spot as she simply watched him walk to the chair, gently move Greta aside, and then shrug into his coat. He hesitated at the door long enough to pitch a sultry nod before he stepped into the hallway.

Some would have considered him overconfident. Some might have thought him cocky, smug, arrogant, or brash. Silja found him to be one of the sexiest men she'd ever met...

Other than Grant Ketchum.

She plopped into the chair. Purring, Greta jumped onto her lap. Caressing the cat's head, she laid her head back against the soft fabric and closed her eyes—thinking about Ballard.

The wine was still working her over, except yes... yes, there was something that niggled at her about Ballard Crafton. There was something about the man's eyes, oh they were enthralling, no argument there, but there was also something dark lurking— dangerous, like a furious thunderstorm about to erupt in churning skies. A shiver found its way down her spine. *Desire or apprehension?* She wondered.

His eyes were nothing like Grant's: soft brown and oh-so sexy. If she were being honest with herself, Grant's eyes could stir like a fierce thunderstorm as well. Then again, she couldn't rightly decide if Ballard's eyes always held that edge because she hadn't gazed into them as much as she had Grant's.

Whoa.

You're not being fair at all, Silja, she scolded herself. *It's not fair to compare Ballard to Grant—they are different people—different men. Ballard is the here and now. Sadly, Grant is part of your past,* she decided.

With that she resolved to give Ballard a fair shot—
but to keep a close eye on those churning skies.

CHAPTER FIVE

Grant woke with a jolt when he heard his cell phone signal that a text message had just been received.

In his line of work, one never slept deeply. It didn't take much noise to wake him. The room was dark. The pearly light of morning crept through a slight gap in the drapes. He had gone to bed in a guest room at First Force headquarter early in the day—the sun had been shining.

Glancing at his watch, he checked the time. It was six o'clock in the morning. Wow. He dragged his fingers through his bed-tousled hair. He'd slept for quite some time.

He snatched the phone from the nightstand, and then, lying back against the pillow, he read the message from First Force's leader, Walt Wabash: *All operatives: assignment. HQ 0800.*

Grant dropped the cell phone to his chest. At least he didn't have to go very far for the meeting—only downstairs.

Sighing, he hoped Anita Salazar hadn't escaped her daddy's security team. If she had, Garrison or Haliday would be carrying her out of harm's way this time.

Rolling over, he tried to find a comfortable spot to lay his head for two more hours. The icy February rain beat softly against the bedroom window. It was a great morning to sleep in. The only thing missing was someone to snuggle up under the blankets and listen to the rhythm of the rain with.

After several minutes of tossing, Grant decided to get up, drink some coffee, and work out at the gym before the meeting.

Leaving two days' worth of whiskers on his face, Grant pulled on a pair of sweats and a T-shirt. He made his way through the hallway and down the winding staircase. At one time, the basement was home to a servant's quarters. Now, it housed the small but well-equipped medical unit and a gym.

When Grant pressed through the door, he was surprised to find Jack dabbing his sweaty face with the corner of a towel slung around his neck while he jogged on a treadmill.

"You're up early," Grant said.

"Couldn't sleep. You got the text message?"

"Yeah, is Walt here?"

"Naw, he's at the house in Rosemount. It's just you, me, Rayne, and Lil. That said, when Lil's around it almost seems like there's twenty extra people in the house," Jack said with a smile in his voice.

Grant chuckled as he stepped onto the treadmill machine next to the one Jack was using. "Yeah, Lil's always a party waiting to happen." He asked, "Do you know anything about the op?"

"I know that it's out of the country, but that's about it. Walt was still gathering intel when he called last night."

"Sure hope it's not Colombia."

Jack snorted. "No, Walt talked to Anita's father. She's safe at home ordering the maids around. I don't think we'll be hearing from her again. At least I hope not." Mopping his face with the towel, he stepped off the treadmill. "I'm gonna hit the shower. I'm sure the team will start to arrive within an hour or so."

* * * * *

Vehicles started arriving at the compound shortly after seven o'clock. The First Force team had gathered by eight sharp in Walt Wabash's office, which was set up like a "situation room" or, as Rayne often referred to it, the "bat cave." Walt and team coordinator, Clark Rhodes, were to brief the team on a mission that would take them to the Ukraine within forty-eight to seventy-two hours.

As they filtered into the office and settled into chairs, Lil delivered a plate of fresh doughnuts to the operatives. However, when she arrived at her father's chair, she held the plate out of his reach in order to present Jack with a multigrain muffin. Taken aback by the action, he winced at it as if his daughter was handing him a dead rodent.

"What's this?" he groused after watching everyone else in the room take jelly filled doughnuts, cream puffs, and cinnamon dipped bear claws from the plate.

"Your blood work results came back with high cholesterol counts from the physicals last week. We need to get those numbers down, Mr. Haliday," Rayne announced from where she leaned against the door jamb with her arms folded under her breasts.

The team chuckled under their breath while Jack looked down at his unappealing breakfast and then up at Rayne. Recovering quickly, the left side of his mouth lifted into an ornery smirk. "I didn't know that you cared, Dr. Lee."

Rayne measured that sexy little grin on his face, but she refused to give him any satisfaction by returning the favor. Feeling the heat on her cheeks, she lifted her chin and squared her shoulders. "I ... I care about all of the operatives, Mr. Haliday."

Jack made a big show of taking a huge bite of the muffin. Around a mouthful, he said, "If you say so, Dr. Lee."

After Lil delivered a doughnut to each operative and made her rounds for high-fives, fist bumps, a stiff wink from Little, and a kiss from her daddy, Rayne shuffled her out of the room to get ready for pre-school. Even through the closed door, they could hear her giggly voice and the patter of her slippers on the marble floor when she scurried to the kitchen. It brought a smile to everyone's lips, except for Little, who rolled his eyes as if he weren't a bit amused by the curly haired scamp. Everyone knew differently. She was the apple of the big man's eye.

After Walt gave them the basic format, he turned the floor over to Clark Rhodes, who brought them up-to-speed with the game plan and the bad guys involved.

Clark had been with the FBI before he joined First Force. Nowadays, he looked nothing like an agent. When Clark joined First Force, he gladly traded in his suit for a pair of worn jeans, polo shirts, flip-flops in the summer, and cowboy boots in the winter. His dark hair brushed his collar and swept across the top of the black squared-off rims of the glasses parked over his dark brown eyes. He was tall and rail-thin with a very square jawline.

Techie or geek or nerd. It didn't matter. No one would want to take Clark Rhodes to task—the man was an expert in the martial arts.

Because it was February, Clark was sporting a pair of Tony Lama snakeskins. The combination of dark-rimmed glasses and snakeskin boots gave him kind of a "Buddy Holly on steroids" look.

Will "Smitty" Smith was the team's field medic who had worked for Special Ops in the Army. Like Grant, Smitty was no stranger to working with explosives, and, judging from Clark's report, it seemed like that would be their part of this mission.

Make things go boom—yeah, they could make it happen.

Because of his medical expertise, Smitty wore two hats while on assignments: whatever his mission was, plus taking care of any wounded. He'd patched up almost every man in the room at one time or another. His quick actions saved Jack Haliday's life after he was critically shot by a biker gang who attacked his home and killed his wife, Laura.

Dan Garrison and Stewart Little munched on doughnuts while intently listening to the objectives and studying the map of the area shown on the large touch screen presentation. Little was a huge man with a rugged look about him. He wasn't a handsome man by anyone's definition.

Some people are born without talent, some without intelligence. The team was quite certain that

Little was born without a sense of humor. Stewart found nothing amusing about the tiny white animated mouse that shared his name. It was a subject that was never mentioned—unless you were on a suicide mission. The stern or terse look on his face seemed to be his default expression.

No one could figure out why Lil didn't turn tail and run when he was around. Instead, the little girl seemed most loving toward him from the very first day she had met him. Perhaps she could sense that he needed the most love of any of them.

Rumor had it that Dan Garrison was married at one time. His wife was brutally murdered like Jack's had been, although no one from First Force knew the details. If Walt did, he wasn't sharing.

Dan never mentioned a wife, but there was a sorrow in his eyes that was ever-present, and it made Grant wonder if there was truth to the rumor. Dan had been a US Marshal before joining the Force.

Jack sat in the wing-backed chair in the far corner of the room with his leg casually draped over the arm.

The ex-Navy SEAL always had a cool air about him—even under fire. Nevertheless, the truth was that he was the man in the room with the most to lose if a mission went FUBAR. He had a beautiful little daughter. Grant was certain that every person in the room yearned for what Jack had—a life

91

beyond the mission—someone waiting for him to come home from the mission—someone to live for.

Grant's eyes fell upon the leader of First Force—Walt Wabash.

The fifty-something ex-CIA agent scared him perhaps more than anyone else in the room. A handsome and fit man with broad shoulders, he had never been married. Walt had no children. He'd been married to the job, its secrets, and its complications to the point that he evidently didn't feel he could share his life or the job with anyone.

After retiring from the CIA, Walt refurbished the Georgian-style mansion that was left to him by his grandmother along with a boatload of money into the First Force headquarters. He didn't keep residence at the mansion. His niece, Dr Rayne Lee, lived on the estate.

Walt owned a lovely English Tudor style home in the suburbs of Rosemount. He had been Jack's next-door neighbor. After the horrid execution of Jack's wife, Walt became involved with Jack's mother-in-law, Dale Martin. Walt wasn't one to share much about his life, but when Dale was around the look in his eyes spoke volumes. Grant wondered if he'd ever take the big leap and marry the lovely brunette.

Sitting on the sofa with her elbows perched on her knees and her long slender fingers steepled under her chin, Grant found himself staring at

Casey Rhodes, Clark's twin sister. The two had shared a womb and little else. Separated at birth, they were raised in two entirely different environments. Clark had been raised in the city by a college professor and his wife, while Casey had been brought up hunting and fishing in a rural setting. Casey was pretty damned handy with a bow as well. The extremely attractive dark-haired woman with an athletic yet feminine build was the team's sniper.

She was soft spoken, but boy how she had an eagle-eye aim accompanied by nerves of steel. She did her job as well, perhaps even better, than any man in the field.

Watching her intense attention to every word Clark was saying, Grant had to wonder if she longed for a relationship or the possibility of children someday, or was Casey Rhodes just like her fellow teammates—lost?

The clap of Walt's hands brought Grant back into the moment. "Okay, you've all got a handle on what our mission is. Be ready to pull out on a moment's notice, although I don't foresee that time coming before Friday or Saturday. Clark's still gathering intel." He picked up a box from his desk and began tossing burn phones to each team member. "Here are your cells for the op. Clark has programmed each number into them. When you are called up, don't forget to leave your personal cells at home." Leaning a hip against the desk, he crossed his arms over his chest. "That's all for now."

A low murmur of voices filled the room as everyone rose to their feet and headed toward the door.

Taking the usual ribbing from Smitty about his West Virginia roots, Grant was bringing up the rear when he heard Walt call out to him, "Grant, could I speak to you for a minute?"

Grant hesitated.

"Close the door, please," Walt added.

Uh, oh.

Grant's eyes flicked to Clark, who was still perched in front of the computer at Walt's desk. He was tapping away at the keys. It didn't matter what Walt wanted to talk to him about, Grant was fairly sure that Clark was so involved in whatever he was researching that he would be oblivious to the conversation.

"Is something wrong?" Grant asked.

"That's exactly what I wanted to ask you. You seemed pre-occupied during the meeting, Grant. Missing details about a mission is a damned good way to get yourself or a team member killed. What's going on?"

Walt's implication caused frustration to skitter up the back of Grant's neck. Succinctly, he said, "I assure you, Walt, that I did not miss any details of our mission. Furthermore, I have never nor would I ever compromise a team member."

"Good to hear, Ketchum. I'll count on that, as will your team."

The two men exchanged steely stares, and then Grant grabbed the doorknob. "I'll be waiting for that call." He marched into the foyer and grabbed the duffle bag that he'd left next to the front door. He could hear the guys talking and joking in the living room, except he was in no mood, so he went out the front door.

As Grant started his Camaro, he could feel his pulse racing. What the hell? Where did Walt get off thinking that he wasn't focused? He had never blown an op. He had never put a team member in harm's way, and he would never leave a man behind. He'd been a member of First Force for almost three years. How could Walt doubt him?

The Camaro whipped along the secluded, winding back road at sixty MPH. Fat raindrops pelted the windshield while the wind whipped the pines that grew close to the edge of the road. Dried oak leaves danced across the pavement in waves.

Okay, okay, maybe he had been drifting a bit during the meeting. For some reason, he just couldn't get Silja out of his head. He had a bad feeling. During the years he'd spent in Special Forces, if there was one thing he learned to trust, it was his gut, and right now his gut was churning with worry over someone that he hadn't seen or talked to in a very long time. She was haunting him, and he couldn't figure out why. One thing was for sure, and maybe Walt was right: he had to get his head on straight before he got on that plane for the op.

CHAPTER SIX

The dancers felt both exhausted and invigorated as they made their way from the stage to the dressing room suite after four curtain calls. Mopping the sweat from her forehead with a towel, Silja limped along the short corridor through the backstage area to bring up the rear.

Unlike after most of her performances, she felt jubilant rather than put off by Ballard's presence in the first row. During her first curtain call, he came forward from his seat to give her a bouquet of orange and red roses. The colors of love and desire—hmmm, it sounded very promising.

Holding the roses to her face to breathe in their alluring scent, Ballard's words from the previous evening swept into her memory. *"I want to make love to you, Silja. I want to take you to bed and make you cry out my name, and then I want to hold you through the night."*

Oh yeah, Ballard Crafton had her fired up. No matter how tired she was or how badly her feet ached, if he wanted to take her home and make passionate love to her—she'd be more than ready.

She was so lost in her thoughts that she didn't notice Eleni pausing to wait for her. She plowed right into the ballerina costumed as the Spanish doll. Eleni staggered backward until Silja grabbed her by the arm.

"Oh! I'm so sorry, Eleni. I didn't even notice that you'd stopped."

Righting herself, Eleni chuckled. "You must be somewhere else, Silja. After we get out of our costumes and makeup, I want to hear more about your evening with Ballard Crafton. I think you have left out some important information. I want to know all."

"Oh Eleni, I've been so stupid. I should've given him a chance long ago, like you and Natalia said. He's so sweet and kind and he's ... *very sexy,* too."

Eleni looped her arm through Silja's as they approached the dressing room door. "How do you Americans say? Better late than never, yes?"

"I'm Russian, Eleni, but yes that is what Americans say."

When they entered the dressing room, the air of celebration had evaporated. The dancers wore expressions of sheer trepidation.

The young dancer from Moscow who'd recently taken Anna Antkowiak's place turned toward them. Her eyes were wide with apprehension when she scurried toward Eleni. Silja could not understand a word. The young girl's Russian was too quick and panicked.

Eleni's expression changed from confused to concerned.

Patting the girl on the arm, Eleni spoke to her softly in their native tongue, and then made her way through the throng of dancers toward the line of vanities where Anna was rifling through drawers and tossing her belongings into a small suitcase.

Placing the bouquet from Ballard aside, Silja drew closer to see what was going on. Gasping, she drew her hand to her mouth when Anna turned to speak to Eleni.

Anna's eyes were blackened. Her lips were broken and swollen, and her neck was brilliant red with bruising, as though someone had attempted to choke her.

Eleni took the girl by the hand, and though she spoke to her softly in Russian, Silja was most certain that she was asking what had happened to her.

Tears burst from Anna's eyes. With quivering lips, she told Eleni and the dancers her story.

Silja watched the dancers' reactions. They clutched their hands to their chest or to their mouths. Some of the girls' eyes welled with tears. They dropped their gaze to the floor as though if they looked away Anna's story would melt into the walls.

Anna became more and more overwrought while her story unfolded for everyone to hear. Stroking her hair, Eleni attempted to comfort the young ballerina—yet to no avail. The girl could not be consoled.

Suddenly, a woman called from the doorway. "Anna ..."

Everyone turned to see an older woman with her hair covered in a babushka. While her clothes were clean, they were worn. Her face was twisted in bitterness and her voice was filled with despair. The woman gestured for Anna to hurry along. Then, she spoke to her in Russian.

Anna nodded to the woman, picked up her suitcase, and hugged Eleni.

The dancers took turns giving her a hug while whispering in her ear. As she made her way to the door, Anna paused when she came upon Silja. Not knowing what she should do, Silja offered her an apologetic smile.

Anna measured her for a moment. She muttered, "Be careful, Silja." With that, she hurried out the door.

The woman tossed the dancers a steely glance before she turned away to follow.

It was only a nanosecond after Anna had left that the dancers were in an uproar. Even if they hadn't been speaking in Russian, Silja was certain that she wouldn't have been able to understand what they were saying. They were panicked. They were horrified, and they were all gathered around Eleni, as if she had the power to do something about whatever had happened to Anna—which was ridiculous, of course. Eleni had no power to stop a rape, which from what Silja could gather was what had occurred.

With both hands Eleni leaned on the vanity. Black lines streamed down her flushed face where her makeup was giving way to her tears. Sniffling, she wiped them with the back of her hand. She plopped down in the chair and grabbed a handful of tissues to clean away the mess while the dancers remained in a tailspin.

Finally, Eleni looked up into the mirror and yelled out a word that Silja assumed translated into "quiet" because the room instantly silenced. She spoke to them with a concise tone. With heads hung low, they shuffled out of the room.

Assuming Eleni wanted some time alone to think, Silja turned to follow the dancers out, except Eleni called to her, "Not you, Silja. I want to talk with you."

As the last dancer was about to slip through the doorway, she spoke to Eleni in Russian while hitching her chin toward Silja. Eleni nodded and the dancer closed the door behind her.

A pinch of fear clutched Silja. What happened to Anna was horrific. A terrible feeling coiled through her that what Eleni was about to tell her was worse—much worse.

"Please sit down, Silja."

Bracing herself, Silja slowly made her way to the vanity chair next to Eleni, who was removing the pins from her hair. Her long dark tresses fell in silky waves below her shoulder blades. She ran her fingers through the tendrils while taking in a long deep breath as though she were trying to cleanse her thoughts—or perhaps the vision of Anna's bruised face.

She did not look at Silja; rather she spoke into the lighted mirror above the vanity. "The Novikov Ballet Company is in serious trouble. Natalia is running out of money."

"How do you know that?"

She turned with the same frigid look in her eyes that she'd displayed days before when they spoke of Anna's disappearance. "All the dancers know...except for you, Silja. How do we know this to be the truth? Because we are trying to keep the company alive—on our backs."

"W-what do you mean by that?"

"You have noticed that all the dancers leave the dressing room in fine clothes after the Saturday night performances, yes?"

"Yes ..."

"We go downstairs to contributors' party. Everyone goes—Natalia, Edvar, and all of dancers from company. We place our pointe shoes in box with our name on shoes. The contributors pay money to attend party. Whoever gives most money will get first choice of shoes. When your shoes are pulled from box, you must entertain that contributor. You must give them anything they desire, and they always desire sex."

Again, Silja found herself gasping and cupping her mouth in her hand. "Natalia is prostituting the dancers to keep the ballet company afloat?"

"Yes, Silja. But it is not just female dancers. Our male dancers must participate as well, except for Dominik because he belongs to Edvar."

"And Anna ... what happened to Anna?"

Raking her fingers through her hair, Eleni turned back to the mirror. She expelled a regretful sigh. "Poor Anna, she is just a young girl. Last Saturday was her first party. How was Natalia to know that she was a virgin? The man who won her, Ivan Belsky, was unhappy because she did not know how to please him. So he raped her and beat her and choked her. That was her mother who came for her. She has no father. Anna's mother worked three jobs to put her through ballet school. This was her first position with a company. Now ... Anna is going home. She is broken. She no longer wishes to dance."

Silja dropped her gaze to her lap. Her eyes welled with tears, and her stomach twisted into a tangle of knots. "My God, who can blame her? This is horrible, Eleni. It must stop."

"Yes, it must. But I have one more thing I must tell you. Ballard is always at all parties."

Silja's eyes widened. "What ..."

Without pause, Eleni brushed her hair away from her ears to reveal a pair of diamond studs. "Don't you recognize these? They are the earrings that you returned to Ballard before he gave you bracelet. He made me wear them the night when I was his prize. He didn't want me. It was your name that he whispered into my ear as he had his way with me. He let me keep them when our night was through. He said I was enchanting. I did not feel this way." Eleni saw the shock in her expression.

Silja was struggling with this revelation.

"I can prove this, Silja." Eleni opened a drawer. She held up a lovely gift box from Cartier's for Silja to examine. "This is box that earrings from Ballard were delivered to you in, yes?"

Silja took the box from her hand. Indeed the delicate gift tag was still affixed to it. The tag read: *For Silja, all my love, Ballard.* Like the diamond bracelet, she had returned the earrings to Ballard by messenger.

How could Natalia use the dancers in such a vile way? How could Ballard Crafton be so charming and tender with her, and yet participate in such a ghastly violation of another human being?

Burying her face into her hands, the vision of Ballard's eyes came to her mind's eye. Yes, they were full of danger. Yesterday, when he was at her apartment holding her close, she couldn't identify what she saw.

Now, it was so clear. She saw deceit and a bellyful of self-indulgence so wicked that she was ashamed to admit she'd kissed him or had anything to do with him at all.

Her first instincts were right—she should have never listened to Natalia—she should have trusted her gut. Ballard Crafton was not someone she cared to be with.

She looked into Eleni's eyes. So many questions raced through her mind, except she could only force a few to tumble from her lips. "Why didn't you tell me about this, Eleni? And why was I never summoned to these ... *parties?*"

"I could not tell you, Silja. I would have lost my position in the ballet—all of the dancers were threatened with this if they told you. That is why they always kept a distance from you. They didn't want to be accused of telling you the secret. As for why you were not summoned, you say that you are Russian, but in the eyes of Russia you are an American, Silja. Natalia has been afraid of ... um, how do you say it ... um, *repercussion.*"

Silja's disbelief soon turned into disenchantment. It didn't take but a second for the disenchantment to swell into fury. She threw the box to the floor like it held poisonous bacteria. "When is the next party?"

"Saturday night, after our last performance of *Coppelia.* What will you do about Ballard?"

"I will have to treat him and Natalia as if I don't know anything about this. But come Saturday night, there are going to be *repercussions,* Eleni."

* * * * *

Natalia leaned back against the sofa in her private dressing room, rubbing her temples while sipping a chardonnay. The headaches and the stiffness in her neck had become an almost unbearable constant. Stress. Even with the contributors paying to spend time with her dancers, she was barely making ends meet. Costume rentals, pointe shoes for each girl for each performance, royalties that had to be paid for permission to perform ballets such as *Coppelia, Swan Lake, Giselle,* or *The Nutcracker* were very expensive, and then there was the payroll. Edvar's paycheck was a killer, but she had to have a choreographer. Edvar Kozlovski was one of the best.

Not only was he the choreographer, but Natalia had also been forced to sell him one-fourth of the company, and still it wasn't enough to cover her mounting expenditures.

She opened a bottle of prescription pain medication, removed two pills, and downed them with the wine.

It was Edvar's idea to have the contributors' parties. She merely wanted to auction the dancers off for a dinner date to the highest bidder once per month. Edvar seemed to be in agreement—until Dominik had gotten wind of the idea. He had convinced Edvar that auctioning them off once per week would bring in more funds. He was right, but it had exploded into an absolute nightmare.

When they started the auctions six months earlier, the contributors were satisfied with a dinner date. Then, they wanted more. Even the wealthy women contributors wanted to lie in bed with a handsome, well-built dancer. Before they knew it, they were prostituting their dancers like common whores on the street.

Poor Anna Antkowiak.

Natalia was the first woman to take the reins of the company—the first woman to be permitted in such a position of power. The Novikov Ballet Company was her father's before her and her grandfather's before him.

In an effort to shield all that was beginning to crumble, Natalia gave Anna's mother some money to help ease the pain, or at the very least to keep her quiet—money that she had to scrape together.

She closed her eyes. She had no idea that Belsky was capable of such a terrible act. He had no compassion for the young girl. He only cared for his own needs, and when Anna couldn't—or perhaps wouldn't—deliver, he turned into a monster.

Moreover, she couldn't report the incident to authorities because the ballet company would be implicated. That would destroy the very thing she was trying to preserve.

That wasn't the only trouble Belsky had caused. Weekly, she received several phone calls from him demanding that Dominik be available for auction. Belsky wanted to have an opportunity to choose from either box, male or female, and he was most interested in an evening with Dominik.

Edvar was furious.

Recoiling, she was shaken from her thoughts by a sharp knock on the door.

"Natalia, I want to talk to you," Edvar called through the door.

She did not answer. She laid her head back and closed her eyes. "Natalia ... I know that you are in there. We must talk."

"The door is open, Edvar. Come in."

Edvar strutted through the door with Dominik at his heels. "I just spoke to Ballard Crafton. He said that he and Silja are seeing each other. While that is wonderful, we just lost a big contributor for our Saturday auctions."

"There will be no auction this Saturday night, Edvar, unless we forbid Belsky from attending."

"What? Why would we do that? Belsky is our second highest bidder!" Dominik hissed.

Her dark eyes filled with anger, Natalia sat straight up. "Because Belsky doesn't know how to control himself! He beat and raped poor Anna Antkowiak because she could not please him. How dare you, Dominik! After all, you do not have to participate in the auctions. I received yet another nasty call from Belsky about this two hours before the party."

Seeing Dominik's indifferent expression toward the way Anna had been treated, she turned to Edvar. "We can't have this, Edvar! We can't have our dancers injured. Anna has quit the company."

With a wave of his hand, Dominik said, "You can replace her easily enough like you did for the matinee, and may I add that Silja is exempt from the parties as well. For that matter, I can't believe that the dancers haven't told her about the parties."

"You know that the girls are reminded on a daily basis that if they tell Silja about the parties, they will be fired. They are terrified—especially the older dancers. They know she cannot be included in the auctions. She was born in Russia, but her paper-work says she is American. It could have disastrous consequences," Natalia bit out.

"Pfft!" Dominik huffed. "We will talk with Belsky and let him know that his behavior was unacceptable—not to do it again."

"And if he does, what can we do? We can't report him to the police. He will simply tell them what we have been doing," Natalia said. "Please, Edvar ... I don't want to have a party this Saturday night. Let the dancers have a rest. They are all on edge."

Edvar caressed his lips with the tip of his index finger. Dominik ran his long fingers through Edvar's spiked blond-tipped hair. He dipped into the touch, and then he said, "I agree with Dominik. We will tell Belsky that it is not acceptable to hurt the dancers. He will abide by our rules. He is a prominent businessman in Yekaterinburg. He doesn't want his reputation tarnished anymore than the company does. The dancers will have two weeks off soon."

"Excuse me ..."

They all flinched and turned toward the open door where Ballard stood. Relief swept through the trio to see the American businessman because they were certain that no matter how much he'd heard, he hadn't understood a word. Besides, it wasn't as if Ballard weren't privy to the activities at the contributors' parties—he'd partaken of the ballet company's fruit many times over.

Natalia noticed that he was beaming like a little boy who had just received a puppy for Christmas. She pasted a smile on her lips and strode toward him with an air of confidence that had gone astray weeks ago. Making a swift change from Russian to English, she said, "Ballard, how good to see you. What can I do for you?"

"I wanted to thank you. Silja has finally come around, and I know that it is in no small part to your influence, Natalia." He took her hand and kissed it. "She is everything I've ever wanted in a woman: beautiful, witty, charming. But I'm afraid I've come to ask you to work your magic on Miss Ramsay one more time."

Natalia pulled her hand from his. "What is it that you want from me now, Ballard?"

"A proposition: Your dancers will never have to attend another contributors' party again, not to mention they won't have to put up with the likes of Ivan Belsky ever again. I will make it well worth your while to help me."

Natalia, Edvar, and Dominik exchanged glances that screamed, *"What the hell? How does he know about Belsky?"*

Ballard snorted at their tentative reaction. He called over his shoulder, "Mikhail ..." Ballard's enormous bodyguard filled the doorway. "You forget, my security staff is Russian, therefore they translate for me. Now, are you ready to hear my proposal?"

"I find that I have few choices in the matter, Ballard," Natalia pointed out. She eased onto the sofa, picked up her wine glass from the end table, and then slid her impassive gaze to meet his. "What is it that you want?"

"I want Silja."

"You basically have Silja. What else is there for me to do?"

"Help me to convince her to move into my home as my constant companion and lover. Of course, she may still dance for your company, but she will be mine exclusively. If you can get her to agree with this, you will never have to worry about the company's expenses again. I will fund your operation completely. How do you Russians say it ... *yes?*"

Edvar and Dominik were practically jumping for joy.

Natalia remained steadfast in her seat. Sipping the wine, she kept her gaze trained on Ballard. "What is wrong with you, Ballard? Have you so little confidence that you will be able to win Silja's affections that you need a third party to ... how does it go ... *seal the deal?* Again, I must inquire: Will Silja meet the same fate as your former lovers?"

Edvar and Dominik froze in place with their mouths gaping open.

Ballard's cheeks instantly turned red, and his eyes heated with anger.

Dominik stepped forward to squeeze Natalia's shoulder in a warning manner. "Please, Natalia, Mr. Crafton is one of our most generous contributors, and we, of course, want to satisfy him in any way possible." He turned to Ballard with a curl on his lips. "Forgive Natalia, she is tired. This production has taken much out of her. We will do everything in our power to influence Miss Ramsay, and we will look forward to your future generosity."

CHAPTER SEVEN

Silja felt trapped by the knowledge of the Novikov Ballet Company's indiscretions. She had a newfound sense of the dancers' disquiet. She was in tune with their apprehension whereas she had been unconscious of it only days before. Moreover, she felt insecure in her surroundings. As Saturday approached, she could feel the trepidation among the dancers mounting.

Ballard had invited her to a late dinner after the Wednesday night performance, but she managed to keep him at bay with the excuse of a terrible headache. He was sympathetic. He kissed her forehead and insisted that he provide her transportation home in his limo rather than allowing her to ride the cold noisy bus.

She feared that he would suspect that she knew something if she rejected his offer, so she climbed into the limo. She tolerated the feel of his fingers caressing her hand along with his endless flirting and chatter while the limo cruised through the city.

It took little effort to fake a headache because Silja struggled with the bile that was rising in her throat at the thought of how Ballard had exploited the young women from the ballet company, including her good friend, Eleni Babinski.

"Would you like me to come in and make you some hot tea?" Ballard asked when they arrived at her apartment door.

"Oh ... thank you, Ballard, but it's not necessary. I think I really just need to take some Tylenol and lay down."

He cupped her chin and lifted her face to meet his gaze. "I'm worried about you. You seem distant, like something's wrong." He ran the pad of his thumb over her cheek and lightly nuzzled the tip of his nose to hers.

She thought she would throw up over his Armani shoes. Swallowing back hard, she managed a feeble smile. "Please don't worry. I always get this way when a tour comes to an end. It's muscle exhaustion and sore feet. I guess I'm just ready for *Coppelia* to be done and to have a little down time," she lied.

His eyes brightened. "That's right, you'll have two weeks off. How about we plan a trip? Let's get out of this cold Russian weather. How does a week or so in the Caribbean sound? Sun and sand and all the margaritas that we can drink. "

God, she had to dig deep for a positive response. If he didn't leave soon, those Armani's were going to be in a bad way. She replied, "That sounds just about perfect. W-where in the Caribbean?"

"I'll surprise you." Taking the key from her hand, he unlocked her door. "Now curl up with Greta and get a good night's sleep." He swallowed her into his arms and pressed his lips to hers. His kiss was as passionate and primal as the first evening they'd spent together, only this night it twisted her stomach instead of tickling her libido.

* * * * *

Thursday evening after the ballet ended, Ballard came to the dressing room suite to fetch her. The dancers were anxious with his presence, which had Silja wondering how many of the girls he had forced into his bed in the name of funding the Novikov Ballet Company.

The girls discarded their costumes, tossed their belongings into totes, and vacated the dressing suite like a formal evacuation had been issued. Most of the girls didn't even bother to wipe the heavy make-up from their faces or remove their false eyelashes before they left.

Ballard seemed perfectly comfortable among the girls. It was as though he'd never laid eyes on any of them other than from his seat in the front row of the theatre.

He even ignored Eleni, and Silja knew for a fact that he'd been with her. Eleni always wore the diamond stud earrings. It was as if they were a scar to remind her of what the ballerinas were forced to do, and yet not once did Ballard glance at the earrings or give any signs that he recognized Eleni at all.

What an arrogant bastard.

Again, Silja managed to avoid intimacy with Ballard with the same excuse of exhaustion. He appeared more agitated by it this evening, but once again he opened the door to her apartment, kissed her, and bid her an empathetic goodnight.

As she closed the door and gathered Greta into her arms, Silja was well aware that her apologies were wearing thin. She knew that she would have to spend some quality time with Ballard Friday evening. Most likely he would expect to stay the night. How would she escape that situation? To think that only three short days ago she couldn't wait to make love to him, and now the mere thought repulsed her.

She almost dropped Greta when her cell phone rang. She pulled it from her purse, and the screen read "Ballard Crafton." She was oh-so tempted to press the ignore button, but with a heavy sigh, she answered instead. "Hello ..."

117

"I hope you will be feeling better tomorrow evening, Silja. I've made reservations at our favorite restaurant, and the chef promised to make his famous cranberry Kissel à la Russe, which is my second favorite after cheesecake."

"Oh ... well ... I wouldn't want to miss that." She needed a moment to steady herself. Running her fingers through her hair, she took a braced breath. "Anyway ... yes, of course ... I'd love to go."

"Good. I'll come backstage to get you about a half-hour after the show?"

"Sounds good. I'll see you then, Ballard."

"Sleep well, Silja. You won't do much sleeping tomorrow night." And with that, he hung up.

Cupping a hand over her mouth, she tossed the phone and Greta on a chair to make haste into the bathroom.

* * * * *

"I am worried, Silja. How will you control Ballard's desires tonight? He is ..." she hesitated. After a breath, she continued, "... Relentless in the bedroom." She zipped up Silja's little black cocktail dress.

"I'm not sure. But if I have to I will puke all over his Armani suit to convince him that I'm not feeling well." Silja pushed the clip of her rhinestone earrings into place.

"You Ameri—"

Silja tossed her a baleful look.

Eleni regrouped. "We *Russian* women can be very resourceful when we have to, but how will you tell him that you cannot see him tomorrow night?"

"I'll manage, Eleni. You just make sure that you don't get caught when you do your part."

"I will be fine. It is you who is taking all the risk."

"Silja ..." Ballard called from the sitting room of the dressing suite.

Silja and Eleni flinched. Quickly, Silja pushed her feet into a pair of silver stilettos. Eleni's face was tight with apprehension. Silja brushed a stray wisp of hair from her friend's eyes. "It's going to be fine. See you tomorrow."

"Silja ... are you ready?" Ballard called again.

"Coming!" She grabbed her clutch from the vanity and hurried from the room.

"You look dazzling," Eleni heard Ballard say as they left the dressing suite. Sinking into a vanity chair, she ran her hands up and down her arms. It wasn't the chill of winter that shivered through her—it was the pure fear of what tomorrow night would bring.

The theatre was quiet. The dancers were gone, as were the orchestra and the stage crew. Only the janitorial staff remained, running the vacuums throughout the auditorium and the hallways.

Taking in a calming breath, Eleni slung her purse over her shoulder and took up a tote bag that rested on Silja's vanity chair.

Eleni scanned the corridor beyond the dressing room door. An elderly man ran a vacuum along the passageway. When she passed him, she smiled, and it seemed to brighten his evening. She turned the corner and pressed through a door that led to one of the ornate hallways along the auditorium. Evidently, the cleaning crew had already worked that section because the lights had been dimmed and it was abandoned.

She scurried along until she came to a winding staircase. The crystal chandeliers that lit the stairwell were dimmed as well. Eleni figured that she wouldn't bump into anyone all the way down to the basement reception room.

She descended carefully down another darkened staircase. She ran her hands along the walls—measuring her steps so as to not miss a step and fall down several flights.

Finally, her nerves got the best of her.

The darkness had taken its toll. She paused to retrieve a small flashlight that Silja had packed in the tote bag in case the basement had been darkened.

Again, Eleni paused to gather her nerves.

Turning on the flashlight, she made her way into the small reception room where the contributors' parties took place each week. Flashing the beam up and down and along the shelves, she inched her way to the bar until she came upon the box that held the dancer's pointe shoes.

With shaking hands, Eleni pulled Silja's shoes from the tote and placed them inside the box. She then returned the box to its resting place beneath the bar.

It was done.

Making sure that she had all her belongings, she made her way around the bar when the room was suddenly flooded with light.

"Eleni ..."

Her head jerked up to find Dominik with his hands planted on his hips and his brows furrowed. "What are you doing in here?" he asked her, tersely.

"I ... um ... I think I left a pair of earrings on the bar last Saturday night. I came to find them so I can wear them tomorrow night."

"Did you find them?"

"No ... no, I did not. Maybe I have them at home. I will look harder when I get there. Good night." Eleni hurried past Dominik and up the stairs.

Dominik watched her anxious exit, and then he glanced around the room.

* * * * *

Silja was nothing less than impressed with Ballard's easy-going demeanor, his light conversation, and his quick sense of humor during dinner.

He didn't seem like a man who had been exploiting … deviations all along.

She had to choke down her dinner and smile brightly as she rewarded the chef with glowing accolades for his Kissel ... or whatever it was called. The food was good. It wasn't the chef's fault that Ballard Crafton was a bastard of epic proportions.

"I suppose that you won't be attending our party tomorrow night, Ballard." A tubby middle-aged man said in a heavy Russian accent when he approached Ballard from behind. Licking his lips, he eyed Silja.

She squirmed uncomfortably in her seat under his fiery gaze.

Ballard turned.

The man added, "It looks like you've got the top prize—Novikov's prima ballerina."

"Ahhh, Belsky," Ballard remarked with a haughty chortle.

Silja's eyes flicked to the man the instant his name tumbled from Ballard's lips. Ivan Belsky— this was the beast who had beaten and raped Anna Antkowiak! The hair on the nape of her neck stood up.

Ballard continued, "No, I don't think I will be at the party. I hope you enjoy the evening."

"I will, but not as much as you, my friend." Looking Silja up and down, he paused at her breasts and then into her eyes. "Not nearly as much as you."

He sickened her, yet this was her opportunity to start her plan in motion. Tossing her napkin onto the table, Silja announced, "Oh, don't miss your party for me, Ballard. I've been invited to a party for tomorrow night, too. I must've forgotten to tell you."

Ballard jerked his body toward her. "What party?" he demanded.

"I don't know, Edvar said there would be a party tomorrow night. Its taking place in that little reception room under the theatre. I suppose we're celebrating the close of *Coppelia*. He said that I should attend," Silja explained in the most casual manner possible.

Belsky let out a loud laugh. He slapped Ballard on the back. Shaking his head, he strutted away while making a grand show of his amusement.

Ballard fell back against his chair.

"What's so funny?" Silja's voice was laced with faux innocence.

"Nothing. At. All."

Ballard was tense during the twenty-minute limo ride back to Silja's apartment. He couldn't have been more tense than Silja. Biting her lip, she tapped her fingers nervously on her velvet clutch bag while anticipating what he would expect from her when they arrived at her place. Dinner wasn't sitting well. It sloshed in her stomach at the thought of Ballard's hands on her. How was she going to get out of going to bed with him?

She glanced at him askance.

Ballard checked his watch and then continued to stare out his window. He was pissed. Belsky had really gotten to him, and he was especially upset to hear that she was going to attend tomorrow night's contributor party. Too damn bad.

The limo pulled up to Silja's apartment building and the driver opened the door. Ballard got out and held out his hand for her. A memory of the night that he carried her to the door flashed through her mind's eye. How enamored she was with him that night—that was before she knew what Ballard was capable of.

Saying nothing, he placed his hand in the small of her back and walked her up the two flights of stairs to her door. This was it. They would go into the apartment, and he would expect her to have sex with him—no, not make love—it was sex, because she couldn't make love to a monster like him. She wasn't even sure how she was going to have sex with him, yet if he was insistent, she knew that she would have to. Otherwise, she could alert him that something was amiss.

She fumbled in her purse for her key.

Ballard said, "Silja ... I know that I've made some promises to you, but ... I need to go back to my office and check on some impending business. I'm so sorry ... I hope you understand."

Freezing in place, Silja slowly let out the air that she'd been holding in her lungs all evening. The weight of the world receded from her shoulders. She dropped the key. Ballard picked it up and unlocked her door. She finally managed to say, "Oh no ... that's perfectly fine, Ballard. I understand. I had a lovely dinner. Will you be at the party tomorrow night?"

He pushed her against the wall, pressed his lips to hers, and shoved his tongue inside her mouth. He ran his hands up and down her sides and then swept them over her breasts. She wanted to shove him away and spit in his face, but she remained in control and let him have his way. It seemed like forever when he finally pulled away—caging her between his arms.

Ballard's intense gaze was burning holes into her. "Most likely," he said, "I will be at the party. And I will expect you to leave the party with me, and we will pick up where we left off tonight. I also want to talk to you about something. Something very important."

He tugged the thin strap of her dress to bare her shoulder, and then he lowered his lips to kiss along the gentle curve of it until he reached her throat. He whispered, "Until tomorrow Silja ..."

* * * * *

Natalia's cell phone rang, vibrating in a tiny circle on her nightstand in the darkness. Groaning, she emerged from the warmth of her blankets, pushed the sleep mask to the top of her head, and reached for the phone.

It was twelve thirty at night.

Involuntarily, she let out another moan when she saw Ballard Crafton's name on the screen of her mobile. No, she had not talked to Silja on Ballard's behalf. In fact, she had avoided the dancer all week. She feared for Silja. Ballard told her that Silja had agreed to a Caribbean vacation, so she decided to see if Ballard could manage to woo Silja into his arrangement on his own. If not, perhaps she would make a feeble attempt to coax her along when they returned from their trip.

Reluctantly, she pressed the *talk* button. "What can I do for you at this very late hour, Ballard?"

"Why is Silja attending the contributors' party tomorrow night?" he demanded to know.

"I know nothing of this." She dragged the sleep mask from her head. "Who told you this?"

"Silja said that Edvar told her to come. It is supposed to be a celebration to close *Coppelia*."

"I will talk to Edvar. He said nothing to me."

"Talk to him immediately, tonight," Ballard said. The line went dead.

Natalia thumbed Edvar's number, but the voice on the other end belonged to Dominik. "Why are you calling so late, Natalia? What do you want?"

"Why has Silja been summoned to the contributors' party?"

"I do not know what you are talking about. We have an agreement with Ballard Crafton. Why would we take a chance on Silja finding out about the auctions?"

"Perhaps she knows."

There was a long silence.

Dominik growled, "I will find out."

Natalia found herself sitting in the darkness with another dead connection and dread tightening the vise in her chest.

CHAPTER EIGHT

The night had been long. Silja tossed and turned in her bed to the point that Greta abandoned her cozy spot on the comforter for a place among Silja's clothes lying in the corner of the bedroom.

Finally, at five o'clock, Silja decided that it was an exercise in futility to remain in the bed, so she went into the kitchen to toss some coffee into her two-cup coffeemaker.

The snow fell gently outside the window. The sky turned dark purple as dawn slowly unfolded beyond the sinewy branches of the trees. The fresh layer of snow that covered the tree branches reminded her of little old ladies with gray hair.

It was a peaceful time of day, yet Silja could not find any peace. With mug in hand, she curled up on the sofa to watch the snow fall. Greta jumped up onto the back of the sofa. Her mistress stroked her ears while she sipped the coffee.

She felt so alone. How she wished she could call her mom to tell her that she wanted to come home. Her father, God bless him, would tell her to sit tight until he could arrive to accompany her on the flight.

They were gone. There was no one to worry about her in a faraway land. Except ...

Silja glanced at the laptop on the desk across the room. *Grant.* If she emailed him that she was afraid she had no doubt he would be on the next flight to the Koltsovo Airport, which was about sixteen kilometers south east of Yekaterinburg.

Nonetheless, what right did she have to contact him? She rolled her eyes at the thought. Oh yeah, his girlfriend would be just crazy about the idea of him jumping on a plane to help out an ex-girlfriend. All girlfriends love that scenario.

She wasn't going to be part of that scenario.

Grant Ketchum was out of the equation.

She was going to get through this, and then she was going to get on a plane and return home to the good old USA where she damned well belonged.

Maybe, just maybe, she'd look up Grant when she got there—in case he didn't have said girlfriend.

Again, she found herself rolling her eyes at her ridiculous thoughts. *Seriously, Silja? He's gorgeous. Of course, he's got a girlfriend.*

As the day dragged on, Silja considered catching the bus to go to the studio to stretch away her stress, except she thought it best to keep a distance from Natalia. She'd managed to avoid the woman all week. If she went to the studio, Natalia would undoubtedly be there.

She turned on the DVR to watch some of her shows. By one o'clock, she gave up trying to concentrate.

She went to her purse to retrieve her cell phone and check her messages—nothing. Feeling lonely and unimportant, she stuffed the cell into the back pocket of her old jeans and decided to satisfy that growl in her tummy by making a salad for lunch.

While she was chopping up vegetables at the counter, there was a knock at her door. Letting out a sigh, she threw her head back and closed her eyes in hopes that it wasn't a delivery of flowers, or worse, Ballard himself. She set the knife on the counter and wiped her hands on a dish towel while she hurried to the door.

When she peeked through the peephole she couldn't believe who was standing in the hallway—Dominik.

What could he possibly want?

Baffled, she watched him through the peephole while he shifted from foot to foot. Dominik tended to be a fidgety man, yet his fidgeting wasn't like most men's—it was as graceful as his dancing.

With his hands pressed into the pockets and his shoulders hiked to his ears, Dominik's tall, slender frame was hidden in a black pea coat with a plaid scarf knotted and tucked into the breast. His muscular legs were accentuated by skinny jeans stuffed in a pair of tall boots.

He topped off the look with a pair of large, square faux glasses. Dominik didn't need glasses—it was all about the style, not necessity.

Perplexed, yet intrigued beyond belief, Silja opened the door. "Dominik ... Whatta surprise."

His Russian accent came out as chilled as the weather he'd come in from. "I need to talk with you, Silja. Please let me in."

"Is something wrong?"

"I hope not." He nodded toward the door with a terse tone. "Please ..."

Lifting a lackadaisical shoulder, Silja stepped aside to give him entry. Dominik went directly into the tiny kitchen. He opened the fridge to survey the contents. "Where is your wine?"

Silja noted Greta's dull reaction to Dominik's presence—she lifted her head and then returned to her napping. Yeah, even the cat remembered what a total jerk Dominik was.

"I don't have any wine, Dominik," Silja said. "What do you want?"

He slammed the refrigerator door closed.

Silja noticed the fine leather gloves on his hands. He had to be cold. While expensive, they were not made for warmth.

Picking up the knife that Silja had left lying on the cutting board, Dominik leaned a hip on the counter while running the blade up and down the leather of his glove. "It does not surprise me that you have no wine, Silja. You were never properly prepared for a lover to drop by."

Silja blinked back. "You're not my lover, Dominik—"

"Is Ballard Crafton your lover?"

"That is none of your business—emphasis on none. I think you should go—"

"It is a shame that the other dancers in the company work so much harder than you do, Silja," he hissed. He felt the knife prick the fine, delicate buckskin.

Being in Silja's presence was bothersome, but the wide-eyed glare that she pitched him was even more agitating. His tone grew more aggressive, accusing. "I think you know what I speak of, yes? I think one dancer has loose tongue. Eleni Babinski?"

"Get out, Dominik!"

"You can make life easier for your friends, Silja. You have the power to make it stop."

She turned to rush to the door, but he grabbed her by the arm and slammed her against the refrigerator. He pressed his body to hers to hold her in place. The cell phone in her pocket *peeped*—it was making a random butt-dial while she squirmed against him.

"Let me go!"

"You are the key to their freedom." Grabbing her chin roughly, he forced her to look into his eyes. "Ballard Crafton wants you to be his constant companion, to move into his home, and if you agree to this, he will give the company all money it will ever need. Your friend, Eleni, will never have to spread her legs for a man that she does not want. Young girls like Anna will never have to bow to abuse if you agree to this simple arrangement." He pressed harder against her.

Silja wiggled and struggled beneath his weight.

"He is wealthy, Silja. You would have everything your heart desires, and your friends would be free of this burden." He pushed away from her to measure the rage vibrating from her body. "You think about what I have told you, Silja." Turning to leave, he hesitated to nod toward the sofa. "You still have kitty. How nice for you on cold winter nights, yes?"

Dominik slammed the door behind him.

Hot tears of frustration trickled down Silja's flushed cheeks. With nothing in her hands, she searched for something to relieve the agitation.

She opened the fridge to grab the first thing she saw: a bottle of water. She snatched the water from the shelf. A screech slipped from deep in her throat when she wielded the bottle at the door. The bottle burst when it hit the wood—splattering the water over the door onto the floor.

Greta jumped from the sofa to scurry underneath and hide. Leaning against the fridge, she decided that she would clean the mess up later. It was only water.

Dominik's words exploded through her head ... he said that Ballard wanted her to what? She wrapped her arms around herself to try to ease the irritation and the anxiety from the unexpected turn of events.

Chop ... she needed to chop the vegetables for her salad. Chopping would ease the exasperation that had trounced upon her. She reached for the knife that she'd left next to the cutting board.

It wasn't there.

Remembering that Dominik was fiddling with it, she searched the counter and the floor—no. Thinking that perhaps he'd tossed it before their push and shove, she went to the sink. Not there.

Feeling a pinch from the disheveled cell phone, she pulled it from her pocket only to find that she'd accidentally dialed Grant Ketchum! "Cripes," she muttered, quickly hitting the end button. She only hoped that he hadn't tried to pick up the call.

Leaning against the counter, she took in several deep calming breaths.

Chopping ... she was chopping up a salad. She scanned the counter and the floor again. Letting out a heavy sigh, she squeezed her eyes closed. *Hokay, the knife is MIA. So calm down and get another one.* She pulled a bigger knife from the block and began hacking at a tomato. The juice oozed over the board and onto the counter.

What the hell? Ballard wanted her to live with him as his companion, and in exchange he would finance the ballet company so the dancers wouldn't have to prostitute themselves anymore?

His constant companion?

Silja laid down the knife.

His constant companion—what exactly does that mean?

She rinsed her hands in the sink.

She grabbed a dish towel.

His *constant* companion.

Her eyes widened.

Her mouth dropped open—she knew exactly what that meant!

Essentially, Ballard wanted her to be his personal sex slave! She could barely catch her breath. It was insane!

Then again, the entire situation with the Novikov Ballet Company was insane. But this—this was an indecent proposal beyond her imagination. Furthermore, how could she turn down his offer? If she did, she would be throwing the dancers to the wolves—there would be no end to their torment, and perhaps more would suffer the same abusive treatment that Anna did.

She stumbled into the living room and plopped down onto the sofa. Leaning her head back against the cushions, she raked her hands through her hair. *Oh my God.* How could this be happening? How could any of it be happening? She had to think—but it didn't appear that there would be any simple compromises on the table.

CHAPTER NINE

The rope dangled and wobbled below his crossed ankles as Grant climbed hand over hand to the top of a platform at a training facility that First Force used to keep the team in prime combat readiness and physical condition. He was well over half-way through with only a few more obstacles left in the grueling course that they worked at least once per week.

Smitty was climbing the rope next to him, and if Grant didn't move his ass, he was gonna beat him to the top. From there, they were to dash across the platform and rappel to the floor. Next, they had to dive to their stomachs and use their elbows and upper body strength to crawl through deep sand under twenty feet of barbed wire to get to the next obstacle.

Managing to gloat and gasp for air at the same time, Smitty jumped to the platform to hurry toward the rappelling equipment at the other end. Right on his heels, Grant landed on the platform. He arrived at the second set of equipment just as Smitty was making adjustments.

Walt called for Jack and Dan to begin climbing the rope—they weren't far behind.

As Grant and Smitty came up out from under the barbed wire, they could see Little holding two guns another fifty feet away. After they ran the distance in more deep sand, they were required to shoot several moving targets.

Grant thought about how his mother had wanted him to follow in his father's footsteps and become the town dentist.

Well, that would've been a helluva lot easier, that's for sure, he thought.

The truth was that becoming a dentist would've been way too dull for Grant Ketchum. Life in the marines, and then working missions with First Force, was more to his liking—although right now he wouldn't mind taking a drill to Smitty's head.

"What's the matter, Ketchum? That West Virginia beer gut slowin' ya down?" Smitty yelled as they plodded through the sand toward Little, whose default expression had gone from ugly to darn right ugly while he timed them.

"Bite me, Smith!"

"Less talkin' and more doin'! Shit, at this rate Rhodes is gonna catch up to ya!" Little growled at them, which really wasn't all that intimidating—Little only had one tone: growl.

Clark Rhodes, the computer geek, and his sister, Casey, were the team behind them after Jack and Dan. The computer guru and the woman on the team—no way were they gonna let them catch up. They would never hear the end of it from anyone, including the computer guru and the woman on the team. Casey was quiet, but she could zing you at precisely the right moment.

Grant and Smitty grabbed the guns from Little. Five paper targets with the dark silhouettes of terrorists glided across a twelve-foot wall of piled straw. The guns were loaded with only five shots—they were required to hit at least two of the targets in the kill zone. No problem; both men hit four of the targets dead on. Good.

They heard Jack and Dan's exerted footsteps in the sand pushing toward the shooting range.

Time to move on to the next and last obstacles: traverse a twenty-foot horizontal ladder, and finally toss a one-hundred pound dummy over their shoulder and hustle to the finish.

The course was demanding, but it had proven to get them through many situations out in the field.

As Grant jumped up to grab the first wrung of the ladder, the cell phone in his pocket rang.

Swinging from wrung to wrung, he listened to the ringing. Reaching the end, he jumped down to hoist the dummy over his shoulder and press on to the finish line with Smitty at his side.

Walt snapped the stopwatch as they stepped over the finish line and pitched the dummies off to the side. "Not too shabby," he said while watching Grant dig madly into his pocket to pull out a cell phone.

The young man's eyes blinked away the sweat and narrowed while he looked at the screen.

"Again, you seem distracted, Ketchum."

Grant couldn't believe his eyes. Silja's name appeared on the list of "missed calls." He hadn't heard from her in so long, yet she'd been so heavy on his mind. Why would she be calling?

"Watch out, Ketchum!" Walt called just as a dummy smacked him in the back.

Grant sidestepped and turned.

"Sorry, Grant," Dan said. "I didn't realize I'd thrown the stupid thing that hard."

"It was his fault, Garrison. He wasn't paying any attention," Walt bit out.

Grant could see the reprimand in Walt's eyes. "Sorry," Grant muttered, "I should've stepped further out of the way, Dan."

Walking away, he pressed the *redial* button. Silja's phone rang and rang, but she didn't pick up. What the hell?

* * * * *

Silja stared at the salad that she'd put together. Problem was that she was no longer hungry. She wasn't sure if she'd ever be hungry again. She tossed the bowl and its contents into the garbage. Her cell phone rang. Glancing down, she saw Grant's name of the screen. *Grant ...*

She reached for the phone, but then she retreated. No—she and Eleni had a plan of action in place, and it could work. She just needed to keep a cool head and everything would work out. She was not going to involved Grant.

Again, her hand reached for the phone, only she quickly pressed the ignore button. That's right, she was not going to drag Grant Ketchum into her trouble.

CHAPTER TEN

"Silja, I am frightened for you. What will happen if this does not work?" Eleni was at the edge of panic. Her face was ashen and her hands were less than steady when she tried to apply red lipstick.

"Don't worry. Once they know that I have evidence of their dirty little prostitution ring, they'll all back down. Natalia won't get any money from Ballard, but the dancers won't have to attend these horrible auctions anymore. If anyone, including Ballard, makes a wrong move, I'll report it." Silja spun around. "Now zip me."

Letting out an apprehensive breath, Eleni zipped up the little black dress that Silja had worn the night before when she had had dinner with Ballard. "I wish that I could convince you not to do this. You are taking such risk for all of us, Silja. If things go wrong, you could be hurt ... or worse. Somehow, we will find a way out of this. Perhaps the dancers should band together and refuse to attend the parties. We have talked about this, but we have not found the courage to go through with it. If we did, Novikov would close. Some of the older dancers are terrified that they will not find work, and that is why they do this." She dropped her gaze to the floor. "I must admit, I am one of them. I am almost thirty-one. How many years do I have left to dance in the ballets? Not many. I have dedicated my life to the ballet. I have no husband, no children, only the ballet. This is why I have done what I have done, like many of the other dancers. But now ... I am ashamed."

Silja touched her shoulder. "Please, Eleni, don't be. I have no one in my life either. Like you, I have given everything to this ballet company. I'm disgusted by what Natalia and Edvar have done, and I'm sickened by the fact that Ballard participated. After the smoke clears, maybe we can sit down with Natalia and see if there is a sensible solution to the Novikov's financial problems."

I hope, she found herself thinking while pushing her feet into the silver stilettos. She studied her reflection in the mirror. She had been so thrilled to take the position as principal dancer at

143

the Novikov Ballet Company five years ago, and now she was wishing that she'd stayed home. She could have danced in Pittsburgh or Charleston or Baltimore. Her life would have been different—her love life would have been different.

She couldn't think in those terms—it was too late. She glanced at her tiny clutch bag on the vanity—and yes, it was too late to call Grant back and ask for help.

After pacing her apartment floors all afternoon, and after the terrible altercation with Dominik, she decided that she had to do something to stop what Natalia and Edvar were doing to the dancers.

Ballard's indecent proposition to be his companion and lover was over the top.

Now she was going to turn the tables on them all. She would show up at tonight's contributors' party and video the auction on her cell phone. When her pointe shoes were pulled from the box, she would make her appearance and announce that she had evidence—but she wouldn't say exactly what kind she had.

Then she would issue her ultimatum: Make one wrong move and the police will know about everything.

She had to admit, the plan wasn't exactly full-proof or anywhere near a professional level, but it was all she had, and she had to do something—

anything. Closing her eyes, she said a silent prayer that everything would go as planned.

Feeling a shiver of unease down her spine, she turned to Eleni. "Are you ready?"

"No, but I suppose there are no more choices."

"You're right, there aren't."

* * * * *

Grant stepped into the shower. He had one hour until he had to be at the private airfield in Harverton, which was only a twenty-minute, ten-mile drive from his condo in the small town of Yeager.

He liked Yeager. It reminded him of the small town of Chester, West Virginia, where he'd been raised. It had a down-home atmosphere where people rooted for the high school football team, and they put on one hell of a Fourth of July fireworks display.

Even though his job demanded that he keep to himself, the people were friendly. They waved at him when he drove past their homes, smiled or nodded at him at the gas station, and always wished him a "great day" after he paid for purchases at the convenience store.

Nice town—nice people.

The water was good and hot. He always made sure he got a shower right before he left because the reality was that while on an op he was never sure when his next shower would be. Sometimes the team would have a place to stay, while other times they made a primitive camp—for weeks. He never knew what the situation would be until he got there.

Once they were on the plane, they would be out of communication until they returned, so he always made sure that he called home to check on his mom before leaving. The conversation was always the same, "When are you going to settle down and have a family, Grant?" she would ask.

Yeah, he wondered that himself. Not any time soon.

He stepped out of the shower, dried, and then made his way to the dresser. He opened the top drawer to fetch a fresh pair of boxers when his eyes fell upon a small red velvet box.

His lips drew into a tight thin line as he picked up the box and opened it. A diamond ring winked at him—the ring he was going to give Silja. Only instead of a romantic proposal, Silja informed him that she'd been accepted into the Novikov Ballet Company and would be going to Russia.

He couldn't tell her no.

His insides had twisted, and he had almost begged her to stay, but ballet was her life. It was what made her tick. How could he take that away from her? The tiny box remained securely in his pocket until he deposited into the drawer, where it had remained for five years. He couldn't return it, nor could he give it to another—it belonged to Sil.

Snapping the lid closed, he tucked the tiny box back in the drawer, grabbed a pair of boxer briefs, and then went about getting dressed to leave, pulling on a pair of camo pants, a black T-shirt, and his combat boots.

Grant made one more check of his go-bag. His jeans were slung over the footboard of his bed. He could see the outline of his cell phone in the back pocket. He had tried to call Silja several times, but she didn't answer, and he didn't leave a message.

Maybe she had just butt-dialed him; after all, they hadn't spoken directly in years. Why would she suddenly call him? It was a miss-dial, he was sure of it. *Hokay—that was fine.* He had to leave the phone behind anyway. He dropped his bag next to the door on his way to the kitchen, figuring he'd better fuel up before he left.

* * * * *

Eleni suggested that Silja hide in the coat check during the party until it was time for her to make her appearance. Eleni volunteered to man the coats for the evening, so they arrived early for the party to secure Silja's position. The room had a small service window that Eleni opened just a crack so Silja could monitor the activity at the party without being detected. Claiming that the service window's roller was stuck, Eleni would check the coats from the doorway. It seemed like a plausible story. No sooner had Eleni closed her in the freezing room than the bartender and the violinist arrived to set up shop.

Hidden in the freezing cold coat room of the theatre's small reception hall, Silja checked her phone again to make sure it was ready. She noted that Grant had called her twice. Her heart sank. She should call him to apologize for the butt-dial, except she was afraid that she would weaken and tell him what was going on. There was nothing he could do for her now. It was too late. She'd made her decision, and the plan was now underway.

Perhaps she'd call him later. Perhaps.

Shivering among the coats for over an hour, Silja was filled with abhorrence while watching the prominent and wealthy clientele of the cultural community fondle the dancers like they were slabs of meat.

She was mostly taken aback by the women—by and large they were in their late forties and fifties, although there weren't very many of them, only six or seven that she managed to count. Then again, there really weren't that many male dancers in the Novikov Ballet Company, and from what Eleni had told her, some of the attendees were unhappy that Dominik was off limits.

Still, she couldn't imagine that the male dancers appreciated the situation anymore than the girls— especially those who didn't care for a woman's company in the first place. They were all trapped by the love of their craft and the fear that they would lose it.

She wasn't sure if she should feel relieved or proud or disappointed that she hadn't spotted Ballard in the group. Where was he? Was he staying away because she said that she would be at the party? She thought for sure that that would be the very reason for him to attend, and yet he was nowhere to be found. Moreover, his seat in the front row of the theatre had been empty during the ballet. She wasn't sure how she felt about any of it.

As she sat among the coats, she suddenly heard Eleni talking very loudly in English outside the door of the coat check. "I can get your coat for you, *Dominik*. Do you have your tag?"

He answered her in Russian, but she continued to speak in English. Silja was certain that it was for her benefit.

Eleni said, "No, it is okay, I will get coat. Where are you going?"

Again, Dominik answered in Russian. His voice sounded agitated, harsh as always, yet Silja had to wonder if he wasn't asking Eleni why she was talking so loudly and in English. The thought made her giggle.

As the door opened, Eleni added, "I will be right out." She quickly slipped inside. "Dominik needs his coat. It is black pea coat."

Silja remembered the coat from his visit. She grabbed it from the rack and tossed it to Eleni. "Where is he going?" she asked.

"Outside for a smoke. Maybe we will get lucky and he will set himself on fire," Eleni stepped out of the closet.

Silja covered her mouth to smother a chuckle.

After what seemed like an eternity, the event that Eleni had described at length was about to begin. She heard Natalia's voice above the thrum of the crowd that then hushed. Gingerly, Silja opened the service window just a crack so she could see what was going on and video it as well. Natalia lifted a box in the air and called out to the guests in Russian. The room became very quiet. This was Silja's cue.

All eyes were on Natalia toward the front of the room standing next to the bar.

With the video running on her cell phone, Silja crept from the coat room to covertly lose herself among the crowd.

Eleni looked at her askance. Her face was tight with anxiety while she waited among several of the dancers.

With measured steps, Silja made her way to stand behind them when she heard Edvar yell out, "Belsky!"

Silja recognized the tubby man who had spoken with Ballard at the restaurant the night before. He skipped and hopped to the front of the room with his hands over his head and an ear-to-ear grin on his face.

Natalia was smiling, except Silja could see the underlying disdain in her eyes when he drew closer. She could feel the tension that vibrated off the dancers while he made a big show of shoving his hand into the box and digging around.

The instant that Belsky pulled a pair of shoes from the box, Ballard entered the room.

Silja's heart stopped. He looked perturbed while he searched the room—undoubtedly for her. She ducked down further behind Eleni and the dancers, and then she heard Belsky cry out in jubilant fervor, "Silja Ramsay!"

The dancers gasped.

Silja couldn't breathe.

Her throat was instantly dry.

Eleni murmured something in Russian—Silja was sure that it was a curse.

The room seemed to stop. Natalia snatched the shoes from Belsky's hand in disbelief, but Belsky danced in place while pointing at the shoes. He shouted out again, "Silja Ramsay!"

Ballard bellowed, "That's not possible!"

Flinching, Natalia spun to come face to face with the irate American. The room fell silent. Natalia said, "This is mistake. Silja Ramsay is not here."

It took every ounce of courage that she could muster. Silja raised her hand over her head. She called out, "I am here, Natalia."

The crowd came to life, chattering to each other as Silja pressed through the group of dancers toward Natalia, Ballard, and Belsky. Frantic, Edvar followed her.

"What are you doing here, Silja?" Natalia demanded.

"I am a dancer for the Novikov Ballet Company. Why shouldn't I be part of your dirty little parties?" Silja asked succinctly.

"Because you belong to me." Ballard grabbed her by the hand.

Silja jerked her hand away. "Really? Did you buy me, Ballard?"

"Silja, I—"

"She is right!" Belsky exclaimed as he stepped between them. "I was the highest bidder tonight! She is mine!" He grabbed Silja by the arm so roughly that she could feel his fingernails biting into her skin when he jerked her out of the room and dragged her down the hallway toward the door.

Trying to break free, she pulled back.

It was time to make her announcement—to give them her ultimatum—but Belsky yanked her out of the room before she could utter a word. She could barely keep up with him in the tall stiletto shoes, yet he didn't try to accommodate her stride. She tripped. He hauled her to her feet and kept right on going.

This wasn't how the plan was supposed to go! She was supposed to wield her warning that she would go to the police if the dancers weren't relieved from their inappropriate duties immediately.

Belsky didn't give her a chance to speak. He grabbed her too quickly, and now she was being dragged off to fulfill the foul obligation that her fellow dancers had been put through for months.

"Stop!" she demanded. "Let me go!"

The tubby man just jerked on her arm harder while tugging her toward the door.

Fear ripped through her.

Maybe this wasn't such a grand idea.

The memory of Anna Antkowiak's mutilated face sent a wave of pure panic churning through her stomach. She glanced over her shoulder—no one was following. She couldn't believe it! She thought for certain that Ballard would protest to the point of a showdown, yet he wasn't even following!

Speaking harshly to her in Russian, Belsky shoved open the door that led into the alley behind the theatre. As he forced her into the alley, she caught a glimpse of a figure smoking a cigarette, but then it was suddenly gone. Several vehicles were parked among pallets and dumpsters. One must have belonged to Belsky. He must have parked in the alley for a quick getaway with his Saturday night purchase.

Snow fell steadily, illuminated against the few dim street lamps that lined the desolate area. She didn't know where Belsky intended to take her, but she had no intention of getting into the sedan that he was shoving her toward.

She twisted her wrist and yanked. "Let go of me! I'm not going anywhere with you!"

Belsky whirled around—bending her wrist until she thought it would snap. He bit out a nasty sentence in Russian and then slapped her across the face.

Yelping, she stumbled to her knees.

He turned to push her toward his vehicle when he bumped into a solid wall of Crafton bodyguard muscle.

Belsky froze. He was terrified, and Silja couldn't blame him. She was just as frightened by the surly Russian brute standing before them as Belsky was. She recognized him as Ballard's bodyguard, Mikhail, except she'd never seen the look of sheer malice on his face. He always seemed so pleasant every time she encountered him—but not this night.

He grabbed Belsky by the throat with his big hands.

Silja let out a scream before she could call it back. Belsky desperately tried to reason or bribe or beg with Mikhail, but he wasn't taking the bait. He tossed Belsky to the gravel like a rag doll, and then he picked him up again to punch him in the face.

Belsky cried out in agony. Although the lighting was poor, she could see the splash of blood over his face.

Terrified, Silja decided that it was time to ditch her plans and make a run for it!

Her ankles wobbled in the stilettos as she slipped and stumbled along the snowy and rutty ground to the end of the alley.

The frosty wind dried out her throat, which made it hard to catch a breath. Even in the chill, the sweat dribbled down her temples.

Finally, she emerged from the dark alley onto the well-lit main street. She could no longer hear Belsky's cries. Forcing her exhausted ankles to push forward, she made it to the bus stop at the same time that her bus pulled up. The doors opened. She fell up the slushy first step while attempting to rush into the bus. The driver spoke to her in Russian, and she suddenly realized that she had no money. Tears burst from her eyes. She glanced over her shoulder to see if anyone had emerged from the alley in pursuit. Not yet.

"I'm so sorry," she told the driver in her poor Russian. "I don't have any rubles. Please ... please I'll bring them tomorrow. I promise!"

She must have looked like she'd crawled out from under the bus because the driver's expression was one of concern. Saying nothing, he hitched his chin toward the seats and then pulled the door closed. "Thank you," she managed in Russian.

She held on to the seats for dear life while making her way to the second row.

There were only three people on the bus: two old women with babushkas wrapped around their heads and necks, and an old man chewing on his gums. They stared at her as if she had just shot the driver, and then they turned away. They didn't want any part of whatever was going on.

As the bus bumped along the street, she looked down at her shaking hands. Much to her surprise, she was still holding her cell phone. She couldn't believe it. With trembling hands, she dialed Eleni's number, but she did not answer. Silja wondered what happened at the party after she was taken away.

Twenty minutes later, Silja stepped off the bus in front of her apartment building. Luckily, one of her neighbors was going inside and held the door for her. She didn't have her purse, therefore she didn't have her key, so she tapped on her landlord's door. At first he was annoyed by the late night intrusion, but when he got a good look at her his eyes filled with sympathy. Dressed in his pajamas and a robe, he ambled up two flights to let her into her apartment. It was obvious that the landlord wanted nothing to do with Silja's situation. She tried to thank him over and over, but he waved his hand at her while mumbling something in Russian before quickly making his way back to his apartment.

Silja closed the door and fell against it to catch her breath. Her plan had totally blown up in her face, and it seemed that she had only made matters worse. *What the hell was I thinking?* Her hands were shaking and her face burned from the frigid wind.

She pushed away from the door to stumble across the room to the bathroom.

Once she looked into the mirror, she understood why everyone had been staring at her with wide-eyed questions that they dared not ask. She looked like an abused twenty-dollar hooker. Her hair was askew. Her dress was ripped. The silver stilettos were dirty and scuffed, and her face was brilliant red from the cold which accentuated the bruise on her cheek where Belsky had hit her. It was swelling toward her eye, and it stung like the dickens, but hey, it could've been worse—much worse. She ran cold water over a washcloth and held it to her face—wincing at the throb.

She had failed the dancers. What now?

As her body warmed, she let out the breath that she felt like she'd been holding since she stepped out of the coatroom. Kicking the stilettos aside, she slipped out of the tattered cocktail dress and pulled on a pair of old comfy jeans, a sweatshirt, and a pair of moccasins. As she sunk onto the edge of her bed, she noticed Greta sound asleep on her pillow. She picked the cat up and snuggled her to her chest. Purring, Greta nuzzled against her as if she knew that Silja was searching for comfort.

Again, she dialed Eleni's number. No answer. Trepidation gripped her. Where was Eleni? Suddenly she realized that someone would come looking for her, if for no other reason than to make sure that she remained silent. She had to get out, and she had to get to Eleni to make sure that she was okay.

She laid her phone on the bed and the cat on her pillow. Yawning, Greta made herself comfortable until her mistress came to bed and claimed it from her, but Silja had no intentions of sleeping tonight. Instead, she yanked open the closet door and grabbed a small suitcase. Hurrying about the room, she pulled things from drawers that she needed, including her passport.

She only had the suitcase half full when she heard the door to her apartment crash open!

From the corner of her room, she could see Mikhail looking about the kitchen and living room for her. She needed time to escape, so she slammed her bedroom door closed, grabbed the chair from the corner of the room, and jammed it under the knob. It probably wouldn't hold for very long, but it would give her time to—to do what? She was two stories up with no fire escape. Russia didn't have the same standard of housing codes that the United States had, so the window was pretty much a bust.

Mikhail began to pound and push on her bedroom door. His Russian accent bellowed through the door, "Silja, I do not wish to harm you. You must come with me. Mr. Crafton wants you to come, now."

The door was giving from its hinges. The chair was rocking in place from the pressure. Silja's eyes fell upon the cell phone lying on the bed—but who could help her? There was no one to worry for her except ...

Grant.

She didn't have the time or the luxury of deliberating over the pathetic ex-girlfriend scenario. She needed help, and she needed it from whoever would give it.

Grant Ketchum was her only hope.

She snatched the phone from the bed as the door bowed and creaked against Mikhail's might. The chair under the knob rocked side to side. A quick text—her thumb raced over the keys. She pressed *send* just as the door burst from its hinges to send shards of wood in all directions and the chair tumbled aside with a loud thud.

Silja threw the phone away—hitting Greta in the head. Startled, Greta jumped from the bed—knocking the phone to the floor near the radiator under the window when the cat scampered under the bed.

The look on Mikhail's face terrified Silja.

Backing away, she thought for sure he would break her in half, but the huge man calmly stepped over the broken chair. He scanned the room. Spotting her suitcase on the bed, he slammed the lid closed, zipped it, and then he grabbed Silja by the arm.

Silja pulled back with all her might, but the bodyguard was too strong.

While dragging her from the bedroom and through the living room, he said, "Do not resist, Silja. I do not wish to harm you, but I will restrain you if necessary. Do not make me do this."

She wasn't going down without a fight. She held onto furniture, but it just squealed against the wood floor when it was dragged along with them until she couldn't hold on anymore. She kicked at him, but he shot her a look that screamed, *Is that all you've got, woman?* It was no use, she was going with Ballard's bodyguard whether she wanted to or not.

As he approached the door, she decided upon one more shot: Silja grabbed a lamp off the end table near the door and smacked him across the shoulder with it. The lamp bounced off of him to the floor.

Mikhail came to a stop, took a deep breath, grabbed her by the waist, and then tucked her under his arm. He closed the apartment door on his way out.

How considerate.

Silja caught a glimpse of her neighbors peeking through gaps in their apartment doors while Mikhail carried her toward the stairs. They must've been curious about what the racket was coming from her apartment and now the hallway. Before Mikhail began to descend the stairs, he noticed the wary eyes upon them. His voice thick with warning, he yelled at them. The doors closed *slam, slam, slam,* as if in a choreographed reply. They wanted no part of being witnesses to what was happening to the young girl who lived just a few doors down.

He carried her through the tiny lobby and out the front door to Ballard's waiting limo parked at the curb. He opened the door and shoved her inside, where Ballard sat sipping a martini.

Ballard looked at her impassively. Dipping his fingers into the glass to retrieve the olive, he popped it into his mouth.

The limo drove forward.

"That's a nasty bruise on your face, Silja. But it will be nothing in comparison to what will happen to you if you ever pull something like that on me again." He turned to her with an expression as cold as the icy winter wind whipping outside the car. "Do you understand?"

Silja said nothing. Rather she stared forward at the back of Mikhail's head through the tinted privacy window.

Grabbing her by the chin, he forced her to look at him. "Do. You. Understand?"

His breath smelled like booze and olives. His fingers squeezed the bruise, making it burn like hell fire.

She bit out, "Yes."

"Yes, what?" he demanded, squeezing even harder.

"Yes! I ... I understand."

He pulled her to him and kissed her hard. "Good. Now there is business we must discuss."

* * * * *

The dishes were rinsed and piled in the drain board. Grant slung his go-bag over his shoulder and opened the door to leave when his cell phone whistled at him from the bedroom. Text message. Glancing at his watch, he had exactly twenty-five minutes to get to the air field to catch the flight with the team. It was probably one of those stupid messages from his cell phone provider informing him of some great offer they had going, and he didn't have time for that crap right now. He slipped out the door and down the front steps to his candy apple red Camaro sitting in his driveway.

CHAPTER ELEVEN

Dominik crept out from behind a car parked at the end of the alley.

His face smashed and bloody, Belsky lay in an icy puddle. Ballard's bodyguard had roughed him up good. With measured steps, Dominik made his way across the alley now covered in a half-inch of snow still falling steadily. Belsky was covered with a thin skiff. He shivered and moaned.

Oh, how he hated Ivan Belsky. When he was a young dancer just out of the Vaganova Academy, Belsky told him that he could advance his career quickly—Belsky had connections in the cultural community. He pretended that his interest in him was purely because of Dominik's talent, but on the eve of his audition with the renowned Bolshoi

Ballet Company, Belsky demanded that he give him pleasure. He demanded that Dominik dump his lover to become Belsky's. Dominik refused—Belsky made him sick—and he walked out of his apartment. The next day when he arrived for his audition, he was told that he was not on the list. He was not permitted to audition. He was unable to get an audition anywhere for two years. His dreams of professionally dancing ballet were diminished—until the Novikov finally gave him an opportunity.

Now Belsky attended the contributors' parties as if he wanted the ballerinas, but the truth was that he made phone call after phone call to Natalia about his desire to spend a night with Dominik. How disgusting would that be? Natalia explained that he belonged to Edvar and was off limits, but the man insisted that it was unfair. Natalia agreed, the witch, but she explained that there was little that could be done.

Edvar Kozlovski was a very high-strung man. When he heard about the calls, he threw a tantrum, which blew his blood pressure dangerously high. It would take Dominik hours to settle Edvar and for his pressure to come back down.

Now that little bitch, Silja, dared to start trouble. It was time for them both to learn a valuable lesson.

As Dominik stood over him, Belsky's eyes opened. Gasping for air, he reached his hand out. "Help me, Dominik," he pleaded.

"Yes, I will help you." Dominik pulled a knife from his coat.

Belsky's eyes bulged. He managed to grab Dominik's hand, except he was too weak to prevent the stab into his shoulder. He kept hold of Dominik's hand—forcing him to yank the knife out as blood gushed from the wound.

The knife was slippery and slimy with Belsky's blood when Dominik rammed the knife into Belsky's chest. His hand slid down the blade—cutting through his thin leather glove on his right hand. Ignoring the burn in his own skin, he pushed the knife harder through Belsky's heart.

Belsky flinched. His eyes fluttered and then his head fell to the side—lifeless.

His face screwed up in disdain, Dominik drew his hand away to pull the glove from his hand. Blood oozed from the slice in his skin. "Swine," he snarled, stuffing the glove into his coat pocket.

Dominik hurried into the theatre and into the men's room to tend to his hand. After he managed to stop the bleeding, he wrapped it in a paper towel and returned to the reception room to find that the party had broken up. The bartender was boxing up bottles of wine that hadn't been opened, and the violinist was packing her instrument into its case.

Sipping a red wine, Natalia was sitting on a love-seat in the corner next to Edvar.

Edvar jumped up when Dominik came into the room. "Dominik, my love, where have you been?" he asked, and then his eyes found the bloody paper towel wrapped around Dominik's hand. He grabbed his hand with a gasp. "What happened to your hand?"

"Nothing ... a simple cut. I am fine, Edvar. We must call the police," Dominik said. Edvar's eyes widened, while Natalia's head jerked toward him. He placed his hand on Edvar's shoulder and squeezed. "You must stay calm, Edvar. I don't want your blood pressure to rise, but I found Belsky in the alley stabbed to death. It is Silja's doing."

Cupping his hand over his mouth, Edvar gasped.

Natalia stood. "How do you know this to be true?" she demanded.

"I saw her running from the alley. No one else was around. I think she planned to kill him for what he did to Anna Antkowiak."

"I don't believe it! Where was Ballard?" Natalia inquired.

"I did not see him."

"We cannot call the police, Dominik. Silja will tell them what we have been doing," Edvar said.

"What are you suggesting, Edvar? That we should leave Belsky out in the alley and not report this to anyone?" Natalia asked.

Dominik laid his hand on Natalia's arm. "I think it is best. The contributors went home unhappy and empty-handed. The dancers are gone now for two weeks on holiday. Let the police find him, and let's get out of here right away before they do."

Edvar rushed away to grab their coats.

Natalia gauged Dominik's reaction. He was shifting nervously from foot to foot. He kept a furtive eye on the doorway. When Edvar returned, he helped Dominik eddy into his coat, and then he assisted Natalia.

Dominik said, "Let's hurry home."

"Why do we need to hurry, Dominik, if we have done nothing wrong? Yet there you stand with your hand dripping blood. A simple cut you claim, and now you are in a hurry?" Natalia inquired.

Dominik glared at her. "Stay if you wish. We are leaving." He and Edvar nipped out the door.

Following, Natalia hesitated in the hallway. She considered going into the alley to make sure Belsky was dead—that he wasn't just unconscious and in need of an ambulance, but when she got to the door she changed her mind and turned to catch up with Dominik and Edvar.

CHAPTER TWELVE

The sound of his cell phone's text message alert nagged at Grant as he tossed the go-bag into the back seat of his Camaro, buckled in, and started the engine.

Everyone on the team knew that he should be on his way to the airfield without his personal cell phone, so why would any of them text him?

His mom didn't like using text messages. She preferred actual conversation, so it couldn't have been her. *Sil?* Was she sending him a text to apologize for the butt-dial or something more important? *Naw.*

Sighing, he shoved the car into reverse. His curiosity was getting the best of him—or was it the bad juju that was coiling through his gut? *Ahhh shit.*

Knowing that he was going to run late, he threw the car into park and got out to hurry back inside. Jogging into the bedroom, he snatched his jeans from the bed, slipping the cell phone out from the back pocket.

The screen read "Silja Ramsay." The text message simply read *"Help!"*

What? His eyes narrowed. Silja was not one to play jokes. She wasn't a prankster. He glanced at his watch—he was now four minutes behind schedule. As he hurried out the door, he thumbed Silja's number. The phone rang and rang and rang.

He jumped into the car that he'd left running, slammed it into reverse to whip out of his driveway, and then peeled out of the apartment complex while thumbing her number again. The phone rang and rang and rang until ... "Hello, this is Silja Ramsay. I can't take your call right now—" He hung up.

What kind of trouble was she in? What kind of trouble could a ballerina get into?

Grant had a problem—a big one.

He was getting ready to leave on an op. Walt was questioning his focus. The team was counting on him.

Silja needed him. She was in some kind of trouble. It had to be important because she would never reach out to him like this if it weren't dire.

He had to calm down. He had to think straight.

He looked down at the speedometer to find that he was traveling seventy-five MPH in a forty-five MPH zone. Whoa.

He slowed the car down. He didn't need the police to pull him over and hold him back for thirty minutes. Rolling to a stop at a red light, he dialed Silja's number again, and again he got the voicemail. Only this time, he left a message.

"Sil, it's Grant. What's going on? Please call me."

Fifteen minutes later, he pulled into a parking spot next to Dan's SUV.

Still, Silja had not returned his call or sent another text. Now what? The team was gathered on the tarmac, ready to leave. He shoved his cell phone into his pocket, grabbed his go-bag, locked his car, and jogged toward Walt, Clark, and the team. He was the last to arrive, but he was right on time.

Walt was checking his watch.

"Glad you could make it, Ketchum," Walt said. He turned to the team. "Okay, load up—it's time to move out."

Dan, Jack, Casey, Smitty, and Little climbed the steps to the plane with their go-bags slung over their shoulders. They were ready to go, except Grant hesitated at the bottom of the steps. He turned to Walt. "Walt ... I've got a problem," he said, and then he handed Walt the cell phone.

Looking over Walt's shoulder, Clark lifted his eyebrows at the urgent message.

"What kind of trouble is this ... Silja Ramsay in?" Walt asked.

"I don't know. She isn't answering her phone."

"Who is she?" Clark inquired.

"Someone who means the world to me."

"Where is she?" Walt asked.

"Russia ..."

Walt studied the message and then studied Grant's face. "What are you asking, Ketchum?"

"I don't want to let the team down, Walt. I know my responsibilities, but she's in some kind of trouble. She has no family to help her, and Russia can be a dangerous place. If you don't want to let me go, I'll understand. But I've got to go to her because if I don't and something happens to her, I couldn't live with myself." Grant could see the contemplation in Walt's eyes. His jaw was tight.

"I'll talk to the team." Walt trotted up the steps into the plane.

Grant glanced at Clark who was gauging the situation over the top of his glasses. "If you need any assistance with intel, call me."

"You'll be busy with the team and the op."

"You're part of that team, Grant. Where in Russia?"

"Yekaterinburg."

"You'll be flying into the Koltsovo Airport. That's gonna be a long-ass flight with several connections." He pulled his iPad from his jacket. His fingers raced over the buttons. "A military charter will be waiting for you when you arrive at the airport. I'll have a private charter waiting at La Guardia to take you on to Moscow, and a shuttle to Koltsovo—you'll have to check your weapon at the point. Sorry."

"Not a problem ... but ..."

"You've never let the team down. They're not about to let you down now," Clark assured him when Walt appeared at the hatch and started down the steps.

"Go," he told Grant. "I'm considering this a mission, so we're picking up the tab on this. Don't hesitate to contact us if you need us."

Grant glanced at Clark, who was wearing a svelte smile as he tapped at the iPad. Grant reached for Walt's hand. "Thanks." He clapped his hand on Clark's shoulder with a nod and then jogged back to the parking area to get into his car.

It would be a long drive to the airport, but at least he knew that all the arrangements would be made and waiting for him when he arrived.

* * * * *

The bedroom that Silja had been locked in for the night oozed elegance. Pale pink walls, an ornate gold curvy headboard with tall bedposts at the foot of the bed, and the huge candlestick chandelier that hung over the middle of the room made for an exquisite prison, but that's exactly what it was—a prison.

The floor to ceiling windows that flanked the bed looked out over a courtyard. A snowy mantle covered the trees and shrubbery, shimmering in the morning sunshine as if God had scattered sequins over their skeletal-like branches. The tables on either side of the bed held large vintage crystal vases filled with roses: orange and red—love and desire—the very feelings she would have most likely grown to feel for Ballard, but now those two emotions were farthest from reality.

Unable to do little else, Silja had spent the night exploring the closets that were filled with designer clothes and shoes and boots and evening dresses in her size. It was as though Ballard had been expecting her arrival.

A beautiful silk night gown had been laid out on the bed.

She was fingering the delicate lace trim when the bed post caught her attention. It was disfigured toward the bottom where it attached to the rail that ran across to the other side. She ran her fingers over deep grooves that molested the wood. The bed-post had been scarred by something rigid that had scratched the surface severely and then dug into the wood. Upon closer examination, the coarse furrow ran the entire girth of the post. Some of the damage looked rather old while newer crevices appeared over top, below, and above the older ones. Her eyes flicked to the other post—it was unmarred. Strange.

When Ballard brought her to the room he said, "I've prepared this room for you because I don't expect you to sleep with me right away. You are upset with me. I understand that. But you will be expected to get over it quickly and serve as my companion and lover very soon."

He closed the door and locked it—leaving her stunned in the middle of the room. Through the door, he said, "Sleep well, Silja."

Silja eased down on the edge of the bed and buried her face in her hands. Sleep? There was no way that she would sleep. She hoped that her text message had gone through. She prayed that Grant had read it and would somehow come to her aide.

God, she needed him now. She needed him all along—how stupid she had been!

By four o'clock in the morning, fatigue and anxiety and the constant pacing had gotten the best of her. They had not given her the suitcase that she was packing when Mikhail burst into her room, so she grabbed the nightgown from the bed. Then, she rummaged through the dresser drawers to find a stack of La Perla panties.

Ballard knew what he liked. If it weren't for the fact that she simply didn't have her own panties, she would never have put them on.

Thinking it would help calm her nerves, she wandered into the bathroom for a hot shower.

When she turned on the light, the room took her breath away. The bath was as elegant as the bedroom. A huge garden tub was situated on a platform in the middle of the room. It was deep and round with a wrought iron trellis overhead balanced on four marble columns that corralled the tub. A warmer filled with large fluffy towels flanked each side, and marble vanities lined the wall to the left, while a shower large enough for at least four people was encased in the wall to the right. Ornate vases atop two marble pedestals at the opening of the stairs that led to the tub were filled with pink and white roses. *Whatever.*

Indeed, Silja was in the lap of luxury. She was where most any woman would want to be, and yet she was a hostage. Ballard expected her to be his companion and his lover—soon. How soon?

How could she give herself to a man who had taken advantage of the ballerinas from the company? How could she give herself to a man who had basically bartered and bought her in exchange for a ballet company? She was nothing more than a slave. She felt tight in her own skin. Her stomach twisted every time she looked at him.

She stepped into the shower and allowed the water to wash over her.

Uninvited, the terse words he spoke in the limo last night returned to her memory, sending a shiver up her spine under the hot spray: *"That's a nasty bruise on your face, Silja. But it will be nothing in comparison to what will happen to you if you ever pull something like that on me again. Do you understand?"*

The warm water hit her chin—causing it to burn. She caressed the sore spot, remembering how he grabbed her face and squeezed the bruises left behind by the battering she endured at the hands of Belsky in the alley behind the theater. She yelped in pain.

Fiercely, Ballard repeated, *"Do. You. Understand?"*

She wished she could erase the memory of how he grabbed her roughly, pulled her across the seat against his body, and kissed her. It was a kiss that sent a vivid message: you are mine. I possess you. When he retreated from the kiss, he said, *"Now we have business to discuss."*

She lifted her face to let the water rush over her bruises. Was she now his property to do with as he pleased? Her fingers gingerly touched the swollen skin on her face. A tear slipped down her cheek.

Please Grant, please help me.

Silja lay down in the bed and pulled the blankets to her chin. Much to her surprise, she dozed off. She was awaken with a start by a brisk tapping on her door.

Ballard's voice called from the other side:

"Breakfast is in ten minutes, Silja, and not a minute more. You can dress casually. We won't be going out in public until those bruises on your face are healed."

She lay in the bed until his footsteps faded away. Is this what her life would be like? Confined to her room until he summoned her for whatever he desired?

Tears welled in her eyes.

He had explained the terms of his agreement with Natalia and Edvar in the limo last night—an exchange: her freedom for financial security for the Novikov Ballet Company.

Again, the hope that her desperate plea for help had reached Grant Ketchum swelled inside of her.

She swept her hair back in a loose ponytail and chose a periwinkle V-neck sweater, skinny jeans, and a pair of Gucci riding boots to wear for breakfast.

Silja made her way downstairs into the dining room. She found Ballard sitting at the head of a long table that was situated in front of two sliding glass doors looking out onto a stone patio that spilled into the courtyard that she could see from her bedroom. A place was set for her next to him. He looked up at her over the rim of a glass of orange juice.

"Tess! Silja is here, please bring in breakfast," he called toward a door on the far end of the room. Then, he smiled at her. "Good morning. Did you sleep well?"

He was dressed in the casual manner that he had been when he visited her apartment a week ago:

jeans, a soft faded denim shirt, and a pair of comfy moccasins on his feet. The Rolex watch on his wrist glinted in the sunshine that beamed through the glass doors when he set the empty glass on the table. Somehow the watch had lost its friendly laid-back persona that it had possessed only days ago.

She was less impressed with Ballard's relaxed appearance this morning. The ugly truth had blown through the facade that he'd portrayed previously. The fact was that there was nothing informal about this man. He was all about business—the business of what Ballard Crafton wanted and needed and possessed.

Right now, he possessed her. It was in his eyes: that self-indulgent authoritarian expression. The thought made her chest clench.

"Silja ..."

Her eyes flicked. She realized that he'd been calling to her for several seconds. He repeated, "Silja ... sit ... have some breakfast. I want you to meet my personal assistant, Tess McMillan."

Silja flinched when she suddenly became aware of a woman standing next to her holding a rather large tray.

Tess was a lovely woman. Silja had her figured for mid-to-late-thirties. She was of average height, and blonde with crystal blue eyes and a bright smile. Her fair skin was flawless, and her figure was alluring in the black sheath dress and black pumps that she was wearing. Even the apron that was drawn over the dress was very complementary.

Silja wasn't surprised. Ballard Crafton only surrounded himself with beauty and elegance.

"Please sit down, Miss Ramsay. I have a very nice breakfast for you." Tess set a plate of eggs benedict, toast, fresh fruit, and yogurt at Silja's place setting. She placed a similar plate in front of Ballard.

"May I have the box that I gave you earlier, Tess?" Ballard asked.

"Of course." She hurried to the other room and returned with a square gold box that was about five inches by five inches.

He covered Tess' hand with his before she withdrew it from the box and something intimate passed between them. Smiling into her eyes, Ballard said, "Thank you, my dear, that'll be all for now."

With a nod, Tess left them alone.

Considering the clandestine exchange between Ballard and Tess, Silja nibbled on a piece of toast while keeping her eyes focused on her plate or the covered patio beyond the glass doors. Pecking at loose sunflower seeds that someone had generously thrown out for them, several Chickadees hopped from the trellis that supported the roof to the short stone wall that corralled the entire courtyard.

Ballard poured a cup of coffee from the fine china carafe on the table. When he poured in some creamer, he said in a stern tone, "Look at me, Silja."

There it was: his first command. She knew that she must obey or pay some kind of consequence. Uncertain of how severe the penalty would be, she dragged her gaze to meet his. Resting his elbows on the table, he peered at her over the coffee cup that he held in both hands.

A week ago she would have found him handsome—the way the morning sunshine glinted off his silver hair, and the way his eyes possessed a sultry yearning only for her.

Today? He was more of an ogre to her than anything else—a troll who's toll for crossing his bridge was way too high.

"I see that you found the clothes that I had Tess purchase for you. I hope that you like them. You look lovely in that sweater, but as I mentioned before, you'd look lovely in a gunnysack." He took a sip of his coffee, and then he favored her with a thin smile.

She stared at him impassively.

"It is commendable that you have agreed to the arrangement that I have made with Natalia and Edvar. Your friends will no longer have to participate in the contributors' parties. For that, they will be indebted to you, no doubt. Are you sure that you understand the agreement that we discussed last night, Sil?"

She looked at him with daggers. Her voice rich with disdain, she brusquely insisted, "Don't ever call me that. My name is *Silja.*"

He studied her before conceding, "If that is what you wish. I will respect that. Again, do you understand the agreement, Silja?"

"I do."

He set the cup aside and reached for the gold box next to his plate. "I know that you need time to get used to our arrangement. I understand completely, and this cold, dreary weather is no place for you to do that. I promised you a trip to the Caribbean. We will be leaving this evening on my private jet."

"But I thought you said we wouldn't be going out in public until my bruises have healed."

"As I said, we will be traveling on my private jet, and when we arrive at our destination, we will be staying on my private yacht."

"I see ..."

He smiled. "You are mine now, Silja. I'm sure that you will find it no surprise that I am a very possessive man. I don't want any man to touch or look at what is mine ... unless it would please me for that to happen. In any case, you will wear this around your neck at all times as a symbol of my possession."

He opened the box and held up a thin silver choker embedded with diamonds.

Silja stopped breathing.

Ballard pushed from his chair and went to the back of hers. Gently, he placed the collar around her neck. She heard a click. Immediately, her hand went to her throat. She fingered the intricate collar while Ballard returned to his seat.

He casually dug his fork into his eggs as if he'd just given her a pencil. Without looking up from his breakfast, he said, "The choker is locked in place. Only I can remove it."

"I'm not a dog to be tied to a post."

"Indeed you are not. As time goes by, and you have earned my trust, you will be allowed to come and go from the house as you please. That said, you will learn the rules as we go along. Your first lessons will take place on my yacht. You'll learn quickly what pleases me and what does not. So please take the time between our departure and arrival to become at ease with our arrangement. Eat, Silja ... you're going to need your strength."

She looked down at the eggs, but she dare not swallow a bite for fear that it would all come right back up.

"Ballard, there is someone at the door to see you," Tess said from the archway that led into the dining room.

"Is it important?"

"I think so, yes."

Taking the napkin from his lap, Ballard wiped the corners of his mouth. "Please keep Silja company while I take care of this."

"Certainly, but I must give you another important message."

"Yes ..."

Tess glanced at Silja, and then back to Ballard. "In private."

Nodding, he hitched his chin for her to follow him. When they were out of earshot from Silja, he turned to her. "What is it?"

"I just received a call from the lab. The subject has died. He had a massive coronary this morning. I'm sorry, Ballard."

"Hmmm, this one died of a heart attack, while the others have died of strokes, interesting. No worries. It just means that we need yet more adjustments to the serum. I have the next adjustment in my notes. I'll call the lab and have them take care of it immediately. We will be provided with more subjects when we need them."

"You don't think the Russian government will be upset that this is the third one you've lost?"

Ballard snorted. "Upset? I'm doing them a favor. Their subjects are nothing more than hardened criminals from their prisons. They have plenty to spare, I'm sure. They don't give a rat's ass what I do to them. The U.S. government wasn't willing to allow trials on humans for another five years or so. I'm farther ahead by miles." He kissed her cheek. "Now be a dear and see to Silja while I take care of our visitor."

"Yes, Ballard." Tess hurried back to the dining room.

Ballard made his way into the grand foyer to find the captain of the Yekaterinburg police force standing next to the beveled glass doors with his hat in his hands. Ballard reached for his hand. "Captain Domashev, what can I do for you today?"

Shaking the wealthy and influential American's hand, Domashev replied, "I am looking for American woman, Silja Ramsay. I have been told that you are at all of her performances and that you had dinner with her the other evening. Do you know where she is now?"

"May I ask why are you looking for Miss Ramsay?"

"Ivan Belsky was found dead in alley behind the Mockba Theater early this morning. We found knife with her fingerprints in his chest. Do you know where she is?"

"I was not at the ballet last night. I had a telephone conference in my office."

"I see."

"Do you have witnesses?" Ballard inquired.

"No." Domashev looked past Ballard for a glimpse of anyone else in the house. "We only have murder weapon. I must admit we have questions as well. Belsky was badly beaten. I cannot imagine that a woman, especially thin woman such as Silja Ramsay, would have strength to beat him so severely. Still I must insist: do you know where she is?"

"I assure you that Miss Ramsay had nothing to do with Ivan Belsky's death," Ballard stated. "How her fingerprints got on the knife is a mystery, but I know that Silja would never hurt anyone. How is your daughter, Captain Domashev? I have heard how ill she has been. I'm sure the medical bills are overwhelming."

The captain cocked his head to one side. "She is in hospital as we speak. Yes, I can barely afford my home because of medical expenses."

"I'm sorry. As always, I will see to it that the fees are paid immediately. Again, I assure you that Miss Ramsay had nothing to do with Belsky's untimely death." Offering his hand to the captain, he added, "Yes?"

Domashev's mouth curved. He shook Ballard's hand. "Of course, thank you, Mr. Crafton."

"Have a lovely afternoon, Captain. I hope your daughter feels better soon. I will be in touch when I'm in need of your...help." Ballard opened the door. Domashev plopped his hat on his head, and then merrily made his way to the police vehicle parked in front of the house.

Closing the door, Ballard bellowed, "Mikhail!"

The bodyguard jogged into the foyer.

185

Ballard asked, "How badly did you beat Belsky? Did you use a knife?"

"I beat him bad, yes. But I did not use knife— this was not as you asked."

"Was he alive when you left him?"

"Yes, Belsky was alive when I went after Silja," Mikhail assured him.

"Who else was in the alley last night?"

"I saw no one."

Ballard crossed his arms over his chest. His eyes narrowed. "Someone was there. Ivan Belsky was stabbed to death. I need to make some phone calls. Have the driver bring the car around in twenty minutes."

CHAPTER THIRTEEN

As promised, Clark had made all the flight arrangements. Grant drove to the Johnstown Airport, flew into LaGuardia Airport, and then flew on to the Domodedovo Airport in Moscow. He then caught a small plane to the Koltsovo Airport.

Grant had left the U.S. late Friday afternoon. It was now Sunday in Russia. He stood in line at the car rental for over a half-hour before retrieving an SUV with a GPS system. Grant was no stranger to working beyond the exhaustion. Grant was accustomed to staying awake for days at a time when he was on a mission, and today would be no different.

First objective: get the GPS chick to speak in English—she was being difficult.

First stop: the Novikov Ballet Studio in Yekaterinburg—about ten miles away.

While he drove along the roadways, he hoped that he would find Silja safe and sound. He was hoping that this was all some kind of misunderstanding, but as time had passed, his faith was waning. She hadn't answered a call or text since he received her plea for help. He even sent her an email while on the layover in Moscow—no response. Because they only exchanged a few emails per year, he didn't have her home address, so he hoped to glean that information from the dancers at the studio.

Grant parked the SUV along the street about a block away from the studio. While he trekked among the Russian citizens huddled in their coats against the icy-edged breeze, Grant realized that they peered at him skeptically from behind the scarves wrapped around their faces. Some made a wide breadth to avoid him completely. They eyed his camo jacket and pants with reservation in their gaze.

The Americans and Russians have always been wary of one and other—it had been ingrained in both peoples' minds from the time they were children. Yeah, it was obvious that the cold war was still being silently fought.

Finally, he came upon the building that housed the Novikov Ballet Company. A slightly built woman was peering in the windows. She wore a long wool coat, boots, a knit hat pulled down over her ears, and a plaid scarf wrapped around her neck and face. Cupping her gloved hands against the glass, she searched intently for something on the other side.

Behind her, he peered through the window in hopes of catching a glimpse of Silja.

Seeing the tall American's reflection in the window, the woman turned. She said in a heavy Russian accent, "You are American soldier, yes?"

Grant smiled politely. "Something like that. Is there anyone here?"

"No. The dancers are on two-week rest. Who do you search for?"

"I'm looking for Silja Ramsay. Do you know her?"

"Perhaps. Who are you?"

"I'm an old friend."

Eleni smiled. "Yes, I recognize you now. I have seen picture of you in Silja's apartment. You are Grant."

"Do you know where I can find her?"

Looking past him, she jerked her head to the right and then to the left, as if she were making sure that no one of significance was about. She lowered her voice. "I am Eleni Babinski, one of dancers for Novikov Ballet Company. I do not know where Silja is. I went to her apartment. She is not there so I came here to see if maybe Natalia, owner of company, could tell me, but no one is here. I am frightened for her."

"So am I." Grant pulled out his cell phone to show Eleni the text message that he received from Silja. Gasping, she drew her hand to her mouth. "Will you take me to her apartment? We may be able to get some idea as to where she is, and maybe you can fill me in on what's been going on."

Eleni had to help this man named Grant. He was possibly Silja's only hope. She said, "Of course."

During the drive there, Eleni told Grant about the contributors' parties and how Ballard Crafton wanted Silja to be his companion and lover. She went on to tell him about how she showed up at the final party to make a video and issue a strong ultimatum, and how Eleni had placed her shoes in the box. She explained that Belsky had plucked the shoes and then dragged Silja from the party before she could say anything, and how outraged Ballard Crafton was by the incident.

"Silja was terrified when Belsky picked her shoes," Eleni told him.

"I would think it would be terrifying for any of them to pick your shoes."

"This is true, but Belsky was a terrible man. The night he picked Anna Antkowiak's shoes, he beat and raped her because ... she was young ... she didn't know how to ... to please a man."

"So he beat her and raped her? Did Silja know about this?" Grant asked.

Eleni nodded.

Grant was exasperated. "What the hell was Silja thinking?" he bit out.

"She had no intentions of going with Belsky," she said. "She wanted everyone to know that she knew about parties and if he made wrong move that she would go to police. All of contributors are important people in Yekaterinburg, so they wouldn't want to be associated with such activities."

"Was that the last time you saw Silja?" he asked. "When Belsky dragged her from the party?"

"Yes," she answered, "but there is more ... Belsky was found dead in alley behind theatre. The next morning, it was on news that police are looking for Silja because they think she killed him, but I have not heard anything since."

"I'd like to kill him myself, but the police think that Silja killed Belsky? Why?"

"He was killed with kitchen knife," she said. "It had her mark on it."

"Marks?" he asked. "You mean like fingerprints?"

"Yes, I believe so. But how can this be? Silja did not have knife with her when she was at party. When Belsky dragged her out she had nothing with her, not even purse. Silja would not kill anyone. Ballard Crafton was furious, perhaps he killed Belsky." She pointed to the building on the right side of the street. "Here is where she lives."

Grant parked and they made their way up the front steps. An elderly woman was struggling with her swipe card to get into the building. Finally, she opened the door. Grant grabbed it, and with a pleasant smile on his lips, he held it open as she made her way through. Eleni guided Grant up the stairs toward Silja's apartment. A portly man was painting the railing at the top of the stairs. Grant knocked on the door. There was no answer. The man at the railing called out in Russian to them.

Eleni answered. "He is landlord," she explained to Grant.

"Tell him that we are friends of Silja's and ask him if he'll let us in."

Wiping his hands on a rag, the landlord approached them. A collection of keys dangled from his belt. They jingled against his thigh with each step. Eleni spoke to him while he kept his eyes fixed on the tall American man. Shaking his head, he replied to Eleni's request brusquely. Turning to Grant, she said, "He said that he cannot open door for us."

Much to Eleni's surprise, Grant simply shrugged his shoulder and turned as if he were going to walk away. She was shocked that he would give up so easily.

Then, Grant spun on his heels, grabbed the landlord by his shirt, and shoved him against the wall with a gun pressed against his cheek. "How about now? Can he open the door for us now?" Grant asked.

Trembling, the man unclipped the ring of keys from his belt. He rattled off a long sentence while Eleni grabbed the keys from his hand. She fumbled through them until the man nodded at the correct one. Finally, she shoved it into the lock to open the door. Grant noticed that the door had been recently replaced when he pushed the landlord inside the apartment.

"Tell him to stand next to the door and not to move," Grant instructed. The words tumbled from Eleni's mouth like a fast-flowing river. The landlord's lips wrinkled in disdain, but he didn't move from the spot where Grant had put him.

The apartment was disheveled. A broken lamp lay on the floor and a stuffed chair was on its side in the middle of the walkway. All in all, it didn't look like a terribly violent struggle had taken place until they came to the bedroom door. It was off its hinges and splintered. A bedroom chair lay on the floor just inside the doorway. *She must've barricaded herself in this room to send me the text,* Grant thought while he ran his fingers gingerly over the broken wood.

He made his way around the bed to the window only to find the reason that Silja did not use it as an out—no fire escape. He looked down at the alley two stories below. He was thankful that she hadn't tried it.

Out of nowhere, a nimble movement caught his attention. Without pause, he brought his gun up from his side. Then he let out a relieved breath when he realized that Greta had leapt onto the window sill. The cat meowed while pacing back and forth.

The corners of his mouth curled as he stuffed the Glock back into his shoulder holster. Grant picked up the cat that he'd given to Silja long ago. "What happened here, Greta?" The cat continued to mew in distress. He tickled her ears, but it did not calm her. "Ahhh, you're probably hungry. She's been gone for a couple days. C'mon, let's see if we can't find some food for you."

When he turned, he kicked something with the edge of his boot. Grant looked down to see a cell phone lying underneath the radiator.

He scooped it up and scrolled through the recently sent text messages to find the one that Silja had sent him. The text had been sent at 10:30 Saturday evening. "Eleni ..." he called out.

She came to the bedroom door quickly. "Yes ..."

"We need to find Greta something to eat." He transferred the cat into her arms. "Do you know where Ballard Crafton lives?"

Eleni nodded.

"After Greta eats, I want you to take me there."

An onset of nerves coiled through her. She nuzzled the cat to calm herself. "Ooh, you are hungry, yes? Come, I know where Silja keeps your food."

She carried Greta into the kitchen.

Grant followed.

The landlord gauged his appearance as though he were the dirty American terrorist that he'd always imagined.

Scanning the kitchen, Grant's eyes fell upon the knife block—all the knives had black handles. He remembered the set—it was Silja's mother's Cutco knives. He remembered packing them up for Silja and shipping them to Russia. Drawing closer, he examined the notches where the knives were inserted—one knife was missing. Not good.

He yanked open the drawers to see if she'd slipped the knife in with the dinnerware. Only butter knives lay neatly in the drawer. He also discovered that the knives in the block on the counter were the only sharp knives that Silja owned.

He opened the apartment-size dishwasher to rifle through the silverware that was in the plastic rack—the knife was not there. It didn't mean anything. The knife could have been broken and thrown away, yet the police had a knife in their possession with her prints on it.

A missing knife from her collection was not a good sign.

Greta dove at the food that Eleni dumped into her dish. The landlord spewed a harsh sentence at the ballerina.

"He said that he is going to call police when we leave," Eleni told Grant, who was now searching the rest of the drawers for the missing knife.

"Ask him if they've been here."

Eleni asked. After the landlord answered, she told Grant, "Yes, they were here yesterday. He also says that Silja owes him money for damages to the bedroom door and the apartment door."

"Tell him that if he calls the police, I'll come back to kick his ass."

Drawing her hand to her chest, Eleni took in a breath. She believed him.

The American was handsome, yummy handsome, and even with the heavy coat covering his body, she could tell he was muscular and strong. Silja had told her that he was an American warrior, a hero, and though he was Silja's former lover, he stirred Eleni's libido.

A curl came to her plump lips when she turned to the landlord and repeated Grant's warning.

The Russian man's eyes grew wide with fear. His spine stiffened. Dropping his gaze to the floor, he stuffed his hands into his pockets while shuffling from one foot to the other. Eleni was certain that they wouldn't hear another word from him.

She turned back to watch Grant move about the kitchen and look through the pantry. She admired his tight buttocks when he bent over. His hands were big and strong. His dark brown eyes were molested by worry and focus, yet when she looked into them she could see softness, compassion, and a sincere benevolence lying deep within the layers of his demeanor.

How could Silja leave such a beautiful man behind?

Silja was now with Ballard, and the thought of that made Eleni's mind wander back to the night that she had spent with Ballard Crafton. A shiver slipped down the nape of her neck. He was a heavy-handed lover, dominant and possessive.

Ballard took her to his mansion. An attractive American woman who he called "Tess" greeted them in the foyer. She was most pleasant. She took their coats, and while Ballard went into another room, Tess led her up a wide winding staircase to an ornate bedroom. The bed had a curly gold headboard and tall bed posts at the foot. The bed was flanked by arched floor-to-ceiling windows. It could not have been Ballard's bedroom; it was too feminine with soft pink walls and vintage vases that were filled with fresh flower arrangements.

Tess laid her coat over a chair, and then casually she asked, "What are you wearing under your dress?"

Eleni remembered feeling rather taken aback by her question. She replied, "Nothing."

Tess went to the vanity and took out a lacy thong, and then she retrieved a sheer white robe with lace trim from the closet. "Please take off your dress and put these on. Mr. Crafton prefers that you wear your hair down. Your earrings are lovely, but he doesn't care for dangle earrings when being intimate. So please remove those as well. Mr. Crafton will be with you in a few minutes." She left the room.

Trepidation vibrated through her.

This was not what she had expected.

Although she had only been summoned to the contributors' parties three or four times prior, the dates had been more spontaneous. She had not been taken to a home. Rather she had been taken to a hotel, where she would strip and spend and hour or so in bed with a man who wanted a blow-job and intercourse.

This situation was more calculated, organized, and she found it most unsettling. It was obvious that Ballard expected more, but what? She had a feeling that this was going to be more than just an hour or so.

While she let her hair down, removed her earrings, stepped into the thong, and slipped into the robe, her stomach twisted into tight knots.

She crossed the room to peer out one of the long windows next to the bed. It looked out over a courtyard. The freshly fallen snow glittered under the soft glow of the solar lanterns. The bushes and small trees bowed under the weight of the snow. Eleni couldn't help but think that she'd rather be strolling through the quiet courtyard than standing in the room waiting for who knew what.

The serenity of the view was interrupted by the sound of the bedroom door opening. She turned to see Ballard enter the room dressed in a pair of lounging *pants and no shirt. He held a small jewel box in his left hand. She was impressed by the fact that his chest and abs were fairly firm for a man of middle-aged years.*

Ballard's eyes slowly measured her. He smiled and made his way toward her. "You have a beautiful body." He brushed her hair to fall behind her shoulders. His lips curled when he opened the delicate jewelry box. In a husky voice, he whispered, "I want you to wear these."

A pair of diamond stud earrings winked at her from inside the box. He placed the box in her hand and then carefully slipped the earrings through the holes in her lobes. Once the studs were clipped in place, he ran his lips along her neck. "You are mine tonight, my beautiful Silja," he murmured into her skin.

Eleni tensed.

Silja? This was to be his fantasy? That she was Silja?

Caressing the sheer fabric of the robe, his hand slowly made its way to her waist. He moved to stand in front of her. "Mmmm, let me see you now."

He slipped the robe from her shoulders letting it fall to the floor. His eyes drank in her round breasts. Her dusty pink nipples stood at attention while he fingered them and then brought his mouth to the right nipple to run his tongue over it. "I want to taste every inch of you. Move back against the bed post."

She did as she was told. He ran his fingers across her jaw and then pressed his lips to hers—pushing his tongue inside her mouth. When he drew away from the kiss, he quietly padded across the room to a closet and went inside. She could hear him moving about inside the closet.

When he emerged, he held a silk cloth in one hand and a pair of handcuffs in the other. He laid the handcuffs upon the bed. Without speaking, he tied the cloth around her eyes.

"Put your hands around the bedpost," he instructed and she did so. "You won't see, only feel my touch, my desires, and if you move at all or make a sound you will feel my punishment," he explained, while he placed a pair of handcuffs to her wrists, securing her to the bedpost.

Again she felt his mouth on her nipples. He moaned, "Do you understand, Silja?"

Her mouth felt dry, and unease scraped through her. She was aware that she was supposed to agree to his terms, but the words simply did not come. She yelped at the pain in her left nipple when he bit down hard.

"Answer me," he groused.

"I will not move!" Eleni felt his fingers caress her nipple to soothe the ache.

"You needn't be afraid as long as you obey me, Silja. I will be gentle, and what pain I inflict will hurt so good, I promise," he whispered while his hands meandered along her ribs, over her tummy, and to her hips. "Mmm, you're skin is so smooth and soft, like silk," he said.

She felt his fingers hook the band of the thong, and the miniscule fabric fell down her legs to her feet. Even though she could not see, she could feel his eyes upon her.

He didn't touch her for what seemed like an eternity. He was silent. She could hear him breathing. There was no movement, and she wondered what he was thinking, planning. She trembled at the thought. Oh God, would he consider that movement? Would he punish her for trembling? His hands grabbed her thighs.

"Open to me," he instructed.

She spread her legs apart. He pressed his finger inside her, moving slowly in and out, and then he pushed in a second finger, and then he pulled away. Before she knew it, his fingers were in her mouth. "You're nervous, I understand, so let's get the first one over with and we'll move on from there. Our night has only just begun."

She heard him tear something. She was certain that is must have been a condom. She was thankful. A moment later, he pushed his erection inside her. The bed post dug in between her shoulderblades as he pressed her against it while pumping into her hard.

He grabbed her legs. "Wrap them around me," he said breathlessly.

The handcuffs nipped at her wrists while he came to the top of his excitement. Letting out a gratifying moan, he feasted on her nipples. "Silja, my dear sweet Silja, you taste so good, you feel so good."

Then he fell against her, used up.

He dropped her legs to the floor. She heard him sink onto the bed.

Tears trickled down her cheeks from under the blindfold. She felt helpless—violated. She had been with several men in her lifetime, but she'd never been ravaged in such a savage manner.

"Tess!" he called out. She heard the bedroom door open and footsteps across the carpet. "Clean her up and strap her to the bed." She heard his body lift from the bed and the woman's footsteps approach.

He added, "Oh Tess, put on that black teddy that I bought you for Christmas and join us, please. I'll be back in a moment. I want a glass of wine."

The night proved to be an exercise in experiences that she'd never had. Her body had been touched in ways it had never been before.

Finally, at three a.m., Ballard's sexual desires had been filled. She lay across the bed—exhausted.

Running his fingers between her breasts, over her tummy, and finally between her legs, he said, "You have been most enchanting, Miss Babinski. Please keep the earrings as a token of my appreciation."

She heard him pad across the room to the door.

He called out, "Tess, make our guest comfortable for the night, see to it that she has a good breakfast, and my driver will take her home afterward. Good night."

The door closed.

Tess did as she was told in complete silence. Eleni wanted to ask her so many questions, but the woman made it most apparent that it was a boundary that could not be crossed.

The next morning, she was served a lovely breakfast that she couldn't eat, and then she was driven to her apartment in a limousine. She took several showers that day.

At the time, Eleni considered Ballard Crafton's deviant sexual desires a product of the situation: he had purchased her for the night. She was no longer a talented ballerina dressed as the Spanish doll dancing about in Dr. Coppelius' shop. She had been reduced to the role of a cheap prostitute. She was his to do with as he saw fit, and the woman named Tess was some kind of servant.

Ballard Crafton was a powerful and wealthy man. His behavior was most likely part and parcel to his manipulative personality.

Now, she completely understood why Silja still held this man, Grant Ketchum, close to her heart. Silja was a strong-willed woman—much stronger than herself. She wondered if Silja had submitted to Ballard's deviant desires, and if she hadn't, what kind of punishment did he wield upon her? Concern washed over her.

Bringing her back from her thoughts, Grant dropped something to the floor while he continued to rummage through the kitchen. She asked, "What is it that you search for?"

"You're absolutely sure that Silja did not have a knife with her?"

"Yes. She wore cocktail dress, no pockets. I have her purse at my apartment. It is very small. Why do you ask this?"

"Because there's a knife missing from the knife block and I can't find it anywhere in the kitchen."

"Perhaps the knife was broken, and she threw it away."

"Maybe." He looked down to see that Greta had finished her dinner. He grabbed several cans of cat food from the cupboard, stuffed them into his pockets, and then scooped the cat up and tucked her inside his coat. "Will you take me to Ballard Crafton's home now?"

"Yes."

"Good. Tell the landlord that I'll make arrangements to have the damages to the apartment paid for. Let's go."

CHAPTER FOURTEEN

Parked along the street in front of Ballard Crafton's mansion, Grant and Eleni waited and watched in the SUV.

Curled up on Grant's lap, Greta was fast asleep. Her tummy was full, the vehicle was warm, and Grant caressed her head.

"Have you ever been inside Crafton's house?" Grant asked Eleni while he continued to gauge the house.

Eleni's gaze dropped to her lap. She wrung her hands.

Waiting for her response, Grant turned his head from the window.

She could feel his eyes measuring her. Finally, she muttered, "Once."

The tensing in her posture signaled that she was uncomfortable discussing her visit at Ballard Crafton's home. Grant realized that she must have been forced to spend time with him. He hated making her feel cheap. He hated that she or any of the other dancers were subjected to such a vile humiliation. It made his blood boil that the young girl, Anna, had been beaten and raped.

Most of all, he was worried sick over what Silja was going through—possibly at this very second. Eleni needed to open up to him. He had to get her to tell him the layout of the mansion's interior without embarrassing her any further.

Grant placed his hand over hers. When she looked up at him, he favored her with a svelte smile. "Can you tell me what you saw inside? The layout of the house. Any detail will help."

His eyes were so compassionate and she could feel the strength that he was trying to transfer from his hand to hers when he gently squeezed it. She didn't want to think about the night that she'd spent in Ballard Crafton's bed. That was not what this empathetic man was asking for. He was asking her to remember the layout of the house.

He needed it. He was going in for Silja. He was going to rescue the woman who he cared about. Yes, she could see that in his eyes, too. Grant needed her help, and he was going to get it.

Leaning her head against the headrest, Eleni closed her eyes. His hand was so big that it completely swallowed hers. It was warm and reassuring.

"We went through front door into large foyer," she said. "American woman greeted us. Her name was Tess. She took me upstairs."

"Where are the stairs?" he whispered.

"In foyer." She took in a cleansing breath. "When we reached top of stairs, we turned right and walked to end of hallway. We passed one or two rooms. It was two ... two rooms. The doors were closed. She took me into beautiful bedroom—pink. It was toward back of house. The room had two tall windows that look out over a garden that is behind house."

She swallowed. That was it. That was as far as she was willing to go. Dragging her eyes open, she turned to gaze at him.

Grant smiled. "Thank you, Eleni. You said there was a woman in the house. Was there anyone else with Crafton?"

"Yes. He has driver and ... um ... how do you call it ... body snatcher."

The left side of Grant's mouth lifted. "You mean bodyguard?"

Eleni's lips curled. She snorted at her missed translation. "Yes, bodyguard. His name is Mikhail. I know this because he used to work at theater before Ballard Crafton came to Russia."

"What did he do at the theater?"

"He was guard."

"I see. So the only people you saw with Crafton were the woman, the driver, and the bodyguard?" After she nodded her head, he asked, "The garden below the bedroom, what's beyond it? An alley? A street?"

"It has gate that opens to next street up."

"Well, isn't that just about perfect?" Grant muttered as he turned his head back toward the house in time to see a limo pulling out of the driveway with two men in the front seat. "Eleni, is the man in the passenger's seat Mikhail?"

Eleni leaned forward. "Yes, that is him."

Grant pulled out the cell phone that Walt had given the team and dialed up Clark.

"What's going on, Ketchum?" Clark asked.

"I've found her. She's being held prisoner by an American businessman named Ballard Crafton. He's got a female assistant. I've got a first name only, Tess. What can you dig up on them for me?"

"I've heard of Ballard Crafton. He's from New York, I think. I'll get back to you A-SAP." Clark was gone.

Stuffing the phone into his pocket, Grant turned to Eleni. "Are you up for a little adventure, darlin'?" He flashed his one thousand-megawatt smile.

Oh yeah, she could see the wheels turning behind those sexy brown eyes. Silja had no idea how lucky she was to have this man coming to save her. Eleni had every intention of making sure that Silja was informed of that fact as soon as she had a chance. Taking in a braced breath, she nodded.

With one last comforting squeeze of her hand, Grant said, "Good girl. Now listen carefully to what I need you to do ..."

* * * * *

Novikov Ballet Studio

"Take the car back to the house. I don't want anyone to see it here," Ballard instructed his driver when he stepped from the limo. "I want you to go with him, Mikhail. I'll be fine. I'll call you when my business here is through."

"Yes, Mr. Crafton." Mikhail held the ballet studio door open for him.

Ballard stepped into the small lobby of the ballet studio and locked the glass doors after Mikhail returned to the limo. The studio was ice cold. It couldn't have been more than fifty-five degrees. Ballard opted to keep his gloves and coat on while he walked down the long narrow hallway that led to Natalia Novikov's office. He peered into the empty rehearsal studios. Huge mirrors hung on the walls that were lined with ballet barres.

His footsteps echoed through the studios and hallway.

He recalled the many afternoons that he stopped by to watch the stunning Silja Ramsay rehearse in the studios. He had ached for her to be his for so many months. Now that she belonged to him, he wanted to make sure that nothing would get in the way.

The visit from police chief Domashev had him unnerved. He didn't want anything to interfere with the operations at his laboratories. He was certain that Domashev was a team player—he usually was when money was flung at him. The last thing he wanted was for his name to be linked to Belsky's murder. Without a doubt, Silja could not be involved. He was most certain that he would find answers right there at the ballet studio.

As he approached the end of the hallway, he could hear voices coming from Natalia's office. They sounded anxious and terse. There was friction among the trio. Yes, he had no doubt in his mind that Natalia, Edvar, and Dominik knew all about Belsky's demise.

Upon opening the door, Ballard announced, "Now that I'm paying the bills for this establishment, I would think that you could turn on a bit more heat. Don't you think, Natalia?"

Natalia, Edvar, and Dominik's heads jerked toward the doorway. The conversation had come to an abrupt halt—how transparent. Smoothing her heavy wool sweater over her lean hips, Natalia agreed, "Of course." As she turned up the thermostat, she asked, "How is Silja? Is she okay?"

"Silja is my responsibility now, Natalia."

"But ... you will treat her well, yes?"

Ballard's lips curled. "How I treat Silja is none of your concern." His eyes rotated around the room and stopped on Dominick who was fussing with the bandage on his right hand. Ballard's eyebrows arched. "I want to know what happened to Belsky." Again, he scanned the room. Edvar exchanged wary looks with Natalia.

Dominik continued to finger the bandage.

Casually, he made his way toward the dancer. "What happened to your hand, Dominik?"

Surprised by Ballard's closeness, Dominik blinked and blinked again. His eyes flicked to Edvar and then to Natalia's anxious expressions. "I cut myself."

"How?"

"How does one get cut? With knife. I was making Edvar salad. The knife slipped on tomato."

Ballard turned to Edvar. "Was the salad good?"

Edvar swallowed hard. With a feeble smile on his lips, he glanced at Dominik. "It was good, yes. Why do you question Dominik?"

"Because I think Dominik knows what happened to Belsky. May I see the cut?"

"I think not," Dominik replied.

Ninja-quick, Ballard grabbed him by his shirt and hoisted him hard against the wall. "Silja is being accused of the stabbing. So I think yes."

Edvar rushed to Dominik's side. "Put him down! Dominik found Belsky's body. That is all!"

The right side of Ballard's lip lifted. "Is that so? You found Belsky's body?" Trembling, Dominik could only manage a nod. "Let me see the cut!" Ballard released his hold—allowing him to drop to the floor.

Edvar scrambled to help him to his feet.

Natalia pulled a bottle of chardonnay and a glass from the cabinet beneath her desk. A slim grin slithered across her mouth while she poured the wine. "Yes, Dominik, show us the cut and tell Ballard why you refused to call police after you found Belsky. I want to know, too."

With daggers in his eyes, Dominik peeled the bandaging away from his sliced hand. The lesion was deep and long and angry red. It had required stitching, which Dominik failed to seek out.

Ballard grabbed his hand to examine the wound. "That must've been one hell of a fat tomato. This cut looks like it had some force behind it for as long and as deep as it is. Enough force to kill a man perhaps?"

"Why would I kill Belsky? Silja did not want to go with him! She stabbed him!"

Laughing out loud, Natalia chided, "Belsky wanted you, not Silja, and not any of the other dancers—"

Edvar yelled at her in Russian. With a defiant sneer, she plopped down in her chair. Edvar urged Dominik, "Tell him you did not kill Belsky."

"It was Silja—"

Ballard back-handed Dominik—hard.

Grabbing his face, Dominik fell against the wall.

"I have the police under control," Ballard told them. He turned to look Natalia in the eye. "But, under these new revelations—I now own the Novikov Ballet Company. I will have Tess prepare the paperwork and send it to you by messenger within several hours. While I'm in the Caribbean, you will find a reason to replace Silja as the principal dancer. I will build her a private studio in my home. She will dance for me exclusively."

Spilling the wine over the desk, Natalia jerked to her feet. "This was not agreement! You promised me that she could dance for Novikov, and I have no doubt that you made same promise to her! It is bad enough that you are stealing my ballet company from me, but do not destroy her like others, Ballard!"

"Don't defy me, Natalia! Don't even try! What makes you think that Silja would even want to dance for your company if she knew what you were involved in? Do as you're told, or I will expose Dominik for the murder of Ivan Belsky. And I'll see

213

to it that you all spend time in a Russian prison for hiding it!"

Natalia's eyes seethed with anger. "And I will tell them how you paid for our ballerinas to spend time in your bed, and for certain Silja will want no parts of you!"

He backhanded Natalia hard.

With a yelp, she fell into her chair and clutched her face.

Edvar and Dominik cowered against the wall in each others arms.

Ballard said, "Tell them anything you want, bitch! My laboratories are far too important. The Russians will not only look the other way, but they will also have a good chuckle when they toss you in a cell! As for Silja—she is mine."

* * * * *

"You barely touched your breakfast, Silja. Is there something else you would prefer?" Tess asked.

"I would *prefer* not to be here at all," Silja replied, tersely. She watched Tess gather the plates onto a tray as if she hadn't said a word. "I'm curious, what is your relationship with Ballard?"

"I'm his personal assistant."

"And what exactly does that entail? You cook, clean, run errands, do paperwork ... anything else? Anything ... personal, intimate?"

Tess hesitated in her task. She dragged her impassive gaze to meet Silja's. Her tone was pleasantly flat. "I do whatever is asked of me. You will be best served if you do the same. Ballard is a very generous man, a kind man, and if you treat him well, he will treat you like a queen. But if you fight him or give him trouble, you will pay a very high price. My advice to you is this: be giving and caring toward him at all times, and you will be completely fine."

"Sounds like you talk from experience. What will he do if I'm a *bad* girl?"

"I do speak from experience, love," Tess said. "I've been at his side for almost seventeen years. As I said before, do right by him or you'll learn very quickly what happens."

Tess' cell phone beeped at her. She pulled it from the pocket of her apron and read it. She then removed the apron and tossed it onto a chair. "Ballard needs some paperwork immediately. I'm going to take you to your room where you can begin to pack for the trip."

Silja tugged at the silver choker around her neck. "Why don't you wear one of these? Or are *personal assistants* not on his list of possessions?"

"I have made a list of the things you'll need for the cruise. You'll find a suitcase and everything else you need, including toiletries, in your room." Tess waved her hand for Silja to follow her upstairs.

Silja was most impressed with the grace that Tess exuded—in the way she avoided her question and in the way she moved. Her golden locks swayed across her spine with her every step while she unerringly glided across the floor in her tall, black pumps. Surely, the woman had some dance training in her background. She wondered how much of a role Tess would play in her arrangement with Ballard. Time would tell.

Tess opened the bedroom door and hitched her chin for Silja to step inside. "I'll check on you in a little while. Ballard plans to leave around seven this evening, and he won't be happy if you're not ready."

"Is that a fact? Tell me, Tess, will you be coming with us?"

"Where Ballard goes, I go. Is there anything I can get for you before I return downstairs?"

Out of nowhere, an epiphany hit Silja like a lightening bolt between her eyes. Greta had been left behind in the apartment! Silja's heart sank into her stomach. Greta must be hungry and thirsty by now. Silja cupped her hand over her mouth.

Noticing the sudden angst in Silja's face, Tess stepped toward her and touched her arm. "What is it? Is something wrong?"

"My cat, Greta—she was left behind at my apartment without any food or water. We need to go get her."

Instantly, Tess removed her comforting hand from Silja's arm. "I'm sorry, that's not possible. Ballard doesn't like animals in his house. He doesn't particularly like animals in general."

"But when he was at my apartment he said that he likes animals—"

"I'm sure he did." Tess stepped from the room and locked the door behind her.

Her hands clenching in fists at her side, Silja felt helpless while she listened to the rhythmic click click of Tess' heels as she walked down the hallway toward the staircase.

Hot tears of frustration burned her eyes until they surged over the rims.

She wasn't the only victim in this nightmare. Greta was probably starving by now, and there wasn't a damned thing she could do about it. She could only hope that the landlord or one of her neighbors would hear her crying and get her from the apartment.

Eleni ... maybe Eleni would stop by the apartment and take care of Greta. All she could do was hope, or perhaps she could convince Ballard to stop at the apartment on the way to the airport. It wasn't like they were catching a commercial flight. Maybe she could appeal to his gentle side and find a drop of compassion for her poor cat.

The lovely woman who claimed to be nothing more than an assistant made it abundantly clear that pissing off Ballard Crafton was a very bad idea. Now, she desperately needed a favor from him. She decided some cooperation was in order. Wiping away the tears with the cuff of her sweater, she went into the walk-in closet to find the suitcase that Tess said would be there—it certainly was.

She dragged the case across the room and threw it onto the bed. Tess' list of "must takes" was lying on the nightstand. The first thing on the list was six bikinis. *Seriously, six?* Silja rolled her eyes. She went to the dresser to search for the bikinis only to find six very skimpy pieces of fabric held together by a very thin string. There wasn't really enough fabric present to even refer to them as "bikinis" at all. Urgh! There was no point in getting upset. She grabbed the scraps of fabric and tossed them into the suitcase with a heavy sigh when a movement beyond the window caught her eye.

She made her way to the window. A black SUV was parked on the street behind Ballard's courtyard. It was running, but from her angle, she couldn't see if anyone was sitting in it. Letting out a sigh, she looked for the next item on the list: negligees and teddies. She could only imagine how skimpy they must be. Ballard had mentioned at breakfast that during this trip she would learn what pleased him and what did not. What the hell was that supposed to mean? What kind of weird stuff was this guy into?

She wrapped her fingers around the choker and gave it a proper tug. It didn't budge. She felt like a trapped animal. How was she going to get through this?

If Grant had gotten her text he would know that she was in Russia, because that was where she had lived for five years. He would find her—and help her.

But what if Grant had gotten the message and he arrived after she left for the Caribbean with Ballard? He wouldn't know where to search for her. She had to find a way to stall the trip. How? She lay across the bed to hatch a plan. Ballard wasn't a fool, and she didn't have much time—it had better be good.

* * * * *

Slipping his go-bag over his shoulder, Grant looked across the cab of the SUV to Eleni. In the driver's seat, she had her fingers wrapped tightly around the steering wheel. Her face was pale with fear.

"Remember," he said, "if I'm not back in fifteen minutes, get out of here. Don't wait for me. I don't want you to get hurt. Keep your hat on your head and your scarf around your face. I don't want anyone to identify you." Peering at her pallid expression, he offered a reassuring grin. "Don't look so worried. I'll be back."

"I am frightened for you and Silja."

"Everything will be fine. It'll be like a cakewalk." he told her.

Not understanding the term, she cocked her head and narrowed her eyes.

"It's going to be fine." When he turned to get out of the vehicle, his cell phone rang. "Yo Clark, talk to me."

"I hope your girl is okay. Ballard Crafton is a real piece of work. He owns Crafton Technologies, which was a drug testing lab out of New York. He did all kinds of sensitive work for the government. I'm still trying to find out what kind. The woman is Tess McMillan. She's his personal assistant, but there's more to the story than that. Crafton took responsibility for Ms. McMillan when she was seventeen years old and living in a juvenile detention home where Crafton worked as a counselor. He became her legal guardian. He even put her through college. Soon afterward he got a job in his preferred field: chemistry. But wait, there's more. He married her about five years ago. She still goes by her maiden name, but she is his wife. Anyway, seems Crafton has a short fuse when it comes to the ladies. There are warrants for his arrest here in the states. That's why he moved his lab to Russia. The government claims to have washed their hands of him, but I'm not sure that I believe that. I'm thinking he works for them like we do—off the grid. I'm still working on that."

"What are you getting at?" Grant asked. "He abuses women?"

"Mmm, it's a little worse than that, my friend," Clark said. "Two years ago, he was involved with an opera singer, Lucinda DeRolf. No one knows exactly what happened because Lucinda can't tell anyone. Her head injuries are so severe that she lives in a nursing home in upstate New York. She's unable to remember much, and she's still learning how to talk again. Her family has pressed charges against Crafton, but his big-time lawyer managed to put up a bunch of smoke screens—until he had a violent break-up with concert pianist, Yung Lo Ming."

"What happened to her?"

"She doesn't play the piano anymore," Clark said. "Ming's attorney claims that Crafton became so angry that after he beat her, he took a hammer to her hands. She spent two months in a coma. By the time she came out of it, he had moved his business to Russia—per his attorney's advice. The Russian government took him right under their wing, and that makes me a little nervous about what kind of testing his lab does."

Grant peered up at the house. He wasn't absolutely sure that Silja was in there. She may have been in the back seat of the limo that had pulled out of the driveway. "I've got to get her away from him."

"Yep, and you might need some backup. If Crafton is tangled with the government, he's definitely got some clout. Looks like the team will be finished with the op within twenty-four hours or so. They'll travel to a hotel in Yekaterinburg and wait for your signal."

"That works. I'll be in touch." Grant shoved the cell into his pocket, and then grabbed the door handle.

Eleni grabbed his coat. He turned to her.

"Where will we go after you bring Silja out?" she asked.

"We'll have to find a secure place to hide until we can get out of Russia."

"I think I know a place," she said. "I will make call while you are in house, yes?"

"Are you sure we can trust the person you're calling?"

"I am sure."

"Good," Grant said. "See you in fifteen minutes."

Staying low, Grant jogged across the street. He ducked behind the stone wall that surrounded the courtyard and then crept along the wall until he came to the gate. He peered through the rungs of the gate into the snow covered garden. Stealthily, he picked the lock and then slipped through the gate into the courtyard. After dropping to his stomach, he crawled behind the shrubbery. The snow was several inches deep, and it soaked into his pants and jacket as he made his way toward the house while keeping an eye on the sliding glass doors beyond the patio.

* * * * *

Lying across the bed with her arm draped over her eyes, Silja let out a frustrated sigh. The simple fact was that once she stepped onto Ballard's private jet, Grant wouldn't know where to begin to search for her. Nevertheless, she was certain that he would find out that she was with Ballard. He would go to the ballet company and find someone who would tell him. She jumped up from the bed and rummaged through drawers in search for paper or anything that she could write on to leave him a clue of where he could find her ... if her text had gone through.

She found a pen and a small notepad in the nightstand. Gratified by the small victory, she plopped down on the bed to write a message. The only problem was that she didn't know herself specifically where Ballard planned to take her. It didn't matter; she would tell him that they flew to the Caribbean in a private jet—Grant would do the rest. He would come to Ballard's house and he would search it to find her note. She was sure of it. She had to be sure—it was the only scrap of hope that she had left.

She was beginning to write her note when she heard the doorknob click. Shoving the pad under the pillow, she jumped from the bed and pretended to toss items into the suitcase. She heard the knob slowly turning and the door easing open. She swiped an errant strand of hair from her cheek. Why was Tess or Ballard or Mikhail taking so long to come into the room? The floor creaked and the door softly closed.

Silja turned around. Her eyes widened and her mouth dropped open. "Grant!" she gasped.

He put his finger to his lips. With a smile in his voice, he said, "You were expecting Batman?"

"Batman-shmatman ... I'm so glad you're here." Relief and hope and all of the old feelings from the past spilled into Silja's heart—propelling her forward. She raced across the room with her arms wide open. He swallowed her into his hungry embrace as her mouth crashed against his. She wrapped around him like a tightly woven vine.

Grant kissed her with a passion that he instantly recognized and had craved more than he had ever realized.

Five years had been too long—an eternity. He could have kissed her for hours, and he wanted nothing more than to lay her across the bed and to make love to the one woman he wished he'd never let out of his life—except time was of the essence.

Drawing away from the kiss, Silja ran her fingers over his bristly face to make sure he wasn't a fantasy, a mirage, but that he was really standing there. His dark brown eyes burned into her with an intensity that was oh-so familiar. They still had the same sultry effect on her that they had always had.

Grant's gut twisted into anger when he saw the bruising on her face. Gingerly, he ran the pad of his thumb over them. "Did Crafton do this to you?"

"No ... the bruises are from something else. I'm fine, really."

"I'm not fine with it. Who did this? I'll make him wish he'd never touched you."

"We'll talk about it later. I'm just so glad you're here. I've missed you so much."

The corners of his mouth lifted when he heard the words. "There'll be no arguments, Miss Ramsay. I'm taking you home to the United States."

"Hey, you'll get no back talk from me. But how did you get in?"

"Oldest security snafu in the book: sliding glass doors. Grab a jacket. We've got a ride to catch." Grant grabbed her by the hand only to turn around coming face to face with the business end of Tess McMillan's forty-five caliber.

She held the gun in her hand steady and true. Tess' lips curled around a sardonic tone. "Don't be rude, Silja. Introduce me to your handsome friend."

CHAPTER FIFTEEN

They were so screwed.

Silja's mouth went dry. Ballard would have Grant killed. Now she was regretting texting him for help. She felt Grant's body gently bump against hers. He was slowly backing up toward the window. Taking his cue, she inched backward.

"I'm an old friend of Silja's, Ma'am," he said.

Tess stepped forward. "Don't move. Keep your hands where I can see them." He raised his arms to expose the gun in his shoulder holster. She added, "Give me the gun."

"This gun?"

"Don't think I won't shoot you. Now give me the gun, smartass."

"Yes, Ma'am." Slowly, he took the gun from the holster and, with a quick flick of his wrist, he threw the gun—hitting her in the cheek.

Falling backwards, Tess fired off a shot into the ceiling. She was dazed, but rage drove her to scramble to her feet. Grant grabbed a vase filled with roses from the nightstand. Throwing it at her, he knocked her to the floor. The vase shattered when it hit the wall above her to send roses and water raining down on her head.

Tess' gun flipped from her hand. He scooped up the gun and grabbed Silja's hand.

"We've worn out our welcome. Time to go!"

They jumped over Tess to run into the hallway. They had descended only a few steps on the stairs when two gunshots whizzed over their heads.

Poised at the bottom of the staircase, Mikhail yelled at them in Russian.

"Well that's just about perfect!" Grant said, "Back up the stairs!"

Bullets sprayed the walls along the staircase while Silja and Grant took cover behind the railing at the top. Grant looked over his shoulder to see Tess coming out of the bedroom with his gun in her hand. He fired off a shot to force her back into the bedroom. She wouldn't stay there long. He wasn't sure how much ammo was in the gun he was using so he needed to ration his shots.

A chunk of the railing above their heads split when one of Tess' bullets made purchase. Hunkering down closer to the floor, Silja let out a yelp. He turned to make sure she hadn't been hit only to discover pure terror in her eyes.

He checked his watch—only four minutes until Eleni would drive away.

Grant asked, "So, are you seeing anybody?"

"What?!"

"Are you seeing anybody? I mean besides this possessive asshole?"

Mikhail was easing up the stairs with his gun aimed for the railing above his head.

"This isn't exactly the appropriate time for this conversation—"

"What makes you say that?" He sent a shot over Mikhail's head to keep him in place.

Mikhail ducked while backing down the stairs.

Grant grabbed Silja's hand to yank her to her feet and then took off running down the hallway toward the bedroom where Tess was hiding. Bullets splintered the hardwood floor behind them. Grant kicked the bedroom door open. He could hear Tess cry out when she fell against the wall with a hard thump. With vases breaking and bullets licking the walls along the hallway, they rushed into the bedroom.

Slamming the door closed, Grant found Tess lying behind the door unconscious. Blood saturated her face. He grabbed his gun from her hand and shoved it into the shoulder holster.

Quickly, he assessed the room. To buy a little time, he pushed the dresser in front of the door. Silja hurried to his side to assist him in the task. Grant felt a surge of pride that she'd gathered herself together enough to lend a hand—even though he really didn't need it.

Once, the dresser was in place, he checked the time on his watch—only two minutes left.

He snatched the nightstand from the floor and pitched it through the huge window to the right of the bed.

Silja looked back at Tess, who let out a slight groan. "Will she be okay?"

"I think so. C'mon, darlin', we're gonna have to climb down real fast." Taking her by the hand, he pointed out the window next to the bed with his other. "See that black SUV in the street past the courtyard?"

Silja was dazed, but she nodded.

"Good. The minute your feet hit the ground, you run like hell for it. You got that?"

Again, she nodded.

"No matter what, you get to the vehicle. You understand?"

She replied, "Yes, but—"

"No buts. Let's do this."

Bullets battered the bedroom door—drilling into the wall across the room. Mikhail kicked at the door. The dresser rocked to and fro.

"No time like the present! C'mon!" Grant insisted, stepping through the broken window onto the roof above the patio. He extended his hand to Silja. "Be careful of the glass and the snow. It's a little slick out here."

He bent down to grab the trellis below the roof and eased himself onto it. "Follow me," he called up to her while he climbed down.

Silja looked over the edge. The ground seemed to be a mile away. She could hear Mikhail's cursing and his heavy footsteps making their way down the hallway toward the staircase. She swallowed hard and then eased onto the trellis to follow Grant downward.

It wouldn't be long until Mikhail was in the dining room and through the glass doors!

Grant jumped the last four feet into the snow. He reached up for Silja. "Only a little farther," he assured her. Soon his hands were holding on to her slim hips. She jumped down from the trellis. He looked through the glass doors to see Mikhail sliding around a corner into the dining room.

Grant yelled, "Run!"

He attempted to take a shot at Mikhail, but the gun was empty. Tossing Tess' gun into the snow, he yanked his from the holster. He pressed out two rounds to shatter the glass. Mikhail dove behind the dining room table.

Silja took off across the courtyard at a dead run while checking over her shoulder to make sure Grant was following. He was, only he would stop every five steps to shoot toward the house. The designer riding boots that she had chosen from the closet that morning were proving to be a bad idea. She slipped and slid over the snow-covered court-yard. The dicey surface brought her to her knees twice. Scrambling, she managed to right herself, and she finally arrived at the gate. Silja fumbled with the latch. She pulled and pulled, but it wouldn't budge. Bullets pinged off the stone wall next to her. She glanced up to see Grant slide like he was going for home plate toward the gate.

He slid into the gate with his boots, busting it open. Then he scurried to his feet.

Mikhail was now on the patio but his gun was empty. He cursed at them in Russian.

"Hurry!" Eleni called from the SUV. She had pushed the passenger side door open. Grant and Silja raced to the vehicle.

"I'll get in the back!" Grant said as he pushed her toward the open door. As soon as his butt hit the seat, he yelled, "Drive, Eleni!"

Eleni pressed down hard on the accelerator. The tires spun on the icy pavement. The SUV fishtailed while darting down the street. She called over her shoulder, "I did not think you would make it!"

Grant glanced down at his watch. "What're ya talkin' about? I made it with thirty seconds to spare."

Dropping her head against the headrest, Silja tried to catch her breath. Her words came out in short hiccups, "I can't believe we made it. Thanks for helping us, Eleni." She wiped her nose with the cuff of her sweater.

That's when she heard a soft *meow*. She hesitated. Suddenly, four nimble paws padded onto her lap. Silja's eyes flew open. "Greta! You got Greta!"

"We couldn't leave her behind. That would be like leaving a teammate behind," Grant said. "Not on my watch."

Holding the cat close to her chest, Silja gazed over her shoulder at the man who had always done right by her. His chin was bristly with two days' worth of whiskers, and his eyes were bruised with fatigue, yet Grant Ketchum never looked as alluring as he did that instant. Why did she ever leave him behind?

She said, "No."

Grant blinked back. "No what?"

"No, I am not seeing anyone, including the possessive asshole."

"Geesh, Sil, is this an appropriate time for this conversation?"

Her heart swelled at the sound of his pet name for her tumbling from his lips. Sil. It was like five years had not passed, even though they certainly had.

Silja giggled. "You haven't changed one bit, have you, Ketchum?"

"Was I supposed to?"

"I had hoped not."

He drank in her brown eyes and her delicious plump lips that still bore a hint of pink lip gloss glimmering in the light coming through the windshield. He found himself fighting the primal urge to drag her into the backseat and to make love to her. He wanted nothing more than to feel the sizzle and burn of her heated skin against his. Swallowing it all back, he favored her with a svelte smile.

Grant's eyes met Eleni's in the rearview mirror. Like it or not, it was time to get down to the business at hand: a secure place to stay until he could contact the team.

Grant asked, "Did your friend come through with a place for us to hide out for a while?"

"Yes," Eleni answered, "Anna Antkowiak's grandmother has small cottage near Rezh. Her grandmother died six months ago. Anna was happy to let you use it. She will meet us at cottage with key and food."

"How far?"

"Eighty-three kilometers. It will take hour or so to get to cottage. It is secluded. You will be safe."

Grant gently squeezed her shoulder. "Thanks, Eleni, you did good. You're a real sweetheart."

Smiling, Silja reached across the center console to touch Eleni's hand. "You're a good friend."

Eleni's eyes filled with tears. "I am not," she muttered through trembling lips. "If I were good friend, I would have told you about parties. I would have warned you about Ballard Crafton rather than encourage you to go to him. I do not deserve your praise. I do not deserve your friendship."

Silja squeezed her shoulder. "It's all going to be fine, Eleni. You and all of the dancers were in a very bad … desperate situation. You did what you had to do to survive. Please don't feel badly. We're all going to get through this, you'll see."

* * * * *

Ballard rushed into the living room. Tess lay across the sofa with a compress to her nose. Her dress was bloodstained, as were the tips of her golden hair, and her eyes were turning black and blue.

With the sleeves of his dress shirt rolled to his elbows, Mikhail was wringing out a fresh compress into a bowl on the coffee table.

"What the hell happened?" Ballard demanded.

Removing the compress from her face, Tess said, "Your newest flame escaped with a man."

"He was professional." Mikhail handed Tess the rag.

Agitated, she snatched it from his hand to plop it over her forehead.

"Was he an American?"

"Yes, he was dressed in military fatigues. He knew exactly what he was doing. Like Mikhail said, he was a professional." Wincing, she added, "He said that he was an old friend."

Thinking back on the photograph of the marine and Silja sitting on the porch swing that he saw in her apartment, Ballard ran his fingers through Tess' hair and across her cheek. "I have an idea of who our intruder could be." He kissed her forehead. "Don't worry, my love,. He will pay and so will she."

He turned to Mikhail. "Get the GPS tracker. As long as she's wearing that choker, we can find her. And get Captain Domashev on the phone. We are victims of a home invasion, and that murderer, Silja Ramsay, has attacked our dear sweet Tess."

CHAPTER SIXTEEN

The roads wove through towns and rural areas. Eleni had driven for about forty-five minutes when she slowed the SUV to pull into a small service station. "We need gas," she said.

"Good," Silja said. "I really need to use a restroom."

They climbed out of the vehicle. Reaching her arms over her head, Silja stretched her back. The choker that Ballard had attached to her neck pinched. Scowling, she wrapped her fingers around it. "I wish I could get this damned thing off my neck," she complained.

Grant's eyes widened when he spotted the silver choker doused in diamonds. "What the hell is that?"

"I don't know. It's some kind of collar that Ballard put around my neck to mark his sick territory. I can't get it off. It's locked."

"Holy shit, Sil! He's tracking our every move!"

"What?" she asked. "What are you talking about? It's only a stupid choker."

"No, it's a symbol of possession, which means it has a GPS tracker in it. We've got to get that off of you right now." He yanked open the back door of the SUV to retrieve his go-bag.

"It is shame." Eleni ran a finger over the diamonds. "It is beautiful choker, yes?"

"Beautiful or not, I want rid of it," Silja told her.

"I don't blame you," Eleni said.

After digging through his bag, Grant pulled out a Swiss Army knife. He flipped through the tools until he came up with a pair of snippers. He carefully slid the jaws of the device through the collar and squeezed. The knife made dents in the silver, but it did not break. Letting out a frustrated breath, Grant reattached the jaws and squeezed again. The grooves became deeper, but still the choker remained in tact.

"It's damned good quality, I'll give him that." Grant tightened the jaws once more. His knuckles were pressing so tightly that they looked like they would burst through the skin. He clenched his teeth while he fought to press even harder.

"Ouch!" Silja cried.

"I'm sorry," he said, "but it's gotta go."

Grant gave another hard squeeze until the choker broke, falling loosely around her neck. Yanking it away, she tossed it to the pavement like it was a venomous snake.

Grant picked it up to examine it. Sure enough, there was a tiny GPS tracking chip among the diamonds. It appeared to be functioning. He turned to Eleni. "How close are we to the cottage?"

"About thirty kilometers, I think."

"That's about twenty-five miles." He eyed up an old beat-up farm truck that was pulling into the lot with a large crate full of goats in the bed. "Okay girls, I'll pump the gas. You do what you need to do in the restrooms, but don't dilly-dally. We need to be on the move."

While they made their way toward the building, Eleni turned to Silja. "What is this *dilly ... dolly* that we should not do?"

Patting her friend on the back, Silja chuckled, "Don't worry, Eleni. I won't let you dilly-dolly."

When they piled back into the SUV, Grant took the wheel.

Silja asked, "What did you do with the choker?"

A wicked curl formed on Grant's lips. He hitched his chin toward the old farm truck pulling out of the station. "The goats in the back of that truck are having a very expensive snack right about now."

Silja and Eleni giggled.

* * * * *

Eleni directed Grant along gravel roads through mountainous farmlands until they turned onto a narrow road that led to Anna's grandmother's cottage. Laden with heavy snow, the trees bowed over the road formed a tunnel-like pathway. Encased in ice, the tall grasses whipped in the wind when the SUV passed.

In the distance, they could see a tiny house come into view. Grant had to take caution not to run over the many sheep and goats that darted and scrambled in front of the vehicle.

A small blue SUV was parked in front of the cottage.

Grant drew his weapon. Touching his shoulder, Eleni told him, "That is Anna's car."

His military training kicking in, Grant kept his gun in hand while he scanned the meager farm for threats. The cottage was nestled in a clearing surrounded by woods. A small barn stood behind the dwelling. In the distance, the Rezh River could be seen. There were no other buildings in sight.

As they approached, the scarred wooden door creaked inward slightly. Then, it opened all the way. Anna stood in the doorway with a shawl wrapped around her shoulders. She spoke to Eleni in Russian and Eleni answered back.

The young girl brushed a wisp of her hair from her face with the back of her hand. With a pensive smile, she said, "Come, I have brought food and built fire in fireplace."

The cottage was chilly because the only heat was from the stone fireplace situated in the middle of the great room. The fire that Anna had built had not yet graduated into a full flame. It snapped and spit sparks while it slowly devoured the short stack of dried logs. A pile of wood and kindling rested on the hearth.

An old stove and a worn wooden table took up the right side of the room. Two old chairs were positioned in front of the fireplace with a rag rug between them.

Grant took note of the windows: one on each side of the door, and one on both ends of the house. The windows were small and single paned with empty wooden flower boxes attached to the outside. A straw broom stood upright in the corner next to the door. The kitchen contained only a couple of cabinets and a small, aged refrigerator.

He also noticed that the lock on the door would hardly hold back any intruders—anyone could kick it in if he had a mind to. He felt confident that he'd sent Ballard and his cronies off to chase their tails, or the goat's tails as it were, in the bitter cold.

"There is only one bedroom," Anna said. "There is bathroom and small shower. It is shame. Bathroom was only built one year before my grandmother's death."

Silja hugged Anna. "You're looking so much better than the last time I saw you, Anna. How are you feeling?"

"I have offer to teach for small ballet school nearby. I will be better soon, I ... I think." She pressed her fingers against her lips to stifle a sob that threatened to slip out.

Hugging her tighter, Silja pressed a kiss to the girl's forehead. "I want to thank you for letting us use the cottage. This is an old friend of mine, Grant Ketchum."

Anna studied the rugged-looking American man tentatively. Grant's heart clenched with anger at the fright that had been put into the lovely young girl's eyes.

Averting her gaze, Anna stepped back from Silja's embrace and tugged the shawl tighter around her body. "I wanted to help," she said. "I must get back to Mama, it is long drive. She does not know you are here. It is better this way. I have put food in cupboard and refrigerator and a kettle is warming on stove for tea." She bowed her head while she made her way past the American man to grab her coat hanging on a hook near the door.

Eleni followed.

"Eleni, where are you going?" Silja asked.

"I will stay with Anna." Her eyes flicked from Silja to Grant and then back to Silja. Drawing closer, she whispered, "I can see fire in your eyes, Silja. You do not want me here tonight."

"Eleni ..."

"It is true. I will be back tomorrow. Now rest ..." She winked, "If you can. Good-bye, Grant."

Giving her a hug, Grant said, "See ya, and thanks again, Eleni." Sympathetic toward Anna's uneasiness caused by his presence, he was careful to keep his distance while he followed them to the door. He told Silja, "I'm going to check out the barn. I'll park the car behind it and see what kind of cell reception I can get. I'll be right back."

"Okay," Silja said. "I'll see what I can do for dinner."

"Sounds good." He pitched a nod and wink before he slipped out the door.

* * * * *

The flames whirled and crackled around the logs in the fireplace. Shadows danced along the open beams across the ceiling of the meager cottage, and over Grant's face. The ashen skies outside dropped a steady snow—casting darkness throughout the dimly lit room.

Warming himself on the floor near the hearth, Grant watched the flames turn from orange to yellow. Embers fell from the wood—glimmering like a bed of red and orange and gold sequins beneath.

Dinner had been simple: a pot of leftover stew and a loaf of bread that Anna's mother had made. As hungry as they were, they guzzled the hot meal down in no time flat.

They spent most of dinner catching up. Grant told Silja what little he could about First Force, and she told him about her years at the Novikov.

She also explained her short-lived attraction to Ballard Crafton. "He was so charming. I had no idea what he was capable of. Eleni was forced to spend time with him. I was forced to agree to the arrangement. In any case, I couldn't let the dancers be put through that anymore ... especially after what happened to Anna."

Anger burned through Grant's veins like an acid drip. "He didn't hurt you while you were at his house, did he?"

"No," she said with a shake of her head. "He didn't touch me."

"I don't understand why he wants other women. His wife is very attractive," Grant mused.

"Wife?"

"Yeah, Tess McMillan is Ballard Crafton's wife."

Silja's mouth dropped open. "I knew there was something between them ... but I would've never ... how do you know?"

"Our team coordinator, Clark Rhodes, gathers intel when we go on missions. He said that Tess has been with Ballard for many years, but he only married her about five years ago."

"How sick is that?"

"Different strokes for different folks." He shrugged. Noticing her silence, he glanced up to find a baleful look on her face. He quickly added, "But not for me."

"Imagine my relief."

Grant laughed. Not wanting to frighten her any further, he opted not to tell Silja about Ballard's abuse of the opera singer and the concert pianist. He stuffed the last of his bread into his mouth and gathered the dishes from the table. Together, they washed them at the old porcelain tub under a window that looked out over the small farm.

Stretching her back, Silja said around a yawn, "Well, if you don't mind, I'm going to check out the shower."

"Let me know how it goes."

She curled up on her toes and kissed his lips. When she pulled away, she whispered, "I won't be long." She made her way toward the bedroom.

Watching her walk away was an exercise in control. He desperately wanted to follow her into the shower, but there was no invitation, and he wasn't going to force anything. He only hoped that she was feeling what he was feeling.

For the next half-hour Grant spent his time with Greta curled up on his lap near the fireplace.

He stroked her neck while contemplating their next move. The little house was in a dead zone. He needed to go where he could use his phone to contact Clark and set up a rendezvous with the team.

He also needed to ask Silja about the knife—a conversation he was not looking forward to having. He couldn't imagine that she could have killed another human being, and he believed that she would have told him immediately if she had. No, Silja had had nothing to do with Ivan Belsky's death. She couldn't have.

The wood floor creaked, drawing his attention from the fire to the silhouette of a beautiful figure wrapped in a towel, padding barefoot toward him. "That's a great fire you've got going," Silja said.

"Yeah ... it's been burning for a while."

The light from the flames illuminated her face enough to see the curl of her lips. "Is it hot enough to throw any heat?"

"Oh, there's plenty of heat."

"That's good. I need to warm up." She let the towel slip to the floor.

He watched the shadows lick over her delicious body as if they were worshipping every delectable inch. Her dusty pink nipples stood out from her round breasts in stiff peaks. Her silky skin smoothed over her ribcage and down to her lean hips, which brought his focus on the small tuft of dark hair at the apex of her long tight thighs.

Oh yeah, he remembered this, and again he cursed himself for ever letting her go. That was all in the past. This was here and now, and if she'd have him, this was going to be his future.

Grant swallowed hard. He didn't know if he would make sense when he spoke, but he knew what he wanted—her in his bed. "Between me and the fire, I think we can accommodate a warming trend."

"I don't see how," she said.

He blinked back.

She smiled. "Studies show that the most effective method of getting warm is skin on skin. You have way too many clothes on, Ketchum."

"Well, I wouldn't want to argue with science. That would be just plain stupid." He tugged the T-shirt over his head and tossed it aside.

Greta leapt from his lap to scurry under a chair.

He locked eyes with Silja as he unbuttoned his camo pants and pushed them down to expose his full erection. His lips curled when she licked her lips. He stood before her naked and aching to touch, feel, and taste every inch of her.

"That's much better," she whispered in a husky voice as she dropped to her knees in front of him. Fingers splayed wide, she ran her hands up his tight thighs and over the clenched muscles of his buttocks and hips until her fingers caressed the length of his arousal. He drew in a deep breath and let his head fall back when her tongue ran up the sensitive place where her hand had just explored—leaving a trail of electricity in its wake.

"Sil ..." he groaned. Entangling his fingers deep into her hair, he pulled her closer to him. He murmured, "Ahhh, Sil ... if you keep going this isn't going to last for very long ..."

"Sssh, we have all night to even the score." She then ran her tongue up his leg where thigh joined groin.

Feeling his resolve wavering, Grant gently grabbed her chin. "Please ... I have a better idea." He scooped her up into his arms and carried her into the bedroom.

The bed wasn't very big, but they he didn't need a lot of room for what he wanted to do. He laid her across the bed. Her damp hair splayed over the pillow. Reaching up to caress his broad shoulder, she smiled at him. He lowered over her to capture her mouth and press his tongue inside.

Then, she wrapped her legs around his hips and opened herself to him.

He pressed deep inside—savoring the warmth of her. Her body was still moist from the shower, but the silkiness of her skin was undeniable.

His lips smoothed down her cheek and neck and chest until he found her hard, pebbly nipple where he feasted.

The steady rush of passion vibrated through him. God how he'd missed this woman. Amidst the rediscovery, the emotions, and the heat of desire, they climbed to their climax together.

Grant's fingers gripped the pillows on either side of her head, feeling the spurts finalizing his desire.

Running his fingers through her hair, he took in her lovely face. Then, he kissed her tenderly to show her that his love for her had never diminished, but had only strengthened over their time apart.

He eased his body onto the mattress next to her. She laid her head on his wide chest. Her fingertips danced over his chest.

Yes, he remembered this sultry ritual of hers. He remembered how much he loved the tingle her touch created over his super sensitized skin. Quietly, they lay in the dark for a long time, holding each other, savoring the moment.

Listening to the thrum of his heart, Silja ran her fingers over the outline of Grant's strong hands. Snuggling deeper into his arms, she whispered, "I missed this."

"I missed us," he replied.

"We've been telling everyone that we're *'old friends.'* But we were never friends ... we've always been ... this ... lovers," Silja said.

"Oh, I dunno. I kinda like you. We're very good at being friends—we're just better at being lovers. We're lovers who know how to be friends. How about that?"

"I like it." Silja pushed up on an elbow to look down into his face. Letting out a long breath, she said, "Grant ..." she expelled another breath. "After Mom and Dad died and I got the invitation to join the Novikov, I felt like it was a sign that I should start new, ya know? I don't think my head was in the right place. I think I made rash decisions during the mourning process—they say that's a bad time to make any decisions at all, and now I feel like I ran out on you. I hurt you. For that, I'm truly sorry." She caressed his face with the tips of her fingers and then gently pressed her lips to his.

He pulled her down to lie on his chest. He rested his cheek against the top of her head. He just wanted to hold her, to feel her close, to breathe in the scent of her. He didn't want to rehash the past, because that's exactly where he wanted to store it—in the past.

The fatigue was getting the best of Silja. Her body relaxed against his and he could feel her breathing slowing into a deep sleep. She was replete with feelings that she hadn't experienced in years.

Clearly, she felt safe in his arms, and for that he was thankful—but he had to talk to her about Ivan Belsky. It was essential.

He whispered, "I know you want to sleep, and I want that, too, but I have to talk to you about something first."

Silja's eyes dragged open to meet his. "What is it?"

"You know that Ivan Belsky was murdered, right?"

Silja jerked up onto her elbows. "What?"

"You didn't know that he was found in the alley behind the theatre the morning after the contributors' party—stabbed to death?"

"Oh my God, no."

Grant dragged in a ragged breath. It was just as he thought. Now came the hard part. "He was stabbed with a knife that somehow had your fingerprints on it. The police are looking for you."

Silja brought her hands to her mouth. "I didn't stab Belsky. I didn't even have a knife with me." She let out a long breath. Her mind raced to revisit the events of that night. She recalled, "He dragged me into the alley. I was fighting back ... that's how I got this shiner. He hit me." Her eyes widened. "That's when Mikhail came into the alley!"

"Crafton's bodyguard?"

"Yes ... he was beating on Belsky terribly, but I didn't care—he was getting what he deserved after what he did to Anna Antkowiak—"

"I totally agree with that."

"Anyway ... I didn't hang around. I ran out of the alley and was lucky enough to catch the bus back to my apartment right away." Dropping her hands to her lap in frustration, she said, "I wish I had my cell phone."

"I have your phone."

"Oh my God! Get it!"

Grant slipped from the bed to retrieve his go-bag. After rifling through the bottom of the bag, he pulled the phone out and tossed it to Silja, and then he sat on the bed next to her. Turning on the phone, her fingers frantically swept over the buttons.

Holding up the phone, her face brightened. "Here it is! I made this video of the evening. It's all here ..."

Grant looked over her shoulder as she pressed the button to play the video that she'd made that night. Obviously, it wasn't a quality Spielberg production, but the recording revealed damning evidence of the auction for sexual services from the Novikov dancers. Grant's eyes narrowed as he observed a tubby man reach his hand into a box and pluck out a pair of pointe shoes.

"That's Ivan Belsky," Silja interjected, pointing to the screen.

Ballard's voice bellowed through the audio. Belsky argued that he'd won Silja fair and square. The video became bumpy and jumpy as Belsky yanked Silja down the corridor and into the alley.

Grant's blood raged through his veins at a white-hot boil as he listened to Belsky yell at her. Then, he heard her cry out when the bastard slapped her across the face.

The audio became scrambled as the wind whipped through the alley and another struggle ensued. It became most apparent that Silja must've hesitated, because the cell phone then recorded the dirty snow-covered gravel on the ground. But the audio then picked up the sound of two men yelling at each other in Russian. A nanosecond later, the recording was a dizzying whirl of movement accompanied by the sound of rushing wind and Silja's feet hurrying along the pavement.

Silja turned off the phone. "That's all there is. After that I got on the bus and made it back to my apartment. It wasn't long before Mikhail showed up. I was able to get that text to you before he broke into my bedroom and dragged me into Ballard's limo, but this is certainly evidence that I did not stab Belsky. Although I can't say I wouldn't have liked to."

"You and me both. Okay, so evidently the bodyguard killed Belsky. Good for him, but that doesn't answer the question of how a knife with your prints got involved. That said, there is a knife missing from the knife block in your kitchen. When Eleni told me that you were a suspect in the murder, I spent a lot of time searching your kitchen for the missing knife."

Silja flopped back against the pillow. "That's right. I was looking for it myself the other day."

"How would Crafton's bodyguard have gotten possession of it?"

"Ballard was at my apartment a week before this all happened ... he brought a pizza over. That's when he was doing his 'I'm nothing more than a charming older man' routine. I've got to hand it to him: he was very convincing. Anyway, I suppose he could've picked up the knife any time during that evening, but I just don't know why he would've—it's not like he knew what was going to go on with Belsky. For that matter, neither he nor I knew that I would be attending the party at that time. So it makes no sense for him to take the knife."

"True ... are you sure that no one else was in your kitchen besides Crafton before Belsky was killed?"

Closing her eyes, Silja raked her fingers through her hair, searching her memory ... *Dominik* ...

Silja's mind went back to the afternoon that she had been cutting up vegetables when there was a knock a the door. She remembered her surprise at finding Dominik on the other side. He was his usual cocky, objectionable self—a real jerk. And then, she remembered the conversation that set everything—possibly even Belsky's death—into motion ...

"You can make life easier for your friends, Silja. You have the power to make it stop," she remembered Dominik saying.

She remembered turning to rush for the door, but he grabbed her by the arm and pressed his body to hers to hold her against the refrigerator. "Let me go!" she had demanded.

"You are key to their freedom," he had told her. *"Ballard Crafton wants you to be his constant companion, and for you to move into his home. If you agree to this, he will give Novikov all money it will need, Silja. Your friend, Eleni, will never have to spread her legs for man she does not desire. Young girls like Anna will never have to bow to abuse if you agree to simple arrangement."* Silja remembered wiggling and struggling beneath his weight.

"He is wealthy. You would have everything your heart desires, and your friends would be free of this burden. You think about what I have told you, Silja."

He had turned to leave, and hesitated as he nodded toward the sofa. *"You still have kitty. How nice for you on cold winter nights, yes?"*

Suddenly, Silja's eyes flicked wide open. She sat straight up. "Dominik! Dominik Potrovic came to visit me! He's the one who told me about the arrangement that Ballard wanted in return for funding the ballet company."

"Who's Dominik?" he asked. "Does he have something against you?"

"He's the principal male dancer for the company," she explained. "He and I...that was some time ago. He came to my apartment to bully me into the arrangement with Ballard. I remember noticing the knife was missing after his visit. I was so flustered that I didn't think anything more about the missing knife—it was one of my mom's *Cutcos*. I know that Dominik didn't have any use for Belsky. Then again, he has little use for anyone—except fpr Edvar."

"Who's Edvar?"

"Edvar Kozlovski is the choreographer for the ballet company, and Dominik's lover. Perhaps Belsky did something to them and they planned to kill him and pin it on me. Edvar isn't a very strong-willed person. I can't imagine him participating in a murder scheme." She shook her head and shrugged her shoulders at the same time. "Nothing would surprise me at this point, nothing at all."

Grant took the cell phone from her hand and placed it on the small night table. After gathering her into his arms he kissed her cheek and lay back down in the bed. "We've got evidence that you did not stab Belsky. Now let's get some rest. I'll contact my boss for some help."

"He can do that?"

"Yeah, Clark is a worker of miracles."

"Are you sure he can pull off this miracle, Grant?"

"Well ... kinda. Clark Rhodes is the coordinator for First Force," he told her.

He looked into her beautiful brown eyes that were full of worry. The last thing he wanted to see in her eyes was apprehension. He wanted to erase it, take it all away, and replace it with only love, desire, and caring. He had already told her too much. The less information that she had, the better off she'd be if things went south.

Pulling her closer, he assured her that she would be okay. "Everything will be just fine. Now close your eyes and get some sleep." Silja settled her head on his shoulder.

Grant was satisfied that they had evidence to clear her of Ivan Belsky's murder, but that wasn't the only factor working against them. Ballard Crafton would be looking for them. Grant wasn't afraid of what would happen to him if Crafton discovered them. He was Special Forces, and he could take care of himself. He was terrified of what would happen to Silja if she fell back into Ballard Crafton's hands—his very angry hands. He had to get her the hell out of Dodge.

He wondered how far he would have to travel to get a signal to call Clark and if Silja would be safe while he was gone. He couldn't imagine that Crafton knew where they were. He was certain that no one had tailed them. Luckily, they had ditched the tracking device Silja had been wearing a good twenty miles back. Considering all that, he decided that she would be safe while he was gone. Taking in her fatigue, he knew that she definitely needed some rest before they were forced to face an escape from Russia.

After Silja had been still and quiet for a long time, Grant eased out of the bed, grabbed his go-bag, went into the main room, and eddied back into his clothes.

While stoking the fire, he noticed Greta sleeping on the chair. He had to chuckle at the kitty lying belly-up, warming her tubby tummy. He gathered the calico up and placed her in the warm bed with Silja. Immediately, Greta cuddled up to her mistress. Silja snuggled deeper into the pillow and let out a gentle sigh.

The right side of Grant's mouth lifted at the sight of the two of them comfy and warm in the bed. He could never let this go again. He had to protect them with everything he had.

The urgency to call Clark swept through him. He pulled on his coat and slipped out the door into the blustery night.

CHAPTER SEVENTEEN

First Force Headquarters, Harverton, Pennsylvania

"Whoa," Clark muttered while running a hand through his hair.

He had been compiling intel from the computer since the previous night. It was now mid-afternoon.

Walt looked up from his paperwork. "I don't like the sound of that. What've ya got?"

"I've been digging around to find out what kind of work Crafton Technologies did for the government, and if they really dumped him after the allegations against him over the opera singer and the pianist. Turns out our government did wash their hands of him after the second incident with Miss Ming, but he moved his labs to Russia because their government wasn't skittish about having a violent man working for them. In fact, they were thrilled to have him continue his testing on a serum for mind control."

"What?" Walt jumped from his seat to look over Clark's shoulder at the laptop.

"Yep, I was able to hack into the feds data base to find out what Crafton was working on. I've heard about stuff like this. They haven't been terribly successful as of yet, but they keep trying to develop a serum for soldiers to make them into beasts that have no fear, and can fight fiercely with the strength of RoboCop. Korea, China, you name the country. Everyone wants their soldiers to be unstoppable. I guess the good ol' USA didn't want to be left behind. Looks like Crafton was getting close to human testing when he got in trouble with the law, and that's when our guys booted him to the curb. Cut all his funding. The Russians were all too happy to pick up where the US left off."

"Is anyone watching the operation?"

The light from the laptop sent a blue hue across Clark's glasses while his fingers raced across the keys. "I'm trying to find out. I can't believe we'd let Crafton go to Russia and not keep an eye on him. There's no way in hell we'd let him walk away with that serum. He had to sneak it out somehow. He's a smart cookie. Maybe he's got an eidetic memory. Regardless, there's got to be operatives assigned to the man. I've sent an encrypted message to a friend of mine, Peyton Mattock, who runs a team in Russia for Hawke Operatives International. Hopefully, he'll know something about it."

"That's Seamus Hawke's group," Walt said. "I worked with him briefly in the CIA."

"That's right," Clark said. "They run a lot of missions in Russia. I'll bet they've got their fingers in this one."

"Good. In the meantime, Grant needs help."

"That's a big affirmative. Unfortunately, I haven't heard from him since yesterday. I sent a text about two hours ago—no response yet. We've got to find him and get him the hell out of there. I'm glad we didn't have our team return home. At least they're fairly close at hand ... I hope."

Scrubbing his fingers across his chin, Walt muttered, "That makes two of us."

Clark's face brightened. Tapping at the keys, he announced, "Well, good golly, Miss Molly, I've got an answer from my old buddy, Peyton."

"So he's got a lead on this?"

"Yes, sirree." Clark narrowed his eyes to concentrate on the message before him.

Walt leaned over to get a look.

"He says his team is watching Crafton," Clark reported. "He confirms that there is human testing going on with the serum, and so far the body count is three—at least that's how many body bags have been carried out of the lab. The government is providing him men for testing who have been doing hard time in prison. He says that they have a mole inside the prison, and are expecting a truck filled with new prisoners any time now. Replacements for the one's they've lost, no doubt."

"Can you arrange a rendezvous with our team?" Walt asked.

"You betcha."

CHAPTER EIGHTEEN

Dusk was giving way to the darkness when the police cruiser pulled into the snow-covered gas station. There were no cars at the pumps. Only a single attendant could be seen at the cash register through the window in the small store. Captain Domashev stepped out of the vehicle while the officer at the wheel lowered the back window for Ballard.

Studying the tracker, Ballard groused, "What the hell? The tracker says they came to this destination, but now it claims that they are going in the other direction—from where we came." He let out a furious growl. "Like the prisoners that the Russians give me to experiment on, this tracker is inadequate. Junk!"

"I will ask attendant if he has seen SUV." Domashev flipped the collar of his wool coat up and pushed his hands deep into the pockets. He walked with nimble steps toward the building.

Through the window, Ballard could see the attendant nodding while pointing toward the roadway. Yes, evidently he had seen Silja and her soldier. After the short exchange with the attendant, Domashev returned to the cruiser.

"He said there were three of them. Two women and one man," Domashev reported. "The man was tall American as you have described. Both women were brunettes. He said vehicle turned right out of lot."

Pitching the device across the cab, Ballard let out a huff. "The American must've removed the collar from Silja's neck. The other woman was probably Eleni Babinski. She is one of the ballerinas from the Novikov and a good friend of hers." Sitting back hard against the seat, he compressed the bridge of his nose between his forefinger and thumb, while Domashev obediently stood outside in the elements to wait for his instructions.

They were traveling into the farmland to hideout. It had to be, but how far and how many twists and turns had they made in their travels? Ballard's deliberation was interrupted by a small blue SUV pulling into the station.

Anna's foot pressed the brake when she spotted the police cruiser in the gas station lot beyond the pumps.

Eleni touched her hand lightly. She told her, "It is okay. Don't be nervous. They know nothing. They are not looking for us."

Swallowing back her fear, Anna rolled the vehicle up to the pumps. She wrapped her scarf around her face before she got out.

Eleni laid her head against the headrest and closed her eyes. It had been a nerve-racking day. She was feeling the fatigue.

Ballard studied the young woman pumping gas, but her face was hidden behind the scarf so he strained to see the woman sitting in the passenger's seat. His eyes narrowed. She looked familiar, yet from the distance and angle he couldn't be sure. He looked up at the captain shivering in the cold weather.

"Ask that young woman to come here, Captain," Ballard said.

Domashev called out to Anna in Russian, "You there! Come here, I want to talk to you."

Anna's spine stiffened. Fear scraped through her. She glanced through the passenger window to see Eleni's head tilted off to the side and her eyes closed. She was dozing.

Anna swallowed hard. Her heart was beating so fast that she thought it would burst. Wrapping her arms defensively around her torso, Anna shuffled through the snow toward Domashev.

"What can I do for you?" she asked in Russian. Her scarf slipped from her face. Quickly, she tucked it back into place.

She wasn't quick enough—Ballard recognized her from the contributors' party. He was fairly sure that this was the young woman that Belsky had won at the auction about a week ago—the one that he'd badly abused.

Smiling at her, he asked through the open car window, "Do you speak English?"

Anna flinched when her eyes met Ballard's. She knew exactly who he was. Her fingers clenched the fabric lining inside the pockets of her coat in an attempt to stop them from shaking. It was little use. She replied, "I do."

"You look cold. Please come sit inside the warm car."

Anna glanced across the lot at her car. Eleni had not moved.

Domashev opened the door for her. Ballard slid across the seat.

Her voice shaking, she asked, "Am I under arrest?"

"Of course not, my dear," Ballard crooned, "we simply want to talk to you, and we want you to be comfortable at the same time. Please, don't be frightened. Come out of the weather."

Anna looked over her shoulder at Domashev. His nose and cheeks were brilliant red. Impatient to get out of the wind and chill, he hitched his chin toward the car. There were no other options; she had to get into the police cruiser with Ballard Crafton, and so she tentatively slid into the seat next to him. Folding her hands into her lap, she prayed that the questioning would be brief.

Domashev hastened into the front seat and placed his hands over the vents to thaw them out.

"You are one of the dancers from the Novikov Ballet Company, are you not?" Ballard asked.

Keeping her eyes focused on her hands, Anna mumbled, "Not anymore."

"What is your name?"

"Anna Antkowiak."

"Yes ... I remember you. You danced in *Coppelia* with Silja Ramsay. You were one of the Chinese dolls. You are a lovely dancer, Anna."

"Thank you, Mr. Crafton."

"Ahhh, so you know who I am. Tell me, Anna, who is the girl in the car with you?"

She drew in a ragged breath. Her hands clenched together so tightly that her nails were beginning to pierce the skin. "A friend," she muttered. Anna was certain that the answer would be no good, and she wasn't at all sure how to help Eleni, but she had to stall for time somehow.

"Poor Ivan Belsky. What a terrible way to die— in a cold dark alley with a knife sticking out of his chest. You know that the police are still trying to figure out who killed him. You knew him, didn't you, Anna?"

The mere mention of Belsky's name made her insides twist and her gut wrench. She was well aware of what Ballard was eluding to. Incensed by his probing, she blurted out, "I have done nothing wrong. May I go now?"

"I don't know, Anna, it seems to me that you have more of a reason than anyone to want Belsky dead. He had no right to beat and rape you, but that doesn't excuse murder. Not even in Russia. Isn't that right, Captain Domashev?"

Domashev agreed. "That is correct."

Anna could barely breathe. What was he suggesting? This couldn't be happening. Tears welling in her eyes, she cried, "No! I had nothing to do with his death! I have done nothing wrong! Let me go now!"

Domashev scolded her in Russian, "Be still, girl! We are taking you to the station for questioning." Turning to Ballard, he asked, "Do you want me to get other girl?"

Waving a careless hand, Ballard smiled. "No need. I think we've got everything we could ever want right here."

"But she will go tell the others."

"Oh, I hope so," Ballard said. "In the meantime, I want round-the-clock surveillance within eighty kilometers of this area, yes?" After Domashev nodded his head, he added, "Good. Let's go."

The cruiser pulled across the lot past Anna's SUV parked at the pumps. The sound of tires crunching against the snow stirred Eleni. Foreboding washed over her when Anna's desperate eyes met hers as the cruiser rolled by. Ballard leaned forward so that Eleni would see him.

Jumping from the vehicle, Eleni slipped and slid in the snow after the cruiser while screaming, "Anna!"

* * * * *

Silja snuggled down into the blankets. It had been so long since she had been made love to with such primal desire. It had always been that way with Grant. His love making was powerful, unyielding, possessive, and oh-so satisfying. Her lips curled at the memory of how good it felt to be back in his arms, how good he felt inside her. After all this time—perhaps because of the passage of time—she knew exactly what she wanted: to return home and be with him for the rest of her life—if he'd have her. Well aware that they weren't out of the woods yet, and that Ballard was using everything at his disposal to find her, she still felt safe with Grant at her side.

Feeling secure, she stretched, yawned, and reached for the warmth of Grant's body only to find his side of the bed empty. Greta was nestled deeply into the pillow where he had laid his head.

Pulling the blankets to her chest, Silja sat up and searched the room for him. She called out, "Grant ... Grant, where are you?" She listened for his response, but instead she heard someone pounding on the cottage door.

Eleni's voice was panicked as she banged on the door while yelling, "Silja! Please let me in! Silja! Grant!"

* * * * *

Grant had driven almost ten miles before the bars on his cell phone slowly started to increase to an acceptable signal strength. The tires crunching through the snow, he rolled the SUV to the side of the narrow, snow-laden road. He looked out over the beauty of the mountainous region. Far below, light glowed from houses wearing a blanket of white under the light of a full moon. He dialed the cell phone and waited for Clark to pick up.

"What's going on, Ketchum?" Clark asked.

"Time to bug out," Grant said. "We're hole up at a small cottage along the Rezh River. We're safe for now, but I'm sure that Crafton is pulling out all the stops to find us. That said, Crafton isn't my only concern. It seems that the police are also looking for Silja. She is on their list of suspects for the murder of a man named Ivan Belsky."

"What's the connection?" Clark hitched his chin toward Walt to alert him that Grant was on the line.

Walt joined him at the computer. Clark placed the call on intercom.

"The ballet company that Sil was dancing for was broke, so the owner, Natalia Novikov, was forcing the dancers to prostitute themselves to big-time contributors to keep the business above water. Crafton was one of those contributors, as was Ivan Belsky, who was found stabbed to death in the alley behind the Mockba Theatre after one of their contributors' parties where they auctioned off the dancers to these wealthy bastards. The bad news is that the knife used to kill Belsky belongs to Sil, and therefore her prints are on the murder weapon. Now here's the good news: we have video of Crafton's bodyguard beating the shit out of Belsky, but Silja doesn't think he killed him. She's thinking it may be one of the dancers, Dominik Potrovic."

"Why is that?" Clark inquired.

"Potrovic was at her apartment not long ago, and that's when she noticed that one of her knives was missing. She says he has an axe to grind with everyone, including Sil." Grant noticed a pair of distant headlights glinting off the snow as a vehicle wound slowly down the road.

"I'll look into the police activity on the case. In the meantime, I'm going to advance our team toward you, and then you'll rendezvous with a team that has been watching Crafton's lab. Turns out that Crafton is testing a serum to turn soldiers into mechanical beasts—and the Russians are letting him test on humans—convicts out of their prisons for now. We're going to help them shut the operation down, and then get you and your ballerina back to the US." Clark tapped at the computer's keys.

Walt interjected, "If at all possible, sit tight at the cottage with your tracking device activated. You've got one in your go-bag, right?"

"I've got it right here in my pocket," Grant said.

Walt glanced at the computer screen to see a small cottage and barn. "Good—use it. I think Clark's got the farm up on the satellite, but it'll make it easier for the team to find you."

"Got it, thanks guys."

"It's what we do," Clark said.

The line went dead.

Grant's brows furrowed when the vehicle slowed—drawing closer.

He was starting his SUV, when flashing lights exploded through the darkness—revealing the fact that it was a police cruiser. Two officers jumped from the vehicle with their guns trained on Grant.

"Well, that's just about freakin' perfect," he muttered to himself. Quickly, his fingers found their way into the pocket of his camo pants. He pulled out the tracking device, activated it, and then tossed it under the driver's seat. Promptly, he tossed his cell phone to the floor and ground it into broken pieces with his heel.

He knew what was about to happen. He would be searched. At least Walt and Clark would be able to track his vehicle.

The officers flanked the vehicle.

Grant raised his hands. The officer at his door tapped on the window while yelling at him in Russian. Grant didn't have to interpret the language.

Keeping his gun aimed at Grant, the officer yanked the door open and gestured—demanding that Grant vacate the SUV.

The sound of sirens filled the night. Flashing lights ripped through the darkness, and a nanosecond later his vehicle was surrounded by police cars.

The officers rushed from their vehicles to corral him. They shoved him against the SUV, patted him down hard, and then handcuffed him. One of the officers talked excitedly on the cell phone before he directed another to stuff Grant into a cruiser, while another found the demolished cell phone lying near the brake pedal. Biting out an angry sentence, he tossed the fragments of the phone into the snow.

By the hand gestures, Grant figured they were all going to follow along—to where, he wasn't sure.

Yeah, the situation wasn't looking good—not good at all.

* * * * *

Whimpering ... the sound of whimpering stirred Grant from the blur of unconsciousness.

When he lifted his head, the room spun. He winced—feeling the sting of swelling to his right eye, and the acrid taste of blood filled his mouth—his blood. The cuffs that secured him to the metal chair pinched his wrists. Fighting through the nausea undoubtedly caused by a concussion, he opened his eyes and raised his head toward the hiccups of weeping.

He prayed that they had not found Silja.

Willing the room to stand still, he finally managed to focus on the woman huddled in the corner of the dank room. Sobbing, she rocked back and forth in a fetal position with her forehead buried in her knees. It took several moments before he recognized her.

He remembered that the officers who had taken him into custody on the road had driven him ... but they had not taken him into the main entrance. Instead he had been roughly ushered through a corridor in the lower level of the station. They had handcuffed him to a chair in a small, dark, dank interrogation room. He searched his memory some more but could not come up with the memory of Anna Antkowiak's presence during their fierce, hands-on interrogation.

Finally, he managed, "Anna ..."

The young woman's head jerked up. She looked at him with terror in her watery eyes.

His head was pounding, and another wave of nausea washed over him as he muttered again, "Anna ... is that you, sweetheart?"

Her wide eyes flicked to the metal door, and then to him. Rolling onto her knees, she answered, "Yes, it is me ... Anna Antkowiak ... Silja's friend. Are you all right?"

It hurt like hell, but he managed a thin smile. "Yeah ... I'm doing great. Where did those bastards go?"

Licking her parched lips, Anna glanced at the door once more before speaking in a desperate trembling tone, "I am so sorry ... I have told them where Silja is ... please forgive me. I-I am so frightened. They will kill us. Please, please tell them what they want to know ... how many more beatings can you take?"

Grant let his head drop back.

She told them where Silja is.

Panic ripped through him. He yanked at his restraints to no avail. The room whirled. He swallowed back vomit.

He understood why Anna gave Crafton the information that he wanted—she was terrified. The wounds from her terrible ordeal with Belsky were far too fresh. He remembered how she could barely stand to look at him when he met her at the cottage. He was a man—and that was enough to petrify her. She was emotionally broken. She had nothing to fight with.

That didn't make the situation any less dire—Crafton would go after Silja, and then what?

Anna scrambled across the room toward him. She reached out her hand to touch him, and then just as quickly, she pulled it away. Tears streaming down her flushed cheeks, she cupped her hand over her mouth. "I am so ashamed for what I have done, but please, you must tell them what they want to know."

With half-lidded eyes, he glanced at her. "Well, darlin', I'm not sure that I remember what exactly that was."

"It was your name and who you work for. I could not remember your name. They believed me, but now they have gone, and I do not know what they have planned to do with us."

The door opened.

Gasping, Anna quickly backed away from him. Grant said, "Well, I guess we're about to find out."

Two officers came into the room followed by Ballard and Captain Domashev. One officer grabbed Anna, shoved her against the wall, and handcuffed her, while the other removed the cuffs from the metal chair that Grant sat on, yanked him to his feet, and then handcuffed his hands behind him.

Everything ached—his ribs, his jaw, and the sudden movement brought on yet another round of nausea. Grant swaggered in place.

Ballard approached to talk close into his ear.

"You're training is impressive. I am most intrigued. You and Miss Antkowiak will be taking a ride in the van to the prison where they will be picking up some other individuals that remain nameless—just like you. From there, you will be transferred to my labs where you will be more ... useful. Finally, I have a subject well worthy of my serum."

Anna let out a horrified gasp.

Ballard turned to her. "Thank you for your cooperation, Miss Antkowiak, but I'm afraid you shouldn't have resisted arrest—at least that's what the media will be told."

He nodded at Domashev, who directed his men to take the prisoners to the van immediately.

Before leaving the room, Domashev turned to Ballard. "I will go for Miss Ramsay now."

"Thank you, Captain. I will meet you at the lab." Ballard said.

CHAPTER NINETEEN

Eleni's words were pierced with panic, "We must hurry. Anna is weak after what she has been through. They will get all information from her. They will know where you are. They will come for you." Her dark eyes were molested with fatigue, worry, and angst.

Silja yanked drawers open in the cupboards, rummaged through them, and then moved on to the next. The snow beyond the tiny window over the sink caught her eyes. Against the solar light over the barn door, she could see the delicate snow falling like fairy dust. Her mom used to call that kind of flurry *"sneaky snow."* It appeared so innocent, a non-threat. Nevertheless, it could pile up without notice and make the roads slick as a whistle. Before you knew it, you had a major storm on your hands.

The calm among the chaos made her lips curl. *Mom.*

Eleni grabbed her arm. "What are you looking for?"

"I don't know what happened to Grant, and I know that we can't wait—"

Eleni took Silja's hands into hers. She spoke softly, except she was unable to suck back the alarm laced in her voice, "I know what you fear. I fear same—that Ballard has Grant, and knowing what he is capable of is ... oh ... how do you say ... *t-terrifying.* But I know this: Grant is good man. He would not want for you to be captured. So what is it that you are searching for? Maybe I can help."

Her heart sinking, Silja turned to stare into the flames of the fireplace.

Grant had left hours ago. He had mentioned that he needed to get out of the dead zone to contact his team.

Why hadn't he woken her up? Most likely he had felt she needed rest after the ordeal at the party and at Ballard's home. It was so like Grant to protect her that way. She would've gladly left the warmth of the bed to go with him.

Eleni was right. Anna's emotional state was very fragile since the beating and the rape. There was no doubt in her mind that the poor girl would feel overwrought with desperation and reveal their location to Ballard. Sooner or later, he would come for her.

Closing her eyes, Silja dragged in a ragged breath. She didn't want to think about the possibility, yet it couldn't be ignored—*unless Ballard had Grant.* She shuddered at the thought.

It was more than obvious that he had the police under his thumb. Eleni had told her that Ballard was in the police car that had taken Anna away. She couldn't bear to lose Grant again—she couldn't bear to lose him like this.

"I wanted to leave him a note. I was looking for paper ... I suppose that's really stupid—"

Eleni folded her into her arms. "No ... not at all, but I don't think there is time to find paper you search for."

Silja brushed a tear from her cheek with the back of her hand. "I'll get my coat. You grab Greta, and let's get the hell out of here. Clark Rhodes ... I'm going to figure a way to get a hold of Grant's boss if it's the last thing I do!"

Eleni's lips stretched into a wide smile. She grabbed Greta from a chair just as the cottage door ripped from its hinges, hurling shards of wood bouncing across the floor. Domashev and two officers burst into the room with their guns drawn.

Protectively, Silja and Eleni wrapped their arms around each other—with Greta tightly cradled between.

Scanning the meager cottage with his eyes, Domashev strolled toward them. "Finally we meet, Miss Ramsay. I am Captain Domashev. Mr. Crafton wishes that you come to his laboratory."

"And if I don't?"

"This is not request. You will come."

"Where is Anna Antkowiak?" Eleni demanded to know.

"Where she belongs. On her way to prison for the murder of Ivan Belsky," he told her in Russian.

Enraged, Eleni pushed away from Silja. In their native language, she yelled, "Anna has done nothing wrong! She did not kill Ivan Belsky! You know this!"

Domashev slapped Eleni across the face, which sent her backward to the floor.

Greta jumped from her arms to scurry into the bedroom. Silja tried to help Eleni, but Domashev grabbed her by the arm. Shaking her, he demanded, "What is soldier's name? The one who helped you! Tell me now!"

"Grant? What do you know about Grant?"

He shook her harder, mercilessly, shouting, "His name is Grant what? Who does he work for? No matter how we beat him he will not tell us. You will tell me now!"

Cupping her hand over her mouth, Silja gasped. Her fears had been realized—Ballard had Grant in his custody! They were beating him for information, and he would not tell. He would not be broken, and neither would she. Fighting through the suffocating dread, she shouted, "I won't tell you anything!"

Domashev came to a complete halt. Slowly, he released his hold from her arm.

Stepping backward, Silja tried to massage away the feel of his throbbing grip from her arm.

His steely glare locked with Silja's apprehensive gaze. A poisonous curl crawled across his mouth. He said to the officers standing near the door, "Take Miss Babinski behind house and shoot her."

Throwing her body over Eleni, Silja screamed, "No!"

The officers grabbed her by the arms and forced her to her feet. Silja kicked and screamed and wrestled with the two men while Domashev laughed. After deciding he'd had enough fun, he said, "We will take Miss Babinski with us. Perhaps Mr. Crafton will have other use for her."

The officers grabbed the women and dragged them through the snow to the police cruiser. The house was now quiet. The only sound was the crackle of the fire and the wind that blew like an icy phantom throughout the tiny cottage.

Greta crept from the bedroom in search of her mistress' comforting touch.

* * * * *

Jack Haliday steered the SUV through the mountainous road with his comrade, Dan Garrison, sitting shot-gun. Smitty sat in the back seat. The conversation had fallen silent about four miles back. Now the three men scanned the snowy roadside in anticipation of a rendezvous with Peyton Mattock—an old friend of Clark Rhodes who was in charge of the team assigned to monitor activities at the Crafton Laboratory.

Jack figured they were approximately two or more miles away from the laboratory located well beyond the city limits of Yekaterinburg. From the satellite photos that Clark had sent them, they could see that the compound that housed the laboratory was surrounded by high-tensile fencing with razor wire stretched in long, sweeping coils across the top. The security staff looked pretty hefty to boot.

Jack's team was short by two. The tracker that Grant was supposed to activate to help them locate the farm actually led them to his abandoned rental vehicle. As per Walt's instructions, the team split up. Stewart Little and the team sniper, Casey Rhodes, were sent to the farm to investigate what had gone awry.

Jack, Dan, and Smitty pressed on to the meeting place with Mattock's team. Jack and his team weren't sure what Mattock had in mind, but they were game for whatever method it took to shut down Crafton's operation.

Off to the left, some bushes fluttered. A man dressed in snow camo with an AK-47 pointed at the windshield stepped into the headlights. Jack glanced at Dan and then caught Smitty's eyes in the rearview mirror. The SUV crunched to a stop. Jack let down the window when the man approached and said, "First Force ..."

Lowering the gun, the man replied, "Peyton Mattock, Hawke Ops International. You boys short a man?"

He was not at all what Jack had expected. He didn't look like the standard Special Forces individual. His thick dark hair was worn in long dreadlocks pulled back into a ponytail. He sported dark Oakley sunglasses even though it was the middle of the night. His face was flushed from the winter wind.

Jack hitched a thumb toward himself. "Jack Haliday." He went on to introduce his comrades. "This is Dan Garrison and Will Smith. We call him Smitty. Anyway, we might be short a man. We were supposed to meet him at a farm near Rezh, but his tracking device took us to his SUV, which was abandoned about thirty miles from there. We sent two of our team members on to a farm where he'd been hiding out to investigate the situation."

"They won't find him at the farm," Peyton stated. "My man inside the prison said that the van came to pick up some prisoners for Crafton Lab's experiments about fifteen minutes ago. He said there was a woman and an American inside. He looked pretty beaten up. He's probably your man. It's highly unusual for a woman to be in the vans."

Figuring that the woman was most likely Silja Ramsay—the woman that Grant had come to Russia to seek out—Jack, Dan, and Smitty exchanged glances.

Peyton continued, "Ballard Crafton arrived at the lab about an hour ago."

"Okay, now what? We need a plan—quick," Jack said just as his cell phone rang. "Haliday ..."

"The farm is empty, but they haven't been gone long. Looks like there was a scuffle. We're on our way to the rendezvous point," Stewart Little reported.

"ETA?"

"Twenty-five minutes, if all goes smoothly."

"We've got a situation, so step on it, Little." Jack turned to Peyton. "We've got two more team members heading this way. He said they should be here in about twenty-five. What's the ETA on the van?"

Peyton checked his watch. "If your guys are here in twenty-five, they'll have about five minutes to get ready. Let's get this vehicle hidden and get back to camp. My team's already got a plan in the works. It's simply a matter of bringing you up to speed. I'll send one of my men down to meet the rest of your team."

Peyton pointed out where he wanted Jack to park the SUV, which they then covered with a winter camo tarp. Jack, Dan, and Smitty suited up and grabbed their weapons.

Peyton would take the lead on the mission. They were on his turf. His team had done all the recon and intel—it was Hawke Op's party. Team First Force would have to follow his orders, and they were okay with that.

Peyton guided them through the wooded area and deep snow to a camp on a hillside above the Crafton Laboratory compound. The snow had stopped and the wind had calmed, revealing a clear, starlit sky. The camp was made up of three tents, and there was no evidence of a campfire. It appeared they'd been camped in this location for weeks, possibly more. Yeah, it looked like it had been a cold-ass existence.

Measuring it up, Jack, Dan, and Smitty knew exactly what they were going through—they had been there, done that. It was totally miserable.

They followed Peyton into a tent disguised with winter camo. The team leader made sure that the flap was closed securely so that no light shone through the gap. A Colman heater burned in the corner, and Peyton's team was gathered around a table with a map and lantern on it.

"A police cruiser with Domashev arrived at the lab while you were out. He delivered two women—both brunettes," one of the men said.

"I'm not sure what's going on. They've never used female prisoners for their experiments." Peyton scrubbed his fingers across his chin.

"Who's Domashev?" Dan asked.

"*Captain* Domashev. He's a corrupt sonofabitch who runs the Yekaterinburg Police Department," Peyton explained. "Crafton must be a new addition to his list of prominent citizens in the area for whom he does favors. In any event, we'll deal with that when we get inside. Right now, let me introduce you to my team." He nodded to each man as he introduced them. "Our field medic, Cole Barnhart. The team explosive expert, Tom Cleaver. Our pilot, Jonas Newman, and our sniper, Billy-Joe Vaughn."

They shook hands all around until they came to Billy-Joe, whose left hand was in a cast. "Broke my hand three days ago," the sniper said. "It's not my shooting hand, but it does add a measure of complications."

"That shouldn't be a problem," Dan said. "We've got a sniper with us, Casey Rhodes."

"Perfect." Peyton turned to Billy-Joe. "Go out on the road to meet their team members. You can brief Rhodes on the target and show him his position. We'll be on serious time restraints by the time they get here, so that's gonna be the best course."

Jack, Dan, and Smitty exchanged sly grins at Peyton's assumption that Casey Rhodes was a man. They opted not to correct the miscalculation. Peyton's team was in for a surprise.

"Will do." Billy-Joe immediately took to suiting up and prepping his weapons. With a gun slung over his shoulder and a knife secured in his boot, he made his way through the crowded tent to the opening, where he then waited.

Peyton turned down the flame on the Coleman lantern to a tiny flicker while the sniper exited and readjusted the flap.

Jack told the team leader, "One of the women might be Silja Ramsay. Our man, Ketchum, came to Russia to get her out of a bad situation with Crafton. I have no idea who the other two are."

"A woman involved with Crafton is always in a bad situation. We'll get all three of them out of there," Peyton said. "I gotta say your timing couldn't be more perfect. The staff isn't on the premises on Sundays and Mondays, and they only use a skeleton security crew on those days. Don't get me wrong though. Security is still tight. Today is Monday. That's when they bring in the fresh prisoners for their testing. That way they only have to house them overnight until they use them."

He checked his watch. "Only thirty minutes until that van goes through. We haven't much time to get our shit together. Let's get down to brass tacks ..."

CHAPTER TWENTY

Their footsteps echoed like a death march as Domashev and his officers escorted Silja and Eleni briskly down a long dark corridor until they came to a heavy metal door. Domashev rapped on the door. A small sliding door opened.

"I am here with the women," Domashev said in Russian to the pair of eyes peering through the opening.

"Mr. Crafton is waiting for you," the guard replied.

The heavy door yanked open.

Domashev shoved Eleni. She bumped into Silja, who stumbled through the door.

The guard added, "Mr. Crafton wants you to take them to the holding area. Cell number four."

"Continue forward," Domashev told Silja and Eleni.

As they walked along the cold passageway, they heard the door slam closed and the heavy bolt fall into place.

Silja fought back the roll of nausea in her stomach. By the look on Eleni's face, she was doing the same. What now? Ballard had them all right where he wanted them. The question was what would he do with them? Guilt was quickly mixing with the fear vibrating through every cell in her body. If she hadn't sent that text to Grant, he wouldn't have been in some cell being beaten or tortured right now, and Eleni would be enjoying her two weeks on hiatus from the ballet company before the rehearsals began for the next production. Yes, she would be sentenced to a life of service to a man that she wanted no part of, but no one else would be suffering.

My God, what have you done, Silja!

Domashev's terse tone broke through her thoughts. "Turn here."

They made a right into yet another long corridor. What was going to be at the end of it?

Conversations from the past week raced through her memory. Conversations that were now a damning reality for not only herself, but also for those she cared about—Eleni, Anna, and Grant.

"That's a nasty bruise on your face, Silja. But it will be nothing in comparison to what I will do to you if you

ever pull something like that on me again. Do you understand?" Ballard had told her in the limo the night she was taken to his home. Only she had pulled something worse than showing up at the contributors' party—much worse.

"Ballard is a very generous man, a kind man, and if you treat him well, he will treat you like a queen. But if you fight him or give him trouble, you will pay a very high price. My advice to you is this: be giving and caring toward him at all times, and you will be just fine." It seemed like a week ago, yet Tess had uttered that warning only the day before at breakfast.

The threats were for her exclusively before she had done anything to piss Ballard off, but now she had done more than that—she had agitated him beyond belief, and she was terrified of what lay ahead for her dear friend, Eleni, and the man she had always loved. Grant.

Silja could only hope that if she begged on her knees and promised to be a perfect servant that Ballard would release Eleni, Anna, and Grant.

But she knew he wouldn't. Ballard would want to punish them all. For Grant, it would most likely mean death!

The long, shadowy corridor became blurry through the tears in her eyes that her horrifying thoughts had produced. She sucked back her tears when another heavy door came into view. If nothing else, she had to put on a brave front for Ballard. He would feed off of her fear and revel in it. She wasn't going to give him that.

Domashev pounded on the door, and a guard opened it. The guard ushered them to the holding cells, unlocked the one marked number four, and held the door open. Domashev hitched his chin toward the cell that was about eight-by-eight in size with a long wooden bench along one wall. A dirty metal bucket rested in the far corner.

"I'm sure your room at Mr. Crafton's house was better than this. You know what bucket is for, yes?" Domashev chided.

Silja said nothing. She stepped into the cell with her head held high. She took a seat on the bench. Trembling, Eleni followed. When the cell door clanged closed, Silja called out to Domashev, "Have you got any magazines?"

Her snarky remark was met with a glower. "Mr. Crafton will call for you soon," Domashev replied. He and the officers followed the guard from the holding area.

After the door slammed closed, Eleni turned to Silja. She was beyond panic stricken. Her words came out so muddled with her Russian accent that Silja could barely understand them. "They are going to kill us, Silja!"

Trying to provide what little comfort she could, Silja wrapped her arm around Eleni. "We have to keep our faith, Eleni. We have to hope that that is not what Ballard has planned for us ... or for Grant."

Eleni laid her head on Silja's shoulder. The guilt for what she'd wielded upon her friend welled up inside her so fiercely that she thought she would burst.

* * * * *

It had been a long night. Grant and Anna had been loaded into a prisoner transport vehicle at the station, and then they had traveled about twenty miles to the prison to pick up three hard-core prisoners.

The Russians weren't into prisoner comfort. The travel compartment of the prison van was made of solid aluminum, which made for hard seating. Grant and Anna were strapped onto the benches and hand-cuffed to the wall. The three men were strapped and handcuffed on the bench across from them.

They ogled Anna hungrily and tormented her by licking their lips and making foul gestures at her. They whispered to her in Russian while she cowered away from their words. Grant wanted to kick their asses into next Tuesday, but there wasn't much he could do about it. Anna's emotional state was deteriorating by the second.

The guard who rode in the prisoner compartment had little compassion for Anna. He scolded the prisoners only once and then left the torture to continue. Grant tried to comfort her by whispering words of encouragement, but Anna only turned her head away and sobbed into her shoulder.

Grant had no doubt about what fate Ballard Crafton had in store for each person inside the vehicle. They were guinea pigs for testing his super-soldier serum. He worried about what Crafton had in mind for Anna.

He was fairly certain that the three prisoners were clueless. They showed no apprehension about where they were being taken. *Poor ignorant bastards.*

The transport bumped along the rocky road. Each bump in the road caused reeling pain through Grant's ribcage. His head was still pounding, and his vision was still slightly blurred. At least, the nausea had settled down a bit.

The bumps and ruts in the road abruptly seemed more numerous. The van swayed hard to the right. The prisoners bounced against each other while calling out their dissatisfaction to the driver in Russian.

That's when they all noticed the blood splatter over the window between the prisoner compartment and the cab. The driver was slumped in his seatbelt with a bullet through his head.

The three prisoners exchanged wary glances. Grant looked to the guard. He shrugged, took out a cigarette, and lit it.

The van rolled into a tree. Grant braced his body so that Anna would have something to wedge herself against upon impact. The prisoners were left to bounce around in their seats.

There was a hard pounding on the door.

The guard very calmly opened it. Several men dressed in white camo stood with their AK-47s trained on the guard.

He blew smoke out his nose. He spoke in English with a heavy Russian accent, "Surprise, surprise, Mattock. The regular guard got sick, so I volunteer to take his place."

"Wasn't that sweet of you, Taka," Peyton said, wryly.

"Don't mention it," the guard said. "I know my way around lower level of lab. It will cost you double."

"Like I said, sweet guy."

Taking another drag from his cigarette, Taka nodded toward Grant. "This is American that you told me about, yes?"

Jack stepped forward to peer into the van. "Hey, Ketchum, how's tricks?" He nodded at Anna. "Hello Miss Ramsay, I'm Jack Haliday, one of Grant's teammates."

Anna cowered as far into the corner as she could get.

"She's not Silja," Grant said. "This is Anna Antkowiak. She was a ballerina in Sil's company. I'm hoping that Sil is still at the cottage."

The men all exchanged remorseful glances. "Afraid not," Jack said. "She must be inside the lab. Two women were delivered there earlier. Silja is probably one of them."

"Shit!" Grant bit out. "Eleni Babinski is probably the other." He pulled and yanked at his restraints in frustration. "We've got to get them the hell out of there before Crafton does something that I'll regret."

"Okay, buddy, take it easy," Peyton said. "That's exactly what we've got in mind. Taka, get in the driver's seat. Haliday, Garrison, and I will switch clothes with the prisoners. Cleaver, I want you to get into the driver's clothes, and then you can take the guard position in the prisoner compartment. Because of the circumstances, we can only take handguns, of course. There should be a storage compartment in the seat under the window. Store your extra ammo in there until we're through security."

"Won't they search the prisoner compartment?" Dan asked.

"Probably not," Taka said. "As long as guard is in place with gun, they will let van go through without search."

"Let's hope they're satisfied with what they see," Peyton put in. "Tom will be handing out earpieces. Hide them wherever you can on your person."

Tom Cleaver opened the driver's door to unhook the guard from his seatbelt, just as Casey, Little, and Billy-Joe wandered out of the woods onto the road. Extending his hand, Tom called to Casey, "Hey, good shooting ..." He stopped to correct himself in mid-breath. "M-Miss Rhodes, but his clothes are all covered in blood."

Blinking back at the lovely woman dressed in snow camo checking her rifle, Team Hawke-Ops froze in place.

"I just drop them," Casey replied. "I don't do their laundry."

Shaking off his surprise at the beautiful yet dangerous woman before him, Peyton brought them back to the situation at hand. "Nice to meet you, Casey. Good work. Now let's get this party started."

Stewart Little stepped forward, "What the hell am I supposed to do?"

Jack cupped his hand on Stewart's shoulder. "Sorry, big guy, but you're gonna have to stay behind at the camp. There's no room in the back, you're not gonna fit in the guard's clothes, and, quite frankly, you'd make one helluva ugly woman."

"I suppose." Stewart wasn't happy with his soft role in the mission, but there wasn't one damned thing he could do about it.

After Jack, Dan, and Peyton switched clothes with the prisoners, they were re-handcuffed and loaded into an SUV. Meanwhile, Jonas Newman and his Glock kept a vigilant watch over them. Stewart made his way to the SUV to assist with the prisoners. He slid into the driver's seat.

Jonas asked, "Not happy about stayin' behind?"

Grimacing, Stewart grunted.

"Me either," Jonas said. "I think they're gonna need a little more backup than they've got."

"Got something in mind?" Stewart asked.

"I've got a few ideas. I'm sure Billy-Joe's up for some extra-curricular activities, too. Let's get these prisoners back to camp."

Billy-Joe cleaned the blood off the seat and the window. Luckily, most of the guard's blood had seeped onto the seat. Only a portion of it had soaked into the right shoulder of his uniform, and since Tom would play the role of the guard in the prisoner compartment, they felt pretty confident that they could get away with the stain.

Anna cringed and retreated deep into the corner of the prisoner van while the flurry of activity buzzed all around her.

Feeling badly about the woman's fragile state, Grant said, "Jack ... Anna doesn't have to go inside the lab, does she? She's been through so much. I don't think she'll hold up."

"There's no reason to put her at risk," Jack agreed.

Grant turned to her. "Anna ... you can get out of the van. They will take good care of you."

Anna stared at him with wide, frightened eyes. She remained solidly in place. Like Grant, the poor woman was still handcuffed. It was little wonder why she was so frightened.

In a gentle tone, Grant assured her, "It's okay, darlin', go with Jack."

Jack stepped into the van to take a seat across from her. He reached his hand toward Anna. "Hi, Anna, my name's Jack. I won't hurt you, I promise. Let me remove those cuffs. I'm here to keep you safe."

Sitting stark still, Anna stared at his outstretched hand as if it would burn her skin as soon as he touched her.

After a long silence, Jack said, "My job is to keep people like you safe. Hey, I'm a dad. I've got a little girl back home. She's four. She's got curly hair about the same color as yours. She'd be so excited to know that I helped a ballerina—she loves the ballet."

Anna looked into his eyes. They were so kind and compassionate. His smile was friendly and inviting. Even with a day's worth of scruff growing on his face, he was oh-so handsome.

Flashing his thousand-megawatt smile, Jack added, "Her name is Lil, and her favorite ballet is *The Nutcracker.*"

Anna managed a weak smile. She muttered, "Most children love *The Nutcracker.* It is such a beautiful story."

"It certainly is." Jack could see her shoulders relaxing a bit. He was getting somewhere. "I took Lil and my mom to see it at Christmas."

Anna studied him more. How could a man who takes his mother and his daughter to the ballet be bad? Feeling a little more confident, she scooted across the seat toward him. Jack carefully removed the restraints that held her against the seat, helped her out of the van, removed the handcuffs, and escorted her to the SUV.

Smitty was waiting to return to the camp to help Cole set up a medical tent in case someone was injured.

Taka looked into the back of the van. Spinning around to see Anna walking away with Jack, he asked, "Where is woman going?"

Peyton explained, "She isn't doing well. We're leaving her at the camp for her own safety."

Taka held up a sheet of paper. "You cannot. Roster says four men and one woman in van."

Jack stopped.

Anna's spine stiffened.

Letting out a knowing breath, Peyton said, "He's right. If we don't show up with her, the Russians are gonna get mighty jumpy."

"No worries," Casey said. "I'll go in her place." Turning to Anna, she softened her expression and her tone. "Anna, can you switch coats with me?"

Smitty stepped forward to help Anna take off her coat. She cowered away from the unfamiliar man.

Patting her shoulder, Jack said, "It's okay, Anna. He's one of the good guys, I promise."

Smitty's stomach twisted at the woman's horrified expression at the simple act of a man offering to take her coat. Someone must've done something terrible to the young woman. The thought made his blood boil. He offered her a gentle smile. "Hi Anna, I'm Smitty. I'm a doctor. I've never been to the ballet, but I'd sure love to hear all about it. Can I please take your coat for Casey to use?"

With trembling hands, Anna relinquished her coat to Smitty.

Casey removed her coat and handed it to Anna. Then, she unbuckled her snow camo pants. She shimmied until they pooled around her ankles to reveal a pair of skinny jeans underneath, which accentuated her lean hips that melted into long, shapely legs. Her lengthy brunette braid fell over her shoulder between her full breasts.

Every man from team Hawke Op's eyes were glued to the gorgeous sniper that stood before them. Each one had a "hooyah" in the back of his throat that he dare not set free.

In contrast, the men from First Force went about their business—they were accustomed to having a woman on the team.

Unaware of the eyes upon her, Casey looked down at her combat boots. They weren't going to do—they simply weren't going to be convincing. She asked, "What size shoes do you wear, Anna?"

"Seven."

"A little tight, but I'll make it work. Let's switch, sweetie." The two women exchanged shoes, and then Casey turned to the team. "Four men and one woman—let's boogie, boys."

Impatience gurgled into Grant's chest. He couldn't smother the fears of what could possibly be happening to Silja inside that laboratory. They were taking too long. They needed to speed up the process. He blurted out, "Could we get moving, please!"

The team climbed into the prisoner compartment.

Taka handed Peyton a pair of keys. He said, "Handcuffs on, please. You may remove them after we get through security. I will give signal. Please be discreet. There are cameras at check point. Please do not get me killed, thank you."

As the van pulled forward, the team packed away their extra ammo in a cargo area under the bench. They had stuffed their handguns down the back of their pants. Several of the ops, including Casey, had knives strapped to the inside of their calves. Tom handed each team member an earpiece. They stuffed them into their pants. Peyton hid his deep among his dread locks while Casey dropped hers into her bra. Before taking up his rifle and his position at the doors, Tom carefully placed a backpack in the cargo bench.

After his earpiece was secured deep in his hair, Peyton went through locking everyone into their handcuffs. Casey was the last.

"I like your hair," she commented while he gathered her hands and snapped the cuff over her wrists. "You don't wear it like most ops—cut close or buzzed. Dreads look good on you."

Peyton's lips curled. Their eyes met.

Clearing her throat, Casey added, "So, you've been camping out in the cold for quite some time, haven't you?"

"Yes, Ma'am."

"I like camping."

"In the cold?"

"As long as the sleeping bag is warm."

"Okay, okay!" Dan said, "Can we arrange our hook-ups in private after the mission is over?"

"We use snow buntings—super expensive, but it's like being hugged by a furnace all night," Peyton supplied.

"Is that so? I'll have to get one," Casey said.

"Do they not see us all sitting here?" Dan said to Jack, who just shook his head, chuckling.

Knocking on the window with his knuckles, Taka called through the shatter-proof glass, "Only three kilometers to go."

The compartment went silent.

They hung their heads to hide their faces in the hope that, if security opened the back, they would not be recognized as Americans.

Dan noticed Grant wincing in pain with each bump and turn in the road. The bruises on his face were swollen and discolored. His lip was cracked and caked with dried blood. Trying to clear the blurriness, he continually blinked his eyes.

Dan whispered, "Are you up for this, Ketchum?"

"I'll admit, this one doesn't look too much like a cakewalk, Garrison, but I'm not coming out without Silja."

"Trouble is it looks like someone already smeared said cake all over your freakin' face."

"I'm good," Grant bit out.

Taka knocked on the window again as the van slowed down. They were approaching the gate to Crafton Laboratories.

It was go time.

$$* * * * *$$

Taka drove the van up to the security check point. Inside the prisoner compartment, they sat silently while listening to the conversation spoken in Russian between Taka and the guard.

Moments later, the van rolled through the gate. It came to a stop again and was instantly surrounded by security guards who walked around the vehicle and peered into the small, round windows located in the door of the prisoner section. There were three knocks on the door.

Tom yanked on the lever and pushed it open.

Smoking a cigarette, Taka stood next to the guard who was studying the roster. He counted the prisoners while another guard ran a scanner under the van to detect anyone who may have been secured to the bottom of the vehicle. The guard commented to Taka in Russian. Quickly, Taka pulled a cigarette from inside his jacket. Smiling, the guard took the cigarette and then slammed the door closed.

Finally, they were waved on.

The team exchanged relieved glances.

The van jerked and rocked while it traveled through the compound.

Taka pounded on the window with the back of his knuckles and signaled with his thumb up. He drove the van around the back of the block building toward a garage door.

The van stopped. They could hear a heavy metal door rolling into its brackets above before the van rolled forward once again. It came to a halt in one of the three bays inside the building. The garage door slowly lowered back into place.

Taka banged on the door for Tom to open up. After furtively looking about, he spoke quietly, "Quickly, get your guns from bench. You can remove handcuffs when we get past the first door. I will give signal." He nodded to Tom. "You will follow behind prisoners. Keep your gun on them. The rest of you, keep your faces down. Come."

Tom jumped down from the van and gestured with his rifle for the prisoners to unload.

Peyton held the bench lid open. Casey passed the guns down to the men. Then each of them swiftly found a hiding place for the weapon inside their clothing. Keeping a tight hold on his ribcage in preparation for jumping down, Grant exited the van first, then Casey with Dan, Jack, and last of all, Peyton followed.

Holding his rifle across his chest, Taka led them up a pair of cement stairs onto what appeared to be a dock. The garage area was massive—large enough to hold a tractor-trailer in each of the parking bays.

At the top of the stairs was a metal door with a square window. Taka peered through the window. Satisfied that no one was beyond the door, he instructed Grant to hold the door for the others. Grant complied. When the prisoners were through, Tom approached the doorway. He hitched his chin harshly for Grant to fall in line behind the rest.

Taka led them down a long, dimly lit corridor. Light bulbs corralled in cages hanging along the ceiling tossed crossed-pattern shadows over the dingy cement block walls. The hallway had a dank warehouse odor about it. When they reached the heavy metal door, Taka knocked. An ominous peep door scraped open. Through a miasma of cigarette smoke, Taka spoke to the guard. The door yanked open. Taka handed a stern-faced guard the roster. As they passed, he counted the prisoners, making note that the woman was present and accounted for, as they past.

When Tom came through the door the guard slammed his hand against Tom's chest.

Everyone froze.

Tom's jaw clenched when the guard spoke to him in Russian.

Taka called out to the guard in Russian, "He is new. Levitsky is sick so he took his place today. It is his first time to escort the prisoners."

The guard took a deep drag from his cigarette while he gauged Tom with a scowl on his face. Finally, the guard said, "Very well. Be on your way." He shoved the roster into Tom's hand.

Tom favored him with a stiff nod.

Taka smiled at the guard and then jerked his head toward the corridor, indicating that the group should follow him.

When they rounded the bend, Taka paused. Gesturing for them to get against the wall, he spoke quietly to Casey, "You can take off handcuffs, but quickly and discreetly. When we go through next door there will be another guard, and then we will be at holding cells."

The group sidled up to the wall while Tom handed the keys off to Grant, who handed them to Dan. Dan removed Grant's cuff, and Grant returned the favor, handing the key off to Dan. Promptly, Dan undid Jack's handcuffs. Jack released Peyton, who freed Casey from her restraints. The operatives retrieved their earpieces from their hiding place and stuffed them into their ears.

The entire process took mere seconds.

"We are ready, yes?" Taka asked.

Peyton gave him the signal.

On a braced breath, Taka continued forward around the next corner to approach the next heavy door. They kept their heads down, and their hands in position as though they were all still restrained.

Taka pounded on the door. The peep door slid open. He informed the guard that he had four prisoners. The tiny door slid closed, and with a whoosh of suction, the door jerked open.

Taka stepped through. As Casey made her way into the area, she whipped her elbow up to strike the guard in the throat. Stepping back, he gasped for air. Peyton cracked him across the head with his handgun. The guard slid down the wall with blood spewing from the gash on his head.

Tom closed the door and opened the peep door to keep watch.

Leading with his gun, Grant hurried past the group to get to the holding area in hopes of finding Silja.

Instead, only Eleni remained in the cell. She rushed to the door and clamped her fingers around the caging. Her face was flushed with anxiety.

"Where's Silja?" Grant asked.

"They took her away a few minutes ago. Oh, Grant, I am so frightened for what he will do to her!"

Jack came up behind him with the keys to the cell that he had retrieved from the unconscious guard. Swiftly, he unlocked the door.

Eleni lurched from the cell into Grant's arms. "What are we going to do?" she cried.

"We're going to get her," Grant said.

"This was not part of plan," Taka intervened.

Grant turned around as quickly as he could with pain jabbing into his torso. He jammed his finger into Taka's chest. "Doesn't matter. I'm going to find her and get her the hell outta here."

"The van must leave within thirty minutes. I don't make rules. They will come looking if I am not gone within time limit," Taka explained curtly.

Peyton checked his watch. "Okay, we've got twenty minutes to get the girl and light this place up like the fourth of July." He turned to Jack. "You and Dan go with Grant. I'll go with Tom to set the explosives in place. Casey, can you cover us while we work?"

"You got it."

Nervously, Taka shifted from one foot to the other. "I will sit in van and wait."

"Not a bad idea, Taka." Peyton nodded toward Eleni. "The lovely lady can sit in the van with you—both of you on the floor of the prisoner compartment where you won't be seen."

Panic seeped into Taka's tone, "How will I get woman past guard at first door?"

Swatting the nervous Russian man on the back, Peyton's lips curled. "You worry too much. We'll take care of the guard." Checking his watch, he turned back to the group. "Everyone needs to be back at that van in ... nineteen minutes. Just so we have our seating assignments ahead of time. Tom will drive the van out. I'll sit shotgun. Everyone else in the back. Let's move."

Taka's finger jerked into Peyton's chest. "This will cost you more!"

Peyton rolled his eyes. "I figured as much."

CHAPTER TWENTY-ONE

Cold hard fear crawled over Silja's skin. Domashev's steely fingers clenched her arm—dragging her through a brightly lit hallway.

Ballard had summoned her from the cell to wield his punishment upon her. No matter how she tried to gulp back the dread of what would come next, it was of little use. The fact was that she was scared—beyond belief.

Domashev said nothing when he came to the holding cell. The guard yanked the cell door open. Domashev stepped inside, jerked her to her feet, slapped a pair of flex cuffs on her wrists, and then fiercely hauled her out of the cell. She could hear Eleni desperately calling to her in the distance when the heavy door slammed behind them.

What would become of Eleni? Where was Anna? What would happen to Grant—assuming something hadn't happened already?

After tripping up a staircase, he dragged her past a long window that looked into a laboratory. The walls were pure white. There were all kinds of lab equipment: tubes, beakers, conical flasks, and several syringes lay upon a stainless steel table next to a gurney with pristine white sheets and restraints dangling over the side. Lab coats hung neatly on a long coat hook near a far door.

The lab was empty—no scientists or engineers were working among the instruments.

Finally, they arrived at a door. Domashev knocked.

Ballard called from the other side, "Come in, Captain."

Domashev opened the door and shoved her through. Silja stumbled to her knees but was able to right herself.

Ballard sat behind a large desk with his chin resting on his folded hands. His expression was impassive. "Thank you, Captain Domashev. You are dismissed. Miss Ramsay and I have much to discuss."

Easing out the door, Domashev left her standing in the middle of the room—feeling exposed, vulnerable, and powerless. Her hands were tightly bound. It was as though the walls were closing in on her—

sucking the air from the room. She kept her eyes focused on the floor—willing it to swallow her up.

Ballard's terse voice filled the suffocating void. "Look at me, Silja."

Slowly, she lifted her gaze to meet his stare.

Those eyes—oh, those dangerous dastardly eyes were like icy hands grabbing at her skin and penetrating her with their white, heated rage. Yet, there was an impressive control over his fury when he spoke, "You've disappointed me greatly, Silja, and for that you will be punished. I love beauty, and I love the beautiful women who are born with gifts far beyond what most are blessed with. You are one of the blessed, Silja. You dance so eloquently. I would have given you anything, everything. But you defied me—just like the others—and you will pay, just like they did."

Silja tried to control the trembling in her hands and the shiver that each word sent through her.

Abruptly, he rose from his chair—letting it roll away to smack against the wall with a sharp thwack.

She let out a gasp before she could call it back.

He opened a drawer, pulled out a gun, and slammed it onto the desktop.

Then, he pulled out a knife—her kitchen knife. Without pause, he flung it across the room. Cringing, a scream escaped her throat when the knife dug into the carpet next to her feet.

She jumped back.

Suddenly, Ballard was right there next to her. She hadn't even noticed him moving across the room. He grabbed her by the hair, yanking her head backward, and then he put his face close to hers. She could feel the heat of his wrath against her cheek.

He caressed her throat with the knife when he spoke, "Recognize the knife? It's the knife that killed Belsky—your knife. Domashev knows that you had nothing to do with the murder. I informed him. We know exactly who killed Belsky, and that knowledge will keep people in line."

"W-who?" she stammered out.

Ballard let out a haughty snort, "I guess it makes no difference if I tell you—that squirrelly little dancer, Dominik Potrovic. He's enjoyed the position of the lead male dancer for quite some time, but that will change soon. I don't want a murderer as the lead dancer for *my* ballet company."

Silja's eyes widened.

His arrogance bubbling over, Ballard smiled. "That's right, I now own the Novikov. The dancers will no longer have to entertain the wealthy contributors, but they will entertain me, if my needs so warrant."

Silja tried to look away. He repulsed her on so many levels. It made her stomach roll with agitation. Forbidding her escape, he tangled his fingers tighter through her hair. She could feel his nails scrape her scalp.

He took the tip of the knife and pricked her skin.

Flinching, she whimpered. A bead of blood seeped to the surface and dripped down her neck.

His whisper was terse, vicious, as if Lucifer himself were speaking. "I warned you, Silja. I warned you not to disobey me."

"Please, Ballard ... please, I'm begging you. I ... I know that I've upset you—"

"*Upset* me?" he bellowed while yanking harder on her hair. He jerked her head back until she thought her neck would snap.

"Yes! I've upset you, but it was my decision alone! Please don't punish Eleni or Anna or Grant for my indiscretions. Do with me what you will, but please leave them out of it." Her eyes betrayed her. Tears forced their way to the surface and slowly began to slosh over the rims to her cheeks.

"Your soldier will pay for what he did to Tess."

"Your wife, Tess?"

Finger by finger, he released her hair—allowing her to straighten. Stepping back just a bit, he announced, "I'm going to give you a chance to redeem yourself, Silja. I'm going to give you an opportunity to buy mercy for your friends, Eleni and Anna, and perhaps for yourself as well."

Silja swallowed hard. Her throat was completely dry. Hoarsely, she asked, "And Grant?"

"His fate is sealed. He is most likely in the holding cells by now with the other prisoners—waiting for the tests to be run tomorrow. My serums haven't been too successful yet. Our subjects have all died of strokes or heart attacks, but *if* he survives the tests, he will be the property of the Russian government. If not ... he will be buried in an unmarked grave like the others. He will make an excellent test subject—a well-trained warrior rather than a disgusting criminal. No, I'm afraid there is nothing you can do or bargain with for him, but for the others, and for yourself, it is ... *a possibility.*"

Hatred boiled through her veins like hot oil. She had no choice but to bow to whatever he demanded of her to save Anna and Eleni.

He knew it.

She was forced to abide by his wishes even though it meant death for Grant. She couldn't bear the thought that he would perform some horrid experiment on Grant—how could she ever live with herself knowing that she'd dragged him into all of this?

Remorse washed over her.

He had beaten them. Ballard had won.

The only thing she could do was conform to whatever he wanted in order to spare Eleni and Anna.

Silja recoiled when she suddenly felt the back of his fingers brush gently over her cheek. His touch made her want to heave.

Regret seemed to fill Ballard's tone. "I wanted you more than any of the others. You are so beautiful, and you dance like an angel. The others were very talented women, but they don't begin to compare to my beautiful Silja." Nuzzling into her hair, he whispered, "Now you have a chance to rectify everything. You have a chance to be forgiven."

Forgiven? Silja wished she could grab that knife from his hand and slam it straight into his heart! Who were the other women that he kept mentioning? And what happened to them when they fell out of his favor? She shuddered at the thought.

Desperation tightened in her chest like a vise. Bastard! There was no way out. Not now, and it looked like not ever. She glanced down at her bound hands. Defeat spilled from her heart into her belly. How long would it take until her spirit would lie on the floor crushed beneath his feet?

On a braced breath, Silja muttered, "What is it that you want me to do?"

"You have defiled our agreement, and now you must make amends. Down on your knees."

Hot tears streamed down her cheeks. If the opportunity ever presented itself, she would kill him—she would kill Ballard Crafton for Grant and for anyone else that he's hurt in the past!

After today, she would bide her time. She would vigilantly watch and wait for that one precious opportunity to kill him.

For now, at this moment, her options were nil.

Silja eased down to her knees with her fettered hands in her lap. She didn't look up at him. She couldn't bear to look into the rancid satisfaction that surely must have been consuming his expression.

She closed her eyes, waiting for instruction, when she heard the zipper on his jeans pull down. Bile rose in her throat.

"Look at me, Silja."

Oh God, she didn't want to, except she knew that she must. From this moment forward she would have to do everything—anything that he desired.

Slowly, she dragged her gaze upward until she came face to face with his solid erection bulging from the opening of his jeans. No doubt her complete and helpless submission excited him beyond simple sexual craving.

Ballard commanded, "Please me, Silja. If you succeed, your girlfriends will be spared. You will still be punished severely, but you will be granted another chance to be my lover and companion."

* * * * *

The teams had separated. Grant, Jack, and Dan headed upstairs to search for Silja, while Peyton, Tom, and Casey escorted Taka and Eleni back to the van. Tom had to retrieve his backpack filled with explosives that he had hidden in the cargo bench earlier.

Tom opened the door that led to the garage where they'd left the van. He scanned the garage to make sure no one was about, and then he waved the rest of his team through. They hurried down the short pair of stairs to the back of the van. Tom yanked the door open, hopped in, and quickly claimed the backpack from the bench.

Peyton turned to Taka. "Get in the back and wait for us." Taka climbed into the back and helped Eleni in. Peyton went to close the door and then hesitated. "Give me the keys to the van." Scowling, Taka dug into his pocket and tossed the keys to Peyton.

"You do not have much time," Taka said. "Hurry."

Shoving the keys into his pocket, Peyton nodded. He closed the doors, and the team jogged up the stairs to begin their mission.

Taka watched them retreat through a small window in one of the doors. He smiled when they were gone and shoved the door open.

"What are you doing?" Eleni asked in Russian.

"I am not risking my life for the Americans," Taka told her. "I am leaving now."

Eleni grabbed the back of his jacket. "You cannot do that! They will have no way out, and you gave them the keys to the van!"

Taka shoved her to the floor and turned back to the door.

Eleni scrambled to her feet to grab him by his thick dark hair. "No!" she screamed. "I will not let you do this to them! They will all die!"

"Better the Americans than us!" he yelled back.

Eleni held on for dear life. She wasn't usually this brave, but the adrenaline was rushing through her like a fire out of control. They wrestled over the floor of the van until Eleni managed to knee Taka in the groin and snatch away the rifle from his grip. Shocked by her dumb luck, she pointed the business end of the gun at him.

"Get on the bench. We will sit and wait no matter how long they take," she said in no uncertain terms.

Writhing, Taka eased onto the bench across from her, pressing his knees together and slowly raising his hands in surrender, he stammered. "Don't be a fool. We can get out. I have another set of keys in the cab. If the Americans are apprehended they will put us on trial for treason. We will spend the rest of our lives in prison or worse."

Angst resting firmly on her shoulders at the thought that the teams wouldn't make it out of the laboratory safely, or that her friends would be injured or killed, Eleni made herself as comfortable as possible on the hard bench while keeping the gun trained on Taka. "I am willing to take the chance."

"Foolish woman!"

* * * * *

319

Leading with his gun, Grant eased up a metal staircase toward the main floor of the building. The door at the top of the stairs wobbled in his blurred view. Hesitating three steps from the top, he squeezed his eyes closed while trying to clear his vision.

Jack grabbed his shoulder. "You need to take the rear, Ketchum. Let me lead. You follow Dan," When Grant started to protest, Jack squeezed his shoulder. His tone was unrelenting. "Stand down, Grant."

Jack was right. His ribs were screaming, and his vision was molested by the blur. He was in no shape to lead them through the door. He would put the team at risk. He would put Silja at risk. He would be a fool. Bowing his head, he let Jack slip past him, followed by Dan. Grant took up the rear, as ordered.

Jack approached the door. Gingerly, he turned the knob and opened the door to peer into a hallway. He waved Dan and Grant through.

To the right of the door, the hallway led to a long window looking out over what appeared to be the employee parking area—only a limo was parked in one of the slots. The driver leaned against the car, smoking a cigarette and chatting with a large man.

Looking down upon them, Dan murmured to himself, "I don't know who those two are, but when this place goes up, they're done for."

Across from the door was another door with a long narrow window above the doorknob.

Dan peered through the pane. The room had a small kitchenette, a rectangular table, and several chairs. It looked like an employee lounge. Carefully, he cracked the door open—the room was still, empty. Turning left, Dan quickened to the end of the wall where the hallway came to a T. He peered left and right around the corner—empty.

Peyton had told them that no employees should be on the premises and that only a skeleton security staff should be on duty. Perhaps it would be more of a cakewalk than they had originally expected. Good. Keeping his eye on the area, he waved Jack and Grant forward. They came to stand behind him against the wall.

"What've we got, Dan?" Jack glanced down at his watch—thirteen minutes left.

"The hallway Ts off. It's clear in both directions. There's quite a few doorways and what looks like a long window. I'll go left, you and Ketchum can check out what's down at the right end of the hallway."

Hesitating, they all listened intently to Casey's voice coming through their earpieces. "So far so good. We've only run into a few guards checking out a snack machine. You okay?"

"We're good," Jack said.

"Hurry, not much time left," Casey cautioned.

"Roger that," Jack replied, and then he nodded at Dan in agreement to his plan.

Taking one last look, Dan slipped around the corner to peruse his end of the hallway. Jack checked around the corner before he and Grant stepped out to make their way down the other end. Only a few feet along the way, they came to the long window. They ducked below it. Grant kept watch over the hall while Jack sneaked a peek into the window. Through the glass, he saw a testing laboratory with a gurney near a stainless steel table. The lab was empty, so he gestured to Grant to move further down the hall. They came to a men's room.

"I'll stand guard. You check it out," Jack said to Grant.

Grant went into the men's room. Walking along the line of stalls, he checked to make sure they were empty. No one was there.

When Grant returned to the hall, Jack whispered, "I'm hearing voices coming from the next door down. It sounds like a man and a woman. He sounds pretty angry. We may have hit the jackpot."

A woman screamed.

* * * * *

Closing her eyes, Silja swallowed hard while trying not to vomit.

"I'm waiting, Silja," Ballard barked out loudly. "You will do as I say or pay the consequences!"

She tried to move toward him, but the nausea bubbled to her throat. Sweat beaded on her face as she gasped for air.

Ballard's anger swelled to the boiling point. He slapped her across the face and sent her backward to the floor.

She cried out.

Zipping his pants, he announced, "You will pay, Silja! And so will your friends!" He booted her hard in the stomach. Curling into a ball, Silja writhed in pain. He lifted the knife above his head. She could see it coming down toward her, but she couldn't move to dodge it, nor could she defend herself against it.

There was a quick *pop!*

Ballard's body flinched. His face brightened in utter shock as he stumbled backward and clawed at his chest.

Bouncing off the corner of the desk, he fell to his knees before dropping to the floor.

Silja couldn't comprehend what had just happened.

Out of the blue, warm arms cradled her. Grant's voice whispered in her ear, "Sil ... are you okay? C'mon, darlin', talk to me."

Through the pain, Silja opened her eyes to look into his. *Oh, God, thank God!* She managed, "I think I'm okay ... B-Batman."

Grant snorted. "God, how much do I love you? C'mon, we gotta get outta here, fast."

He was pulling her to her feet when she collapsed. Pain shot through her ribcage like he'd jammed the dagger into her. She shrieked.

Grant didn't wait. There wasn't any time. He scooped her up into his arms to head for the door where Jack was keeping watch, only he couldn't hold her. His ribs throbbed in agony. His head spun, and his knees buckled. He simply didn't have the strength to carry her.

Seeing Grant struggling, Jack hurried to his side to grab his arm. "Put her down, Ketchum! I'll take it from here!"

God, he didn't want to. He wanted to carry her to safety—it was his place, yet he knew that it wasn't going to happen. Grant let Jack steady him while he set Silja's feet gently to the floor.

Another *pop* exploded!

Pain like Silja had never known shot through her right leg—a burning sensation as if someone had just lit a torch to her calf. Crying out, she crumbled to the floor—clutching her leg.

Ballard had crawled up the corner of his desk to retrieve his gun and had managed a single shot that hit Silja in her right calf! Jack spun around to shoot Ballard, nicking him in the shoulder. Ballard rocked backward but managed to hold on and take refuge behind the desk while firing off another shot that whizzed past them.

When Jack turned around, Grant was on his knees over Silja. Whispering words of comfort, he applied pressure to the wound. Blood gushed between his fingers. Pallid, Silja was gulping for air. Shock was already setting in fast, but they were forced to take cover when another shot fired past them from the doorway.

A huge Russian man stepped into the room to join the fight.

Jack scooped Silja up. With Grant on his heels, Jack shot toward the man and then the desk to keep their assailants so busy dodging and ducking that they were unable to get another shot off.

Jack and Grant managed to secure a spot in the far corner of the office between the wall and a set of filing cabinets.

"Security's here," Jack stated.

"No, that's Ballard's bodyguard," Grant told him while a bullet pinged off the cabinet above their heads.

Silja's face was covered with a sheen of sweat. Jack hovered over Grant, whose fingers were soaked with Silja's blood where he was keeping pressure over her wound.

Behind the desk, Ballard clutched his chest with one hand while searching for a clear shot with his other. Blood drenched his shirt. Sweat dripped from his face. Sheer rage fed the adrenaline rush that was keeping him upright, alive, and determined to annihilate the warriors and the woman that be-longed to him.

He could feel his heartbeat pumping through the top of his head. As it did, the blood gushed through his chest cavity onto the fabric of his fine clothing. He would die. He knew it now, but he would take them all with him—especially the ballerina and her lover. They were stuck—they were cornered like rats with no way out, but the only way he could take them down was with one bold action.

Gathering the last of his strength, the last of his gall, he stood to take aim at the corner.

His bloodied hand gripping the gun as he raised it, he pushed up to his feet while trying to breathe past the blood now purging from his mouth.

Jack was faster. He pumped three quick rounds into Ballard's chest to send him staggering backward and tumbling over his office chair to the floor.

Jack spun to take a shot at the bodyguard in hopes of catching him off focus, but the bodyguard was already lying on the floor in a pool of blood.

Dan filled the doorway. Lowering his gun, he asked, "What the hell happened?" Then his eyes fell upon Jack and Grant gathering a wounded woman from the corner. "Shit! I can hear guards coming. We've gotta bug out!"

After shoving his gun into the back of his waist-band, Jack scooped Silja into his arms. "I couldn't agree more. C'mon, sweetheart."

Grant and Dan flanked Jack as they rushed down the hallway toward the T. They could hear the rumble of hurried footsteps. Pinning themselves against the wall, Dan peered around the corner to the door that led to the stairs. He nodded that the coast was clear and waved Jack forward first. Wrapping his arm around Grant's waist, Dan helped his injured comrade around the corner.

They were almost to the door when a voice called out, "Stop!"

CHAPTER TWENTY-TWO

With his gun firmly trained on the three Americans trying to escape with Silja Ramsay, Domashev demanded, "Drop your guns!"

Team First Force had no choice. One by one, the guns dropped to the floor. They raised their hands. Domashev smiled. How they managed to gain access to the compound and free the one known as Grant, he did not know. It didn't matter now. He had them in his custody. They would make excellent subjects for the following day's tests. They were strong, well-muscled specimens. He had heard the gunshots. He only hoped that Ballard Crafton was still alive to show his appreciation for his quick actions and loyalty.

"Put woman down," Domashev told Jack.

"I can't. She's badly injured, and I think she may be unconscious. She needs medical attention immediately." Protectively, he tightened his grip on Silja slumped against his chest.

"She will not need anything very soon," Domashev chided.

Three out-of-breath security guards jogged around the bend to join the captain—guns drawn.

"I don't think we're making it back in time—only two minutes," Dan murmured under his breath.

Feeling quite confident now that security had arrived to back him up, Domashev locked eyes with Jack. He lowered his gun and walked toward him.

Grant eased closer to Jack.

Domashev yelled in Jack's face, "Put woman down or I will have my guards shoot you where you stand, soldier!"

Everyone's eyes were on Jack—waiting for him to obey Domashev's orders or for the captain to give instructions to shoot him.

Grant didn't waste the opportunity. He grabbed the gun that Jack had shoved into the back of his waistband and shot one of the guards, then another.

Domashev whipped his gun up. Swiftly, Jack wrapped his right leg around Domashev's left and yanked it out from underneath him. After knocking him to the floor, he stomped on his throat to hold him in place—denying him air.

A bullet zipped past them from the remaining guard who now wore an "oh shit" expression at the loss of his support.

Dan dove to the floor, swept up his gun, and shot the guard in the chest.

"Looks like we're gonna make our ride after all." Jack stepped away from Domashev lying motionless on the floor.

"What about him?" Dan asked of the police captain.

"He's out. The explosion will take care of him. Let's go," Jack said.

They rushed toward the door when it jerked open.

Casey had a baleful look on her face. "Do you always have to cut it so close?" She pointed her Glock in their direction.

The guys came to a dead stop.

Jack said, "Shooting us seems like a really tough punishment for tardiness, Rhodes."

She pulled the trigger. The bullet whipped past her team. They ducked and spun around to see Domashev slide down the wall with a bullet hole in his throat.

Hitching her chin toward the door, Casey said, "Clearly, he wasn't incapacitated."

"I'd kiss ya, Rhodes, but I'm afraid you'd kick me in the balls," Jack said as he past through the door.

"And you'd be right, Haliday," she confirmed. "What've we got here?"

"She's been shot in the right calf," Grant said with his left arm wrapped around his torso. He clung to the railing with his right while they hurried down the stairs toward the van that was surrounded by team Hawke Ops.

"I've got some quikclot in my pack." Tom shrugged out of the backpack and tossed it to Grant.

Peyton yanked the back doors of the van open so everyone could hop in.

Taken aback at the sight of Eleni holding a rifle on Taka, he asked, "Was it something he said?"

"He was going to leave. He had extra keys," Eleni explained.

"She is mistaken. It was joke," Taka claimed with a roll of his eyes.

"We haven't got time for this. I'll deal with you at camp," Peyton told them. "C'mon, load the girl quickly, you'll have to administer the quikclot on the move—this place is gonna blow!"

After jumping into the van, Dan held out his arms for Jack to pass Silja to him. She moaned as he carefully laid her on a bench to be coddled in Eleni's lap. "Easy does it, sweetheart," Dan said.

Eleni took in a ragged breath. Stroking Silja's hair, she whispered words of reassurance.

Grant was already ripping the bag of quikclot with his teeth when he got in. Casey grabbed the knife that was secured to her ankle and cut away Silja's blood-soaked pant leg. The van lunged forward. Freezing, Casey pulled the knife away. She tore the rest of the fabric with her hands.

Wincing, Silja let out a groan.

Abruptly, the van moved backward toward the closed garage doors. Jack said, "Hold tight, we're going straight through the doors."

Eleni, Grant, and Casey held onto Silja when the van crashed against the garage doors. The deafening sound of metal tearing and bending reverberated through the garage as the van burst into the daylight.

Taka was huddled in a corner, sweat pouring from his brow, while he tried with shaking hands to light a cigarette. Eleni and Casey struggled to keep Silja as still as possible while Grant poured the quikclot over her wound.

A barrage of bullets pinged off the sides of the vehicle. Peyton returned fire from the cab. The van swerved and swayed through the compound toward the security gate while the occupants in the prisoner's compartment braced against the walls.

Dan struggled to make his way across the cubicle to examine Silja's wound. The quikclot had done its job. The bleeding had stopped, although Silja had lost quite a bit of blood.

Wiping what blood he could away with a clean rag that he'd found in Tom's backpack, Dan said, "It looks like a through and through. Let's just hope the bullet didn't damage any major tendons or ligaments on its way out." He ran the back of his fingers over her bruised face. "Her skin is clammy, and her breathing is shallow. She's definitely in shock. We need to get her to camp A-SAP so Smitty can take care of her."

Wincing in pain, Grant climbed onto the bench next to Eleni. Carefully exchanging places, she helped him gather Silja into his arms in an effort to transfer as much warmth as he could from his body to hers. He peered into her ashen face.

Her eyes opened only slightly. Her face was beaded with a cold sweat. She was weak, but she managed to squeeze his arm with her fingers, and her lips curled slightly. "I need to tell you something—"

"Lay still, Sil. We're almost there. You're gonna be just fine," he vowed.

"Please, Grant, let me tell you ... B-Ballard told me ..." she fought to stay cognizant. "He told me who killed Belsky ... it was Dom—Dominik Potrovic."

Grant pulled her close. "Okay, I got it. Now rest, just rest," he said into her hair.

Peyton banged on the window, and then slid it open. "I'm out of ammo. Someone give me their gun!"

Jack passed his gun to Peyton. Through the windshield he could see a line of approximately ten guards near the gate with assault rifles. Their firepower simply didn't match the guards, and Jack wasn't sure that the van would make it through the gate.

Out of the blue, two guards fell forward to the ground. Then, two more fell. They were being shot from behind.

Keeping the van trained on the gate, Tom accelerated while Peyton shot at the guards out the passenger window.

Jack handed Dan's gun through the window. Another guard met his demise from seemingly out of nowhere.

Jack turned to the group. "Hold on! We're almost to the gate—it's gonna be one helluva ride!"

Eleni and Casey wedged themselves against Grant to provide extra stability for Silja. Dan and Jack scrambled across the floor at Grant's feet to provide what steadiness they could from below.

They heard Tom shout out from the driver's seat, "Four ... three ... two ... one!" He pressed the button on the ignition switch in his hand to detonate the explosives with a hearty, "Hooyah!"

The laboratory exploded.

The ground rocked and knocked the remaining guards off their feet into the snow. The van bucked against the blast. Tom pressed harder on the accelerator, charging toward the gate. In the short distance beyond the gate he could see Stewart, Jonas, and Billy-Joe emerging from the snowy tree line, firing their AK-47s into the compound to provide cover for the van while it burst through the gate and pitched metal in all directions.

Stewart, Jonas, and Billy-Joe ran toward the van, grabbed hold of the handles on the door, and hoisted themselves onto the built-in steps on the bumper for a ride back to camp. They sprayed the fence line with gunfire while the van bounced and bumped down the roadway.

Jack alerted the camp in his radio. "Bringing in one wounded. Gunshot to the leg."

With the compound engulfed in flames, the team was certain that what few guards that remained in good condition had their hands full, so they drove along the road until they came to where the SUVs were hidden under snow camo tarps in the brush. As quickly and delicately as they could, they transferred Silja into the back of one of the SUVs and drove through the brush to the camp. Grant held her as tightly as possible as they traveled over the rough terrain.

Cole and Smitty were waiting at the edge of the camp for them when the SUVs arrived. Dan took

Silja from Grant's arms and followed the med team to the tent they'd prepared for such an emergency. Dan laid her upon the bed they had prepped. Smitty grabbed her arm to clean and sterilize it so he could run an IV while Cole cleansed and examined the wound on her leg.

"Is there anything I can do?" Grant asked.

"We've got it from here, man," Cole told him.

"Is she gonna be okay?"

Smitty tossed him a reassuring look. "We'll do what we can to stabilize her, and then she'll have to be moved to a facility. I think she'll be fine."

"But the police are looking for her," Grant said. "She can't go to a hospital. They'll be all over her."

"Talk to Peyton. He's got a friend that we use when we need medical care that's off the grid," Cole said over his shoulder as he carefully dabbed at Silja's leg with Betadine solution. "Smitty ... get me more gauze."

Taking in Grant's battered appearance and his crunched posture while he held his torso, Smitty said, "Don't go too far, Ketchum, you're next."

Grant stepped out of the tent. They needed to work on Sil, not answer a bunch of questions. As he backed out of the tent, his strength faltered. He was coming down from his adrenaline high, and the pain was becoming more piercing with each passing moment. He stumbled.

Jack grabbed his arm to steady him. "As soon as their done with Silja, you need attention. You might have some broken ribs, and we don't need a punctured lung—if it's not already a done deal. Let's get you to one of the warm tents and have you sit down."

"I want to make sure Sil's okay."

"I'm sure you do," Jack said. "She's in good hands. Smitty will keep us informed. Now, get some rest and a hot bowl of soup, or you're not gonna have to worry about Silja. C'mon."

Grant felt a hand on his left arm. "Come, Grant, your friend is right," Eleni said. "Anna is serving soup. It will be good for you to have some nutrition. Silja would want this, yes?"

Grant glanced back at the tent where two men were working on the woman he loved. Quietly, he relented, "Yes, Ma'am." He let Jack and Eleni lead him away.

Peyton met Stewart, Jonas, and Billy-Joe when they climbed out of their SUV. "Thanks for the backup, boys. Good timing. But where the hell are the prisoners that you were supposed to be guarding while we were gone?"

Jonas said, "The murderer, the serial rapist, and the other murderer? Yeah, I can identify with the Russians for sending these guys for some testing. We won't be hearing from them for a while. Smitty gave them a heavy sedative right before we left. They're handcuffed, and their feet are bound with duct tape. They're good to go for several more hours."

"Nice. And where's the young woman we left behind?"

"She's in the middle tent," Billy-Joe said. "Smitty has her warming soup for you guys on the Coleman stove. I think she was happy just to have something to do to keep her mind occupied. She's pretty skittish around men. I don't know what she's been through. I hope she'll be okay, in time."

Casey poked her head out of the tent. "Hey, you'd better come and get some soup before it's gone. It's really good." Shooting Peyton a naughty grin, she ducked back inside.

Peyton muttered to himself, "I'll bet it is." He took several strides toward the tent when a hand clapped his shoulder. He turned to find a frantic Taka standing behind him.

"What am I supposed to do with the van?" Taka lit a cigarette with trembling hands.

"Take it back to the prison with the prisoners."

"They will arrest me!"

"What for? It's not your fault that you were commandeered," Peyton pointed out. "We took you hostage. You had no choice but to help us. That said, you'd better be in too much shock to describe any of us." He poked his finger hard into Taka's chest. "You got that?"

Taking a deep drag from the cigarette, Taka nodded.

Peyton said, "We'll load the prisoners into the van after we have some soup. Then you can be on your way, and so can we. C'mon."

Taka shook his head. "No ... I do not think I should do this on full stomach."

"Suit yourself, dude." When he entered the tent, Peyton took a seat next to Grant. Casey handed him a warm bowl of soup. "Thanks." He asked, "How's the girl doing?"

Grant said, "They're getting her stabilized. Cole told me you have a friend that runs a clinic?"

"Yeah, near Rezh. It's for low-income individuals. His name is Dr. Rick Stone. He was the medic in my unit when I was in the marines. He met a girl here in Russia. She's a doctor, too. He married her, and they opened the clinic about six years ago. They've taken care of us many times when things were a bit beyond what Cole could do in the field. Don't worry. No one will know she's there—there will be no record of her."

CHAPTER TWENTY-THREE

Two days later

Natalia tossed back two pain killers with a gulp of pinot noir. Her head was pounding.

It had been all over the news that the Crafton Technologies laboratory had been blown to smithereens. They were investigating the cause of the explosion, but no terrorist groups had claimed responsibility as of yet. The news went on to say that the police believed that Ballard was inside the building at the time and was suspected to be dead along with Captain Domashev of the Yekaterinburg Police Department. They did not know what he was doing at the lab.

Natalia hoped that Silja had been far from the blast.

Her eyes fell upon the papers that Tess McMillan had delivered to her office two days ago. They still sat on the far corner of her desk unsigned. Her lips curled. She picked up the papers and tossed them into the waste basket.

One of her problems had been eliminated, but not all. She was still faced with mounting bills. She refused to condone any more parties for the contributors.

Then, there was the issue that Dominik had murdered Ivan Belsky, which made her head pound and the stress in her neck throb.

Ivan Belsky deserved whatever he got after what he did to Anna Antkowiak, but that was not for her to say. That was not Dominik's motive for killing him. His reasons were personal, selfish, and, quite frankly, shallow. How could she get her life or her ballet company back on track with a murderer in her company?

Something had to be done—whether Edvar was on board or not.

She dug her fingers into her stiff neck while trying to rub away the stress and the shame of what had become of her company—her career. Burying her face in her hands, she massaged her forehead with her fingertips.

Her office door opened. She was taken aback when she found two very large men filling the doorway.

Stiffening in her seat, Natalia asked in Russian, "May I help you?"

"We don't speak Russian, Ms. Novikov, but we know that you speak English. We're looking for one of your dancers, Dominik Potrovic," Peyton said.

Her chest tightened. "What do you want with Dominik?"

"We want to take him to the police so he can tell them that he, not Silja Ramsay, killed Ivan Belsky," Grant told her.

"Who are you? You are not Russian. You are not police. Why should I tell you anything?"

"Because I don't think you want Silja to be charged with a murder that she didn't commit," Grant said, "and I think you know how deeply Dominik is involved. I'm a close friend of Silja's. I want to take her home to the United States, but I want her name cleared before she leaves Russia."

Natalia tossed him a knowing look. Her tone softened. "You are the one...the one she left behind to chase her dreams of the ballet, yes?"

Grant said nothing.

"Is Silja all right?" Natalia asked. "She wasn't hurt by Ballard or the explosion, I hope."

"Silja is fine. Like I said, I'm taking her home."

Relieved, Natalia relaxed against the chair. She studied Grant. His jaw was set, but she could see in his eyes that he cared deeply for Silja. He was right. Silja needed to go home with him, and she needed to make all things right in order to pick up the pieces of her broken ballet company before it could have a future—before she could have a future.

Feeling stronger with the fact that there was a means to an end, she pushed up from her seat.

Lifting her chin and squaring her shoulders, Natalia told them, "I will not tell you where Dominik is, but I will go to the police with you and tell them what I know. This way I can be confident that he will be arrested properly, and he will be forced to pay for what he has done. And, most likely, so will I."

* * * * *

Silja's eyes dragged open. For a moment the room was a blur. She blinked several times, and her vision soon cleared. To her surprise, she was in what looked like a hospital room.

When had she arrived here? She remembered her leg burning like hellfire while being carried from Ballard's office enveloped in strong arms, except she didn't think that the arms that cradled her belonged to Grant, although she remembered Grant whispering in her ear.

She searched her mind. She remembered a tent. She remembered being laid onto a cot. She had no idea who had carried her to the tent. Moreover, she didn't recall being transferred from the tent to a hospital.

How long has she been unconscious?

A sudden panic washed over her.

Hurriedly, her hand made its way down to make sure that her leg was still there. Wiggling her toes, she let out a breath.

A warm hand slipped over hers. A familiar, friendly voice spoke softly to her, "Silja ... how do you feel?" Eleni asked.

Silja looked around the room. Grant was nowhere to be found. Her heart sank. Feeling parched, she said, "I'm very thirsty."

Eleni lifted a cup of water to her mouth. "We can fix this."

After Silja took several sips, she asked, "Where's Grant?"

"I do not know. He said he had some business to tend to. He asked me to sit with you until he returned."

"How long have you been sitting here?"

"A couple of hours. This is first time he has left your side for two days." She patted Silja's hand. "He will be here soon, I'm sure. He is anxious to take you home. How do we Russians say it? Better late than never, yes?"

Silja managed a weak smile. "No, Eleni ... that is what we American's say."

Eleni's eyebrows rose. "But I thought you are Russian. Let us review: You were *raised* in America, but you were *born* in Russia, and that makes you *Russian.*"

Letting out a snort, Silja closed her eyes. She shook her head against the pillow. "I was born in Russia, but in my heart I am an American, and that is where I belong." She squeezed Eleni's hand. "You should come to America with us, Eleni. It would be so much better for you there. I'm worried for you here."

"No, Silja. Russia is my home. It is where I was born. I love Russia. I could never leave. I will be fine, and maybe I come visit you someday, yes?"

"Yes, I would love for you to visit me."

"Hey, the patient is awake." Grant strolled through the door with the doctor at his side.

"I'm Dr. Stone. How are you feeling, Miss Ramsay?" the doctor asked.

"The leg is a little sore. I haven't tried to move it yet," Silja told him.

"The nurse will have you up on crutches later today. You were very lucky. The field doctors did a great job. Your leg is healing quite well. As far as I can tell, the bullet did no major damage, but I've recommended to Grant that you see an orthopedic doctor as soon as you return to the States. I'll have the nurse bring in some pain medication. There's no reason for you to be in discomfort." He shook hands with Silja and with Grant.

"Thanks for everything, Doc," Grant said.

The doctor smiled and then made his way out of the room.

"Where've you been, Mr. Ketchum?" Silja asked.

He kissed her on the forehead. "I've been a busy boy. First, I went to the cottage to retrieve your cell phone. We needed it for evidence, and then there was the matter of a missing ..." He opened his coat and Greta sprang from his chest into Silja's arms. "Cat! I found her hiding under the bed. I was glad she hadn't left the cottage, although there were some indications that the farm is missing a few mice."

Tears filling her eyes, Silja hugged Greta tightly while stroking her head. She murmured, "No man left behind."

"That's our policy," Grant noted. "Anyway, Peyton and I visited with Natalia Novikov. We gave her your cell phone and then dropped her off at the police station so she could tell them what she knew about Belsky's murder. Dominik is probably in custody by now." He turned to Eleni. "Peyton is waiting in a black SUV outside to give you a ride to Yekaterinburg. On the drive to the police station, Natalia asked for you. She's pretty sure that she'll be spending time behind bars for her participation in the prostitution ring. I think she wants you to run the ballet company while she's away."

"You didn't stay with her while she talked with the police?" Silja asked.

"We couldn't do that, Sil. We would've had to identify ourselves. In our line of work, that's not an option."

"I suppose ..." Silja noticed the apprehension filling Eleni's expression. She reached for Eleni's hand. "You can do this, Eleni. You are a fabulous dancer, and the dancers all love and respect you. It won't be easy, but I'm sure you will make a wonderful director. Go see her."

Cupping her cheek in her hand, Eleni murmured, "I do not know ..."

"Eleni, remember what you said? That you were running out of time as a dancer—you're getting too old. Here is your chance to continue your dance career. Don't hold back. Talk to Natalia. What have you got to lose?"

Eleni looked to Grant. He winked at her and then hitched his chin toward the door, indicating that Silja was right. She should trust in herself and spread her wings.

Eleni stood up. "I will go to hear what Natalia has to say, and then I will think it over."

"That sounds like a very smart decision," Grant said.

Eleni kissed Silja on the forehead, stroked Greta's neck, and gave Grant a hug before she hurried out of the room.

Grant took Eleni's seat next to Silja. He brushed his fingers through her hair. "The team is on their way to a private air strip for the flight home. Clark is getting you a fresh passport, and he checked out the regulations for bringing Greta into the United States—there are no strict regulations in place. As long as she's healthy, which she appears to be, they'll let her through. So we'll go home in a few days on a commercial flight, when you're feeling stronger."

Silja caressed his bruised face lightly with her fingertips. "And you? Are you all right?"

Smiling, Grant rubbed his torso. "Eh, I've got a cracked rib or two. Doc Stone has me bandaged up like a mummy under my clothes. He said my head is way too hard for any real damage. I'm good as gold."

"Said the badass marine," Silja snorted.

"This badass marine loves you, and I want you to be with me, Sil, really I do, but ..." His gaze dropped into his lap.

Silja's heart sank. What was he trying to say? He didn't want her? Were they going their separate ways when they got back to the States? She hadn't prepared for this scenario. With her heart in her throat, she managed, "But what?"

"I don't know if I can make you happy. I live in a little place called Yeager. It's a small town outside of a small town called Harverton, where the First Force headquarters is located. I don't know if there are any dance facilities there, Sil. I want you to be happy, and I know that dance makes you happy. On top of that, I'm away on missions a lot, and—"

Silja placed her fingers over his mouth. "Don't you know? You make me happy, Grant Ketchum. I'm never letting you go again. And besides, dance is everywhere. If there isn't a dance school in Yeager or this Harverton place, guess what? I'll open one."

Squaring her shoulders against the pillow, she lifted her chin. "As a matter of fact, that's exactly what I intend to do: open a dance school. That should keep me busy while you're off saving the world."

Grant couldn't hold back. He planted a kiss on her lips. Silja wrapped her arms around his neck and pulled him in tighter until they heard a nurse scolding them in Russian from the foot of the bed. Grant jumped to his feet.

The nurse's brows were furrowed. After setting the pain medication on the table, she grabbed Greta from the bed and shoved her into Grant's chest while spewing a reprimand in Russian.

Helplessly amused, Silja cupped her hand over her mouth.

Grant shrugged. "I think that's a very strong hint that the cat has gotta go."

The nurse continued to protest loudly while chasing him from the room. Doing his best Arnold Schwarzenegger impression, Grant called to Silja over his shoulder, "I'll be back!"

The nurse slammed the door in his face. Silja tried, but she simply could not smother the giggle that bubbled to the surface.

Once in the hallway with Greta tucked under his arm, he pulled out his cell phone and dialed. "Hey, Casey, are you still the keeper of the keys to operative's apartments for emergency?" He listened to her response. Smiling, he said, "Good, I need a favor..."

* * * * *

Four days later

The Koltsovo Airport was a throng of hurried travelers.

Much to her dismay, Silja was still walking with the aide of crutches. The bruises on her face were changing from black and blue to a yellowish tone, which was a bit easier to cover with make up.

She and Grant made their way through the terminal until they came to their gate. Silja was amazed at how quickly she tired. They had to fly to Moscow to catch a flight to La Guardia where they would stay the night before flying on to Pennsylvania. She was grateful to take a seat and wait for their flight to be called—until she looked up to see Tess McMillan roll her carry-on bag to a seat across the seating area and sit down. Agitation crawled up Silja's spine.

Tapping Grant on the shoulder, she whispered, "Do you see who's here?"

"Tess McMillan? Yeah, I saw her at the check in earlier while you were in the ladies room."

"Why isn't she being indicted like everyone else?"

"What for? She really hasn't done anything wrong. Ballard had the blessing of the Russian government to perform testing on those prisoners, and she had nothing to do with that. Ballard attended the contributors' parties—not Tess. Ballard attempted to kill you and me—not Tess."

Silja's whisper grew more indignant. "What are you talking about? She was shooting at us in the house."

Grant shrugged. "I was an intruder. I didn't belong, nor was I invited into their house. She was only protecting her home. Even in Russia, you're allowed to protect what's yours—as long as it's not against the Russian government. At any rate, no one knows about those things, because then they would know that we blew up the lab. That would be a very bad thing."

Hunkering deeper into her seat with a scowl planted on her lips, Silja crossed her arms over her chest. "There's got to be something that she did that she could be indicted for," she muttered under her breath, and then her eyes widened.

Slapping Grant across the chest with the back of her hand, she announced in a panicked undertone, "Oh my God, she's coming this way!"

Tucking his chin into his chest, Grant chuckled at Silja's alarm. Before they knew it, the lovely blonde woman was standing in front of them.

"May I have a moment of your time?" Tess asked.

Silja stiffened in her seat.

Grant straightened in his chair. "What can we do for you, Ms. McMillan?"

Folding an errant strand of hair behind her ear, Tess lowered her gaze to the floor and then sunk into a chair across from Silja and Grant.

After taking in a long cleansing breath, she slid her gaze to meet Silja's. "Do you remember that morning at breakfast when you asked me why I didn't have to wear a choker?"

"I remember."

Tess pulled down the collar of the red turtleneck sweater that she was wearing to reveal three small stitches in the right side of her neck. "Ballard traded in the choker five years ago for a subdermal tracking chip—I had the chip removed two days ago." She slipped the collar back into its place. "You see, I have been with Ballard since I was seventeen years old. He was a counselor at the home for juvenile delinquent girls that I was living in at the time. I was young and stupid. I had participated in a convenience store robbery. He was assigned to me, and we became ... close. After a year, he finally decided to go to work for his father's company, Crafton Labs, as a chemist. He took charge as my guardian and removed me from the home. He taught me discipline, and I learned quickly that if I was disobedient, the punishment was brutal. He chose and paid for my college and my car. He controlled my every move. For a long time I went along with it. When I was twenty-nine, I met another man. I wanted to be with him. I tried to escape." She dragged in a ragged breath. "I had to have plastic surgery to repair the punishment, and that is when I was forced to marry him, and the chip was implanted."

"He *forced* you to marry him?"

"He threatened to arrange an accident for my lover if I refused, so yes, I married Ballard under duress."

Silja was most taken aback by her story. Involuntarily, her fingers covered her mouth.

Grant could see the remorse simmering in her eyes for her earlier remarks. Leaning his elbows on his thighs, he dropped his gaze to his clenched hands between his knees and listened intently.

Tess glanced around the area. Most of the passengers were busy chasing after impatient children or reading a book or newspaper. Smoothing her fingers over her black slacks, she continued, "The good news is that I am now free to live my life as I wish. I am a very wealthy woman. I am the benefactor to Ballard's fortune. I made sure of that one day when he was signing a pile of paperwork. Crafton Technologies will cease to exist. I don't want anyone else to be a victim of that awful serum ever again." She nodded toward the small travel case that she was keeping close at hand. "I have his notes—they will be destroyed."

"I don't understand," Silja put in. "You're so beautiful. Why did Ballard need other women?"

"Ballard demanded perfection in his life. He loved and craved talent and beauty. He had no use for mediocrity. While he considered me a beautiful woman, I have no talent, other than my keen organizational skills. He respected that, but he didn't lust after it—he just needed to own it. That's why when we married I was instructed to keep my name, so that the women with whom he had relationships thought I was his personal assistant—like you did. He hated the fact that the Russian's would only provide him with prisoners for his testing. He wanted soldiers—Special Forces types," she nodded at Grant, "like yourself."

"What are your plans?" Grant asked.

Tess favored him with a feeble smile. "I'm going home to Albany, New York. I haven't seen or spoken to my parents since I was seventeen. I have so much to apologize for—so much heartache to repair. I spoke to my father last night. They were very excited to finally hear from me ..." Her voice trailed off. She swiped a tear from her cheek. "Anyway, I wanted to apologize for what Ballard did to you, and for the fact that I had no choice but to participate. I want you to know that I made a large donation to the Novikov Ballet Company to help Miss Babinski keep it going. I wish you both well." She pushed up from her seat, grabbed the case, and turned to walk away.

Silja scrambled to her feet. She pulled Tess into a tight hug. "I hope you find the happiness that you deserve, Tess."

She looked into Silja's eyes full of compassion where there was once resentment. "That means so much to me, thank you."

EPILOGUE

It had been a long, tiring, journey, but one that she had welcomed. Grant and Silja were finally driving along the highway in his Camaro toward home—a place called Yeager.

With Greta curled up in her lap, Silja breathed in the sights and sounds of home, America. It felt good to be back, even though it was flurrying as it almost always was in Russia. Ahhh, but what else could one expect from the final days of February in Pennsylvania? No matter, it would only be a few more weeks until the March winds would blow spring their way and encourage the crocuses and daffodils to bravely push through the earth from their graves.

Grant's cell phone whistled at him. Text message: *Casey Rhodes—Got package. At HQ watching hockey w/team.* His lips curved upward. Shoving the cell into his pocket, he said, "We're not far from First Force headquarters. Everyone's there watching a hockey game. Do you feel up to stopping by for a little while?"

"I owe them my life, Grant," Silja replied. "Of course I want to stop by and meet them. You've told me so much about them. I'm ashamed to admit that I don't really remember any of them at all."

"Actually, that's understandable. Okay, we'll drop in, but only for a little while, and if you get tired you're gonna tell me right away, right?"

Silja rolled her eyes. "Yes, Sir, Mr. Ketchum, Sir." Grant chuckled.

* * * * *

"They're here! They're here!" Lil shouted from the foyer of the Georgian-style mansion that housed the First Force Headquarters. With her nose pressed against the glass, she watched intently through the window while Grant helped Silja Ramsay—a real honest-to-goodness ballerina—out of his car.

The little girl blinked back. Grant tucked something furry into Silja's arms. The child's face lit up. She turned to her father and Rayne, who had come into the foyer.

"She's got a kitty cat! She's a real ballerina and she's got a kitty cat!" Resounding joy filled Lil's words.

The fuchsia tutu that she was wearing bounced and danced around her waist, while her pink ballet slippers pattered lightly across the marble floor to the huge beveled glass door. She pulled and yanked until the heavy door slowly opened.

Chuckling at his daughter's enthusiasm, Jack said, "Here ... let me help you." He opened the door to find Grant, Silja, and Greta on the other side. Jack reached his hand out to Grant. "Welcome back."

Shaking Jack's hand, Grant said to Silja, "This is Jack Haliday, he—"

"I remember you ..." Silja broke in. "You were in Ballard's office and ..." Her voice fell away. The memory of kneeling at Ballard's feet, swallowing back the disgust of what he was demanding that she do in exchange for her redemption and her friends' freedom, scraped through her. Embarrassment at what the man may have witnessed before he shot Ballard washed over her. She could feel the heat rising in her cheeks.

Understanding her unease, Jack said, "Welcome to the First Force Headquarters, Silja. I'm glad you're feeling better," he turned to Rayne. "This is Doctor Rayne Lee, our head team medic."

Silja shook hands with the lovely dark-haired woman.

Sweeping Lil onto his hip, Grant said, "And this little ballerina is the irrepressible Lil Haliday, Jack's daughter."

"I'm not irritable!"

Laughing, Jack checked his watch. "Well, it's not bedtime yet. Little Miss Irritable usually shows her face around eight fifteen. But he's correct, most of the time you are irrepressible."

Bemused, Lil cocked her head.

Brushing one of the many stray curls from the child's face, Rayne rescued her. "Why don't we go into the living room? The team is looking forward to seeing you again, Silja." While they made their way through the foyer, she added, "I hope you're a hockey fan."

"And a football fan," Jack interjected.

"And a baseball fan," Grant put in.

Silja and Rayne exchanged amused glances at their men: spot on sports fanatics.

The living room was a bustle of cheers and jeers as the Pittsburgh Penguins and the Philadelphia Flyers fought for goals on the large flat-screen TV.

The camaraderie among the group was unmistakable. Jabs of teasing and high fives showcased the exuberance that filled the room.

Walt turned to see Grant and Silja enter the room along with Jack, Rayne, and Lil, who was enthralled with the cat in Silja's arms. Grabbing the remote, Walt muted the TV and called out to the team, "Hey everyone, look who's here: Grant and his ballerina."

Everyone turned to greet them.

Setting Lil down, Grant proudly introduced the

elegant woman at his side. He nodded to each as he introduced them to Silja. "Everyone...this is Silja Ramsay. Sil, this is the leader of First Force, Walt Wabash."

Taking her hand into his, Walt said, "It's a pleasure, Miss Ramsay."

"This is Dan Garrison."

Dan stepped forward to shake her hand.

Grant added, "Will Smith, or Smitty, as we call him—he's one of the medics that worked on you when you arrived at camp."

Smitty reached out his hand, but Silja wasn't having it. She wrapped her arms around him in a warm hug. With watery eyes, she said, "I can't thank you enough for taking such good care of my leg."

"You're very welcome, Ma'am, but I didn't work alone. I worked with another medic named Cole Barnhart. I don't know if you'll ever meet him, but he did a great job in poor conditions."

Silja smiled. "I hope I do meet him someday. Thank you."

Grant continued, "You may be surprised to meet our sniper, Casey Rhodes."

Grinning, Casey shook Silja's hand. She certainly was taken aback by the very attractive, dark-haired woman dressed in a pair of jeans and a ribbed tangerine sweater—she hardly looked like someone who would hide in the bushes, take careful aim, and kill. Casey did not match what she envisioned as a sniper.

Grant said, "Last, but not least, Stewart Little, our pilot." Stiffly, Stewart shook the ballerina's hand accompanied by the best friendly expression that he could rally.

Searching the room, Silja asked, "It's wonderful to meet all of you, but where is this Clark Rhodes that I've heard so much about?"

Grant looked around the room.

Indeed, Clark was absent. From the hallway Clark called, "I'm here." Tugging his coat from his shoulders, he stepped into the room.

Carrying a large package, Peyton Mattock came in directly behind him. Peyton's mouth arched into a salacious grin when his eyes met Casey's raised eyebrow reaction from across the room.

Clark reached his hand out to Silja. "Nice to meet you, Silja. I'm Clark Rhodes, the team coordinator, and this is Peyton Mattock. He was instrumental in your rescue from the lab."

"*Instrumental?* I was the freakin' team leader, dude," Peyton quickly pointed out.

Clark chuckled.

"What's in the package?" Jack noticed the electricity shooting across the room between Peyton and Casey.

"Oh ... it's just a little something for Miss Rhodes." Peyton made his way around the sofa toward her. He handed the package to Casey. "It's a bunting. In case you should decide to go camping in the cold any-time soon."

Casey took in Peyton's wide smile, the dreads pulled back in a neat ponytail, and the Oakley sunglasses parked on top of his head. Attempting to not make too big a show of her delight, her lips tightened into a thin line. "Is that an invitation?"

"I could demonstrate some winter camping skills, if you'd like," Peyton replied.

"They do know that we can hear their conversation, right?" Dan asked Jack.

"I don't think they give a rat's ass, Garrison," Jack said.

Lil couldn't contain her excitement any longer. She tugged at Silja's jacket, "Can I please hold the kitty?"

"Of course. Her name is Greta."

Jumping up and down merrily in place, Lil clapped her hands.

"You've been standing for a long time, Sil," Grant said. "C'mon, sit down on the sofa." He helped her eddy out of her coat, and then he held her elbow as she eased onto the sofa. Lil immediately took a seat next to Silja.

Grant said "I'll get you something to drink."

"Thanks."

When Grant weaved through the team toward the kitchen, Casey tapped him on the shoulder. "Is this the box that you wanted from your apartment?" she asked while discreetly revealing the red velvet box in her hand.

Furtively, Grant looked over his shoulder to see Silja gently placing Greta into Lil's arms. The little girl's eyes gleamed as if Silja had just handed her the most precious thing in the world.

Slipping the box from Casey's hand into his pocket, Grant whispered, "Thanks Casey."

"I was touching your underwear. I especially like the navy striped low-cut tighties. Personally, I had you pegged as an olive green boxer brief man." She lifted her shoulder. "I'm a little shocked."

"Again ... thanks, Casey."

A wide smile stretched across her face. She slapped him on the back. "Go get her, Ketchum. She's a great gal. I wish you all the happiness in the world."

With the box tucked away in his pocket, Grant made his way to the couch where Lil was cuddling Greta in the spot next to Silja. The grin on her lips hadn't diminished one bit. He knelt down in front of the little girl.

"Well, it looks like you get along really well with Greta. She seems to like you very much."

"Oh I just love her, Mr. Grant! She's so soft and cuddly." Lil placed her ear on the cat's shoulder. "And she's purring! That means she likes me, too!"

As always, the joy that Lil exuded from such simple everyday things was purely contagious.

Playfully, Grant tapped the tip of Lil's nose. "What's not to like, darlin'?" he looked up at Silja and with a chuckle in his voice, he said, "Somehow, I think Jack will be out searching for a kitten in the very near future."

Nodding her head in agreement, Silja giggled.

Grant held out his hand to Silja. "C'mon, I have something I want to show you." Without hesitation, Silja took his hand, and, keeping a firm hold on her, he lifted her from the couch. Her cell phone beeped. Silja pulled it from her pocket, and upon looking at the screen, she smiled. "It's a text from the new director of the Novikov."

"What's Eleni up to?" Grant inquired.

Silja's eyes brightened. With a chuckle in her voice, she replied, "You're not going to believe this. Well, after everything that went on, maybe you will. They apprehended Dominik and Edvar at the airport just hours ago. Seems they were trying to get on a flight for Spain dressed as little old ladies—they had fake passports and everything." Continuing to read the text, she laughed. "Eleni says that they showed Dominik being tackled by a police officer on TV—the little old lady was wearing a cheetah print Speedo under her dress!"

"Well that's just about perfect," Grant joined in the laughter while he led her into the foyer. The last rays of the day's sunshine burst through the beveled door, shooting swirls of light throughout like tiny diamonds glimmering all around them.

Taking in the grandeur of the marble floor and the tall hand-painted vases that dotted the circular area complimented by the sweeping staircase, Silja slid her arms around Grant's waist. Turning, he pulled her in closer to feel the warmth of her body against his.

She said, "By the way, that whole little interaction with the four year old ..."

"Yeah ..."

"It looked really good on you."

"Ya think?" He kissed her lightly on the lips and then pressed his forehead to hers. "Sil ... I want this more now than ever."

"So what are you gonna do about it, Ketchum?"

He looked into her smiling eyes. "Well, first I'm gonna take you to my apartment and make crazy passionate love to you, and then I'm gonna call my mom and tell her there's gonna be a spring wedding." He brushed a frock of hair from her cheek with the pad of his thumb. "What do you say to that, *Swan Hilda?*"

He pulled the ring box from his pocket and into her view.

Opening the delicate lid, the diamond ring practically jumped from the box with its dazzling radiance to remind him that the love that was present five years ago was still ever so strong.

Yes, it was right to give her *this* ring—the original ring that he had purchased—because his love had never dulled—like the gleam of the diamond.

Tears glistened in Silja's eyes as her jaw dropped open. "Oh my God, Grant, it's absolutely gorgeous," she whispered while he slipped it onto her finger. She added, "How lucky can a girl get? I've got a beautiful ring from a wonderful man who actually knows the name of the principal character in *Coppelia*. I'm very impressed."

Clearing his throat, he confessed, "I googled it."

Silja tossed her head back in laughter. It felt good to be in his arms—laughing. It felt like home. It felt like love. It felt like where she should always be. "You're research is much appreciated, and a spring wedding sounds perfect to me."

The End

Thank you for reading **To the Breaking Point***e. I hope you will read the next book from the First Force Series,* **Into the Dark***, coming in 2015. Let me entice you with a short synopsis to whet your appetite ...*

INTO THE DARK

Four years ago, Dr. Rayne Lee lost her husband and her four-year-old daughter, Sierra, to a group of hostile guerrillas in the Amazonian Valley of Peru. It had taken every bit of her constitution to rebuild her life and to join her uncle's security firm, First Force, as the team's head medic. She still desperately missed her husband and her daughter, but all in all everything was back on track—until the phone calls started.

A young girl was calling claiming to be Sierra. The tiny trembling voice claimed that the guerrillas were holding her captive, and there was only one way for them to be reunited: Rayne needed to travel to Peru and give them something that she had. Moreover, the guerrillas had another stipulation: She had to come alone.

Suddenly the ghosts from Rayne's past are chasing her down a dark road.

What could they possibly want from her?

Was it really Sierra calling?

Could she return to the place where her family was murdered and she was brutalized for seven horrible months?

Rayne knew that she had to take the risk—she had to find out!

*Sign up for Cindy's newsletter on the homepage at her website, **www.cindymcwriter.co**m, and you will receive the first chapter of Cindy's latest book delivered directly to your inbox as a thank you!*

*Cindy does not share email addresses.

ABOUT CINDY McDONALD

For twenty-six years Cindy's life whirled around a song and a dance. She was a professional dancer/choreographer for most of her adult life and never gave much thought to a writing career until 2005. She often notes: Don't ask me what happened, but suddenly I felt drawn to my computer to write about things that I have experienced with my husband's Thoroughbreds and happenings at the racetrack—she muses: they are greatly exaggerated upon of course—I've never been murdered. Viola! Cindy's first book series, Unbridled, was born.

Cindy is a huge fan of romantic suspense series, and although she isn't one to make New Year's resolutions, on New Year's Day 2013 she made a commitment to write one, *Into the Crossfire* is the first book for The First Force Series.

People are always asking Cindy: Do you miss dance? With a bitter sweet smile on her lips she tells them: Sometimes I do. I miss my students. I miss choreographing musicals, but I love writing my books, and I love sharing them with my readers.

Cindy resides on her forty-five acre Thoroughbred farm with her husband and her Cocker Spaniel, Allister, near Pittsburgh, Pennsylvania.

For more information, book trailers, and excerpts for all of Cindy's books please visit her website:

www.cindymcwriter.com

GET TOTALLY UNBRIDLED!
CHECK OUT CINDY McDONALD'S
UNBRIDLED SERIES:

It's really quite simple. The Unbridled Series is
Thoroughbred racing steeped in murder, suspense, and a
generous dose of romance—hey, what more could you ask?
Available in print or ebook at amazon.com, BAM,
barnesandnoble.com and where all fine books are sold.

ACCOLADES FOR CINDY McDONALD'S
UNBRIDLED SERIES:

"I love this series!" ~**Wanted Readers**
"McDonald continues her dazzling writing style that keeps
the reader in suspense from beginning to end."
~**The Book Nerd**
"I couldn't put it down. I finished the book in two days—
something that I never do." ~**Socrates Book Reviews**
www.cindymcwriter.com

Be sure to sign up for Cindy's newsletter at her website,
www.cindymcwriter.com, and you will receive the first
chapter of Cindy's latest book delivered directly to your
inbox as a thank you!
*Cindy does not share email addresses.

www.ingramcontent.com/pod-product-compliance
Lightning Source LLC
Chambersburg PA
CBHW060155260626
47160CB00001B/275